<small>THE</small>RAINBOX

By the Author

THE SOUL COLLECTOR
a.k.a. THE MAN FROM MYSTERY HILL

RESTITUTION

THE PROTEUS CURE
with F. Paul Wilson

THE COLLECTION AND OTHER DARK TALES

MY NAME IS MARNIE

MISSING

THE RAINBOX

JUST STORIES

TRACY L. CARBONE

The RAINBOX

SHADOWRIDGE PRESS

THE RAINBOX
First published March 2017
by Shadowridge Press

Book layout and design by Robert Barr

ISBN: 978-1-946808-01-1

shadowridgepress.com

To Abby and Robert,
and Mom and Auntie Robin,

- my family and my kindred spirits,
no matter what time we're in

THE RAINBOX

"The distinction between the past, present and future is only a stubbornly persistent illusion."
- Albert Einstein

"Whatever you do, something else gets undone."
- Barry Ford

ONE

- 1 -

Please stop screaming. Danny ducked in the corner of the porch, his hands tight over his ears as Barry and Dad yelled at each other inside the house. When glass shattered on the floor, he moved his hands and cocked his head to listen. He wanted to run in and do something but Mom ordered him to stay outside no matter what. So he waited. He covered his ears again but it did little to block out the sounds of violence. Anyway, he needed to hear in case it got worse. *Please hurry and come out, Mom. Please.*

"You're not taking my wife and my son, you bastard," Dad said. "No one is taking my family." Danny knelt and peeked through the window to find Dad standing in the kitchen doorway, facing Barry, who was inside by the counter. "I'll kill you before I let that happen!" Dad ran from the kitchen, past the window, and toward his office. His gun was in the office. *Shit. He's gonna shoot Barry.*

Panic and helplessness seized Danny. Dad was drunk and didn't know what he was doing. If he had a gun and Danny tried to stop him he could get hurt. Or worse.

"Mom!" Danny pleaded from the porch through the window. "Mom, get out here!"

He hoped to God she heard him. She'd make this all okay. She'd come downstairs with her suitcase and Danny's new backpack, their getaway bags. She'd grab Barry from the kitchen, and any second they'd both run out before Dad came from his office. Before he ruined everything.

"Mom!" he called again.

He ran to the door and held the doorknob but stopped. If he betrayed her orders and went in—

Mom screamed.

He stood and waited. Listened. *Smash.*

No gunshot but maybe Dad threw a chair. He'd learned to stay away when Dad got violent. He never raised a hand to Danny or Mom but he broke stuff, punched walls, and Mom said they could never be sure when he'd progress to hitting them instead.

His hand was trembling when he let go of the knob and slowly backed away from the door. He turned and saw Mom's car was unlocked. He'd hide there until they came out. He could see from here the door was unlocked. Danny moved from the porch, stopping on each step, waiting for a signal, a hint of what happened, and what he was supposed to do next.

By the bottom step, he knew there was trouble.

Silence from the house.

No one moved inside.

"Oh my God!" Barry's shout carried out the window and gripped Danny.

Fuck it, I need to go in.

Danny barreled in and tripped over a pair of shoes. He fell on his knees. When he looked up—

Mom was dead. Barry sat on the floor Indian style with Mom's bloody broken head on his lap. *Dad shot her!*

He looked to his left. Dad stood by his office on the other side of the room. He didn't have his gun. He didn't shoot her.

Barry? No, he couldn't have. He loves Mom, would never have—but she's dead and he's there.

Barry looked guilty as hell as he stroked Mom's red-stained wet hair.

Dad strolled across the room not saying anything, not showing any emotion. He numbly picked up the phone, then his half-empty beer from the table.

Danny tried to make sense of it. *Mom's blood is all over Barry.*

"You killed her! You were supposed to love us and you killed her. You bastard!" Danny yelled.

Dad was off in a corner holding the phone and beer and not doing a goddamned thing.

"Dad? Do something for God's sake!"

Dad stood frozen, holding the phone.

Mom had just given Danny the new backpack this morning, his escape bag that she was going to pack with all his favorite things. He didn't know what it contained, but he trusted her. They'd come back to the house and get more once they were settled. She'd promised that just a few minutes ago.

And then this.

Danny didn't know what to do, who to run to. Who to trust. He eased toward Mom, hoping she was still alive, that she'd just banged her head. She wasn't moving, not even a little, except for the puddle of blood that streamed its way down Barry's shorts and eventually into a growing circle under him, seeping into the edges of Danny's new backpack. The one filled with everything he needed to escape.

"I didn't do this, Danny. I swear to God, I didn't. It was accident. She fell down the stairs," Barry said through tears.

Bastard.

The boy bent down, looked at Mom's face up close. Her fixed dead eyes stared at him. *Run away, Danny. Run away.* That's what she would've said if she could talk anymore. He was sure of it.

"I thought you loved us," Danny said quietly to Barry, out of earshot of Dad who was finally talking to the police on the telephone.

Then he grabbed the bag and ran out the door.

Danny was the top runner in the sixth grade and knew he'd be safe. He'd played in these woods his whole life and knew where to hide, how to get away. He'd hide until the police came or Dad sobered up. He'd hide and he'd be rescued and then— he didn't know what but he had to hide. Had to close his eyes really tight and try not to see Mom dead on the floor, try not to see the man he'd grown to love as a father running his fingers through her bloody hair. *Why the hell did he do it? Maybe because Dad said he couldn't have her? If he couldn't have her he'd kill her? No, no, no!*

Danny ran past his best friend's house but knew she was away with her family for the day up in the mountains. *Shit.*

He ran into the woods, down the hill. All he could see in front of him was Mom's face. Her dead look. *No!* He wiped his eyes but it didn't help. *How could Barry do this? He said he loved us.* That thought only made him cry harder.

Still he ran, darting between the trees, his backpack banging against shoulders. The sounds of his breathing and his heart pounding drowned out everything else except the faint distant call of Dad's voice. "Danny, come back! Please come back!" He didn't sound angry. Sounded like he was crying. Danny ran faster, wondering if he had it all wrong. If Dad did love him enough to quit drinking and—

Ugh!

Someone punched him in the back. Or kicked him. He didn't know which, but it hurt like hell and he fell face first into crusty dead leaves. Danny tried to get up but something hit his head. A rock? He reached back and felt blood in his hair.

He pushed up and lifted his head from the dirt.

"Dad!" He yelled as loud as he could. "Dad! Help me!"

He saw the shadow of a branch under the moonlight, a giant black claw coming at him, a second before it slammed into his side.

▲▲▲

Danny couldn't see the hands that pinned him under the water in the icy lake but he felt the hard grown-up fingers dig into his shoulders. Crushing pain so strong he couldn't move his arms at all. *I'm sorry, Dad, I'm sorry I was gonna leave you. Please help me.*

He held his breath as long as he could, until his limbs went numb and his mind forced him to—

His nose and lungs burned as the water burst its way in. He gasped and even more water flooded into his mouth and lungs. He knew it was wrong to keep sucking in, that it would kill him, but he couldn't stop.

The hands held him firm while he cried out for Mom and Dad in his mind. *Please help me!*

The moon crept up behind the figure drowning him but he still couldn't see. Just a silhouette. *Doesn't matter now. I'm dying.*

The panic left. The pain went away He relaxed. Floated in darkness.

I'm dead. Nothing hurts anymore so I must be dead. Mom are you here? I'll miss you, Dad. Sorry I was gonna leave you.

And then large hands grabbed his jacket and pulled him out of the water. Giant man hands ripped him from death and threw him hard on the dirt. Punched him in the stomach and pushed his chest. This man rolled Danny on his side and he puked up water. Everything hurt like hell again and Danny knew he'd be okay. No matter what happened, he'd live.

He gasped for air and that hurt now as much as the water did. He puked more water up.

Then the man threw Danny over his shoulder and ran with him.

He couldn't talk, just coughed and gagged. Everything hurt so badly, and his head was bleeding just like Mom's. He started crying again when he remembered.

"Don't be scared, kid. I'm rescuing you," his savior said.

Danny watched behind them. No one followed.

▲▲▲

Danny awoke in a hotel room. He could tell because it was one room with two beds and a weird looking TV on top of a bureau. The frayed flowered bedding smelled like cigarette smoke. Danny had been in a lot of hotels. Mom and Dad and him used to go on family trips. Maybe now they were—Then he remembered. Mom, dead on Barry's lap. And a person trying to drown him.

He pulled the blanket back and swung out of bed to run but his legs buckled and he fell onto the scratchy carpet.

"Whoa, kid take it easy. You got pretty banged up. Back to bed."

The man who had saved him helped him up.

"You okay?"

The man was an adult but young. Maybe twenty. Tall and strong, dirty and scraped up.

"Where am I? What happened?" His voice was hoarse and it hurt to talk.

"Somebody tried to kill you," the man said. "You're safe here, and will have to stay until I can fix what happened."

"Is my Mom dead?"

"I'm afraid so."

Danny started crying again. *Screw being brave.*

"What about my dad?" he asked through tears.

"He'll be all right."

"Is he mad?"

"No," the man said. "He loves you very much and he's going to feel a lot better when you're home safe. You're all he's got now."

Danny wiped his nose with his sleeve. His own pajamas, from the escape bag. He spied the backpack across the room.

"Are you a cop?"

"No," the man said. "But I'm on the right side. You don't need to be afraid of me. I'm here to help you if I can. "

Danny pulled the blankets up closer to his chin.

The man held out his backpack. "I emptied it and dried it on the heater over there. The rest of your clothes will be done soon. I used a hair dryer to do your pajamas."

The boy pulled it to him. His stuffed elephant, Mr. Peanut, would have been better, but this is all he had.

"What else was in here?" he asked. "My mom," he started but couldn't talk suddenly. He burst out crying hard now, like he was four years old. "My mom packed it for me and I don't even know what was in it." It was then he saw the bottom of the bag, the dark stain. Mom's blood.

The man sat down and put his arm around him. "It's okay. Cry it out. Nothing wrong with crying." When Danny had calmed down the man brought over a plastic hotel bag. He dumped the contents on the bed. "Besides the clothes drying over there, this is everything."

A toothbrush, comb, a videogame that was ruined, and a piece of red sea glass. He picked up and held the sliver in his fingers. "This was supposed to mean something," Danny said. "He's a fucking liar." He looked at the man. "Sorry I shouldn't have said that."

"It's fine. It's true, right?"

Danny nodded. "What about the book? Did she pack it?"

The man pointed to a swollen hardcover novel drying on the heater next to the clothes. "It got wet like everything else but it'll survive."

Danny handed the man the sea glass. "I don't want this and I don't want that fucking book. Throw them away!" It felt better being mad than sad. *Fuck everything!*

"Let's not get carried away with the swearing, huh? Anyway, I can't throw it away."

"Why? It's a bunch of crap."

"We need it to get the person who did this to you and who killed your mother. Can you help me do that?" The boy didn't speak. "Because he's done way worse than that and I think that the reason I'm here, that I have the ability to save you, is because he needs to be stopped. It's the only thing that makes sense." The man looked as scared as Danny felt. He looked freaked out and nervous, like he didn't really know what the hell he was doing. Not like a kidnapper at all.

Danny nodded. He was sore and terrified but this guy seemed honest. Messed up maybe. But genuine. That was a word dad only used on a few people and he said it was about the best thing you could say about somebody. A person could be crazy or hopeless but genuine meant deep down honest and trustworthy. There was a quality about this stranger that made him feel safe. Dad said you had to go with your gut.

The man kept closing his eyes, then he'd blurt out stuff like he was surprised he was saying it, then he'd close his eyes again. It was weird but Danny had a feeling about him.

"You remember the stories your dad told you about going undercover? All the times he did it, how it was about playing a part, just like in the movies?"

"You know my dad?" Everything he held against his father was gone now, all the stupid stuff his father did and said; none of it mattered. He just wanted to go home.

"Yeah I know him. I didn't but now, now I do. I guess." He closed his eyes again like he was trying to remember something on the tip of his tongue. "Remember all the things he did to catch the bad guys? He told you about at least a couple of them right?"

"Yeah," Danny wondered where this guy knew Dad from. Maybe he was an undercover cop and just couldn't divulge it.

"You and I need to work together to solve this case. Like he always did."

"And then I can go home?"

"I hope so. I'd bring you back now if it was safe but it's not. Not yet anyway. So, can you play undercover for a while? Play a part to get the bad guy?"

"Yeah, I can do that."

This seemed legit and like the guy said, it wasn't safe to go home. After seeing Mom like that, and almost dying, he knew it was true. His shoulders still hurt where he was held underwater. The man promised to bring him back to Dad as soon as they took care of things, and Danny didn't have a choice but to go along.

"Good boy. Okay, get some sleep. You need it. Tomorrow we'll start, and before you know it you can go home again," the man said. He tousled Danny's hair, just like Dad always did.

"Ouch," Danny said, rubbing his head. The man pulled his hand back.

"Sorry about that. Forgot you got hit there."

Danny wanted to run away but didn't know where he was

or where to go. This man had saved his life and he figured right now, this was about the safest place he could be.

- 2 -

Barry Ford's car pulled up and stopped in front of Bradfield Books. Barry watched out the window as the rain hit the glass, and the drops danced in the puddles. A crowd gathered outside the store. The patrons wore long raincoats and carried black umbrellas. "Are we at a funeral?" Barry asked his driver.

Mr. Blue Sky by ELO blared through the car's stereo speakers. The driver didn't hear him over the song so Barry listened, lost in the lyrics. His speech pathologist, and memory helper extraordinaire, Amy said music was the best way to jumpstart his memory into rebuilding itself. He met with her weekly since his accident and little by little she'd helped him to heal and to rebuild. She was a good friend too, an impartial third party who had the patience and kindness of kindergarten teacher and the body of beautiful woman. If she wasn't so damned professional and he wasn't so messed up he'd have let himself fall in love with her.

He rapped his knuckles on the inside of the car door to match the loud fast beat. This particular song brought him back to the best day of all time. He'd held the love of his life, with her Sugar Daddy colored hair and bright blue eyes, in his arms and told her he'd loved her for the very first time. This song, which was old even then, had played from the radio of his old truck. It was the period in his life when he was writing *The Rainbox,* before he was rich, when he still believed in magic and love. He hummed the song quietly as he looked out the window again. The memory faded away.

The driver lowered the volume. "We're here, Mr. Ford," he said. "Your book signing. You remember. Your collection of stories."

Barry turned to the driver. Recognized him. *Jerry. My driver for over ten years. His son goes to . . . BU. Business major.* "My book signing. Yes, I remember now."

That was a lie. Barry didn't recall planning this at all. Didn't remember the ride over. He'd been sipping cocoa in his living room in front of the fire. The Memory cards Amy recommended were spread on the coffee table and he'd been playing alone, flipping the cards over, trying like hell to find the second monkey. Then he was here, listening to *Mr. Blue Sky* and thinking of lost love.

"Those people are anxious to see you. Mr. Ford. Standing out in the rain like that, a line out the door. You should go in now."

"Yes, yes you're right. Of course. Can't keep them waiting."

"Let me get the door for you. Just waiting for this cab to pass me then I'll—"

"I've got it. My head might be a little scrambled but I can still open a door and see myself in. I'm fifty. Not an old invalid." Barry was often frightened by his confusion but mostly he coped with it the way a seasoned drug addict or functional alcoholic would. He learned to move along with the situation and for the most part no one could tell. Amy said he compensated very well and over time would improve.

"Of course, Mr. Ford. Younger than me, sir."

Barry grabbed his cane and umbrella from the seat beside him and turned the handle.

"Joyce is inside waiting for you," Jerry said.

Joyce. Barry smiled. *Joyce Tuttle.* His assistant and only real friend since Della died. She always took care of things for him. Always had. He pushed open the door and opened his umbrella. "Thank you, Jerry. You go on now."

"I'll just wait until you're inside, Mr. Ford."

Barry nodded and walked to the front of the store. Using his cane and umbrella proved cumbersome but he managed. *Damn leg.*

The customers smiled and waved as he arrived. Their hellos and nice-to-meet-yous blurred in his head until they sounded like a swarm of bees. He stood under the awning and stared at them, suddenly confused by their presence, by his own.

"Who are you people?" he asked. "What do you want from me?"

They rushed him, buzzing excitedly, their hands grabbing at him. Barry batted at them with his wet umbrella. "Get away from me!" There were too many of them, he couldn't fight them all off. He started to hyperventilate and his chest tightened. *Close your eyes and breathe in for a count of five, four, three, two* . . . Amy's voice. He took the breath, held it, counted.

The door opened and out stepped Joyce. She smiled at Barry and all was well again. He relaxed as she hugged his arm. "Sorry about that, folks. The man of the hour has arrived. Just give us a minute or two."

She closed his umbrella and ushered him in. He wanted to go home.

"You can't treat your fans like that, Barry, or you won't have any."

"Fans?" He looked at their smudged demented faces through the wet store window. Looked like a pack of demons to him. "What the hell am I doing here?"

Joyce rolled her eyes. "You're signing books. For the first time in two years, you're signing books, and you're late. Not to mention combative."

"I didn't know who they were. Now I know." *I remember and feel like an utter ass.*

"I'm going to have a word with Jerry about being late," she said as they neared the back table. A large poster of his book cover stood beside the table, reminding him again why he was here.

Barry limped to his seat. His cane kept him from the embarrassment of a walker but still left him feeling like a cripple. Hardcover books with a neat blue jacket and a photo of a piece of red sea glass adorned the table. "My collection," he said with pride as he removed his coat and sat. Two black pens and a glass of water rested by the books.

"Can't blame Jerry. I was—well I don't know what I was doing but I can bet it wasn't his fault."

"Are you all right?" she asked as she held his chin up and inspected his face, locked in on his eyes. "Maybe it was too soon with the accident and all."

"It's fine. It's been two years. Time to live again right? That's what the doctors say."

Joyce studied him the way she always did. A cross of a mother hen and a schoolgirl with a crush. "I'll be right over there if you need anything. Just relax and enjoy it. People are excited to see you again."

"Even though I just attacked them with an umbrella? I could have hurt someone." He worried all the time he would inflict harm when he was in one of his confused states. He detested what he'd been reduced to, a forgetful useless man.

"They understand," she said. "They're anxious to see you, trust me."

Joyce disappeared into the crowd until she reappeared in the drama section off to the left. Barry took a big breath, uncapped a pen, and faced his fans.

There were quite a lot of them and they seemed nonplussed by his less than stellar entrance. All waited patiently, copies of his books in their hands.

"Okay, who's first?" he asked. Fans were wonderful.

A ragamuffin in her twenties stood first in line. She was uncomfortably thin. Brown hair, chocolate colored eyes, and hollow cheeks. A Dickens orphan. "Can you sign it to Bonnie?" she asked as she slid the book toward him. As she did, he saw track marks on her arm from beneath the frayed wet wool coat.

"Of course," Barry said. *Poor little thing.* He was always surprised at the diverse group of people who read his novels and stories. Mainstream with a sci-fi edge is how the media labeled him now. Last year he was a supernatural mystery author. Depending on the market for any given day, his publisher rebranded him. Didn't matter a hill of beans what they called him so long as people read his books and the royalty checks arrived.

He considered a moment and then wrote, "Keep your chin up, Bonnie. Tomorrow and yesterday can switch places and change your life." That was a line from *The Rainbox*, his first novel, the one that put him on the map.

He handed her the book and faced the next customer. And

the next and the next. At one point, he grew confused again. Forgot what year it was. He flipped open the book before him. Copyright 2015. Seeing the date got Barry back on track.

The brain damage was his own damn fault. That was the worst part. Not that he was both messed up and cognizant of his limitations, but that he caused it. When Della died of cancer, after twenty-seven years of marriage, Barry stopped caring. Didn't give two shits anymore. Didn't care about a goddamned thing. So he bought a motorcycle and drove ninety-five miles an hour on route 2 until a tree stopped him. He wanted to die but instead ended up with a gouged out right leg and short-term memory issues.

Joyce got him back on his feet, literally and figuratively. She worked tirelessly with his speech and physical therapists to get him out of rehab and back on his own. She was the one who found Amy for him. He was doing research on a book and wanted a memory specialist. Until then, he assumed it would be a neurologist but Joyce explained that speech therapists also worked with people to improve memories. It was shortly after he'd contacted the woman that he had his accident. He never wrote that book or any others but Amy had been first in line to help. Joyce had gotten him the best doctors all around and pushed him hard to make it as far as he had, even if he wasn't a hundred percent yet.

Continuing in her role as his personal assistant in his writing career, Joyce pulled together fifteen of his old stories for this collection and sent them to his publisher. She arranged this local book tour. Baby steps. No signings out of New England, she insisted. What a dream she was, Barry thought. He searched the dwindling crowd for her and saw her talking to a clerk up front.

He checked his watch. Ten minutes until the end of his signing and then he could return home, have his cocoa, and relax. This had been a stressful night for him but admittedly fun. He'd missed signings, and the crowds, the fans. Joyce was right about that. This had been really good for him.

The ragamuffin sat off in the distance, drinking a coffee, clinging onto his book like it was a treasure and not an overpriced collection of reprints by a man who would probably never write again. No doubt she would stay in the warm and cozy store as long as she could to stave off the cold.

The front door blew open then. In walked a new customer visiting the signing with mere minutes to spare. As the young man drew closer, his feet making wet prints on the tile floor, he scowled at Barry. His walk was deliberate, measured. He stopped behind the last two fans, waiting in line, but the whole time glared at Barry.

Barry searched for Joyce but she was nowhere in sight. He managed to make small talk with a heavy old man, and a teen boy, and scrawled his name in their copies. When they left the only fan remaining was the latecomer.

He was in his twenties, handsome despite the wet hair and rainwater trailing down his face. He didn't have an umbrella, only a very old and now wet copy of *The Rainbox*. The man slapped it down on the table. Not only was it soaked, but it had clearly seen water damage before, and had dried, swollen and warped.

"Do you remember me?" the man asked, sneering.

Barry looked at him more closely. He looked vaguely familiar but—

"I had an accident. On a motorcycle. I'm afraid my memory isn't up to snuff anymore."

"When did you have an accident?"

"Two years ago, give or take."

"Two years?" The man looked confused and Barry pitied him. Must be a drug addict. Or maybe served in Afghanistan and had PTSD. He stared at the man, trying take in his features, to make himself remember. Amy told him the most important way to force memories to stay in his brain, to move from his working memory to the long term, was to make associations. Strong ones. The man's eyes reminded him of—

"I'm sorry, but have we met?"

"What year is it?"

Barry consulted his book again to be sure. *2015.* Barry had a strong feeling of déjà vu. He hadn't gotten that since before his accident. He'd have to make sure to tell Amy that at his next visit. It could mean an improvement. Or, he feared, a sign the brain damage was manifesting itself in a new way.

The man didn't answer, only looked off into space, as if he were trying to make sense of something. But then he shook his head, dismissing whatever it was. He pointed wordlessly to the book in a way that reminded Barry of the Ghost of Christmas Yet To Come.

Barry couldn't shake the odd feeling he had about this mysterious young man. "We've met," the man said, the sadness palpable in his voice. "A long time ago it seems. In another time. Maybe it was a dream."

It was a line from *The Rainbox*, one he knew well. Barry took a deep breath, felt relief. *Just an old fan, a crazy fan from years ago, no doubt. Nothing to worry about.*

But his trembling fingers belied the unease this man stirred in him. He cursed Joyce for leaving his side. Stress made his memory worse and she was supposed to stick by him to protect him from situations like this.

He looked around but she was still absent.

Barry spread open the soggy cover of the book and noticed it was a first edition of *The Rainbox*. A copy like this in good condition was worth money.

"How do you want me to inscribe it?" Barry asked. The sooner he got this kook out of here the better.

"You already did. A long time ago," the man said.

Barry turned the page and saw words in his own writing, in penmanship straight and clear.

To Danny-the son I always wanted. Whatever happens, we will forever have our Rainbox-Love Barry.

"Danny?" Barry looked at the young man. It had been so long. He'd be all grown up now, but the resemblance—

Then he remembered the horrific truth.

No. Danny's dead. Drowned. Fifteen years ago.

"You tried to kill me," the man said. "You killed my mother and tried to kill me."

"No. You're not Danny." He stood up, used the table for support. "Joyce!" he called out. "Joyce!"

"We're not done," the man said. "I don't know what the hell is going on but you're not getting away with it. Any of it. You're a murderer and you're not getting away with it." He grabbed his book and rushed out the front door, just as Joyce ran to Barry from the back. She held two paper cups in her hands.

As she set the steaming drinks on the table, the front door slammed. All that was left of the man was his trail of wet footprints, mixed in with those of all the others.

"What is it? Are you all right?" Joyce held his hand.

"It was little Danny Brundige," he said. Words he never thought he'd speak again. "All grown up. He said he was at least. Had the book I gave him." Barry picked up the cup and tried to take a sip but dropped it. The safety lid failed and scalding coffee poured all over the table and his books. He swung out of the way just before it hit his legs.

The store clerk ran over and frowned. "We'll pay for those books," Joyce said. "Just please go get a towel."

Barry flinched at the mess. "What just happened?"

"You spilled your coffee. You were all upset and dropped the cup."

He leaned on his cane and closed his eyes. Tried hard to remember but it was all slipping away. "A man came in with a copy of *The Rainbox* but, but that can't be. This signing is for my short story collection isn't it?"

Joyce nodded. "I didn't see anyone here, Barry. I left for a second but there was hardly time for—"

Barry stared at the front door, at the mess of muddy footprints. At the stack of *Collections by Barry* on the table. He had a snippet of a memory. *A sad man. No. Not real. I just had a little slip that's all. A little memory slip.*

He squeezed Joyce's hand. "I don't know what I'd do without you, Joyce I really don't."

Joyce smiled. "Come on, let's cash you out and I'll drive you home. I'll tell Jerry he's not needed tonight."

Barry walked from around the table and headed for the register. Off in the distance he saw the ragamuffin. She stood by the door, forced to leave by the store staff. She hesitated, delaying entering the cold wet night.

"I saw him too," she said to Barry, as she opened the door. She popped her umbrella and held it up against the driving rain. She turned and looked back at him. "I saw him too if that means anything."

Barry nodded. "Thank you. It does mean something. It means everything."

- 3 -

Fred Brundige slammed his refrigerator door. The beers were gone. Just as well. They were making him fat, he thought. He reached into the cabinet above the stove and pulled out a half bottle of bourbon. He was unsteady on his feet but what did it matter? No one would care if he died right now. He filled a water glass with the liquor right to the brim. Not even room for an ice cube.

He moved into his living room, careful not to spill his drink. He set it down on a wooden TV tray and crawled into his recliner. He squeezed the arm, the one with a hole worn through. He'd bought this chair and that couch just two weeks before Helen and Danny died. *Two fucking weeks.* He'd made a major drug bust after months of hiding undercover, and was finally cleared to come home.

He took the family out to the furniture store to celebrate. "Sky's the limit," he said. Helen wasn't interested. "What about you, kid? You like this set?"

"I don't care," Danny said. "It's just a couch and chair."

"What's going on with you two?"

Helen and Danny faced him. They sat on the couch and Helen spoke. "You've been gone three months, Fred. Three months. You missed his first day of sixth grade. You missed everything!"

"Keep your voice down," he said. "People are staring."

"I don't think I can stay in this marriage anymore," she said, grabbing Danny and walking away.

Fred was younger then. Stupid. Had no clue how much damage his absence had caused. He bought the set thinking he could make it all okay. In the car on the way home, no one spoke.

The couch and chair were delivered a week later.

Helen and Danny got to enjoy it for a week. *One fucking week.* And then they were gone.

He took a gulp of his whiskey and welcomed the warmth.

He looked around at the walls of his shabby one bedroom apartment. He'd let the bank take the cabin years ago after he lost his family, then his job. That was his own fault too, he admitted, as he took another drink.

When his life fell apart, he started hitting the bottle harder than before. He ran a stop sign and crashed his undercover car into a park bench. No one was sitting on it, thank God, but he failed a breathalyzer and his captain said he couldn't cover for him anymore.

Fifteen years he'd been hanging around, relegated to performing low paying, low profile jobs as a private investigator. It paid the rent and kept his mind occupied but it was pointless. His bread and butter was divorce attorneys and insurance companies who hired him as a snoop. To supplement that work he moonlighted doing background checks on customers' neighbors, and digging through pasts of prospective Internet dates. No one trusted anyone anymore. But it was a job and it beat welfare.

Losing everything changed him.

The kicker was that when Helen and Danny were still alive, they were the lowest on his priority list. Once they died they escalated to the most important. *You don't know what you got till it's gone.*

He'd spent ten years trying to prove Danny was murdered or kidnapped, trolling that lake on his own every single night. Not for the whole ten years but enough of them. Checking databases all over the country continually for a little boy who was eleven, then twelve, then thirteen. No one found a body and Fred clung to that hope.

Danny would be twenty-six now. *He's dead. I can admit it now. Otherwise he would have escaped from wherever he was. Would've come home.*

Fred rose from the chair. He took his drink and walked to the corner of the living room that served as his office.

He sat his stocky ass on a warped desk chair and wiped thin blond hair out of his eyes. He had a scrapbook of old articles, including Missing posters. Danny had even scored the back of a milk carton. Fred had cut that out too, planning to show him when he came home. They'd talk about how hard Fred had looked for him, how he'd left no stone unturned. He flipped through the heavy pages. So many articles and calls for help. Ads in papers coast to coast.

All for nothing. Today marked the fifteenth anniversary of his disappearance.

Why do I even keep this shit anymore?

He walked to the kitchen and grabbed the trash barrel. He picked up the first pile of papers and held them over the trash. He couldn't release them, couldn't bring himself to toss them away. *Jesus, Fred. It's time to let it go, you pathetic shit.*

Someone knocked at the door. He dumped the papers onto the counter and headed to the entrance. "Just a minute!" He peeked through the window on the side of the door but there was no one in sight. Whoever it was ran down the outside stairs.

He opened the door and discovered a piece of paper, folded over and sticking from out from under the doormat. Fred picked it up. Handwritten on the outside was the singular word *Dad*.

"Oh my God."

He looked around outside, ran down the steps himself. "Danny!" It was just like that night all over again. Drunk and useless, chasing after a ghost.

He went back in and carefully opened the note as he shut the door with his foot.

Don't give up. I'm not dead, the note read.

He sat on his desk chair, the closest place he could collapse. Conflicting waves of grief and joy fought for the forefront.

It was Danny's handwriting. He was sure of it.

"He's not dead! I knew it! I knew!"

He went into his kitchen, and proceeded to pour every ounce

of liquor in his house down the drain, then dumped the empties into the trash.

He looked around at his filthy kitchen and the general condition of his house. "Time to live again," he said. "Time to bring Danny home."

- 4 -

Barry sat on his couch in front of his gas flame fireplace. He'd bought the brownstone almost thirty years ago and it was the only place he truly felt safe. An empty cup of cocoa rested beside a completed game of Memory. All the cards were matched and Barry smiled with great pride. Classical guitar music played softly from his Bluetooth speakers. Despite the events earlier in the evening, many of which were quickly dissolving into fragments like a partially remembered nightmare, he was at peace now. The good thing about his memory, he considered, was that most things before the accident were right there at the vanguard. Clear and sharp.

He could remember the smell of a woman's perfume, hear the rustle of her shirt, the way one laughed timidly and another snorted. He smiled at the images. He could recite entire passages from his novels, and quote cult movie lines like any good American.

But then there were the holes. He could almost feel the vibration of a woman's heels on a wooden floor but when he searched for a face? Blank. And what he ate for breakfast or the last movie he saw? Nothing. There was no logical sense to what his mind allowed him access. Amy said it *was indeed* logical. And then she's go off on a diatribe of the brain and neurons and connectivity. Big technical words which meant nothing to Barry.

In essence, most of the day to day happenings that occurred in his life were lost within a short time as soon as new stimuli entered his mind. His brain didn't properly move things into his long term memory, and unless he wrote everything down or worked very hard to remember right away, it was gone. Amy called it encoding. If he snapped an elastic band on his wrist that helped a little, but Joyce said it made him looked retarded. Joyce was old school and wasn't up to the standards of political correctness.

He glanced behind him, at the large white board hanging on the wall of his dining room/living room area. On the left, he kept lists of things to do, tasks to complete: lock the door, take your vitamins, things of that nature. The right side was where he recorded his big memories of the day. Simple things that he pushed himself to recall later. From earlier today he'd written: sound of rain on cars outside, bit my tongue eating Subway, new Geico commercial. Since he got home he'd added: déjà vu, lunatic fan named Danny with 1st edition Rainbox, scruffy prostitute.

Not only did he have the white board, which Joyce often used to write his tasks even though he asked her not to, he also wrote down everything he could remember in a notebook, every time he returned home. In addition he carried a small notebook with him when he was out, just in case.

Tonight was a crazy night and much of it was still lodged in his mind, which surprised and encouraged him. He almost called Amy when he arrived home, but he'd blurred and crossed the lines in their doctor-patient relationship already and needed to accept she was his memory coach, not his daily sounding board.

He opened the notebook to his most recent entry. *A man named Danny came to the book signing. He was angry. Joyce didn't see him. A girl whose name I can't recall said she saw him. I couldn't remember why I was at the store and got violent when the crowd came at me. Joyce said I hit them with my umbrella. I don't recall. Inside, I got my time mixed up and thought it was 2000. How did the man have his book if he wasn't Danny?*

He strained to remember the young man's face but to no avail. The phone rang. *Joyce.* He set the book down.

"Hello," he said.

"*Hi. How are you doing? Are you settled in for the night?*" she asked.

"Yes." He set the phone on speaker, placed it on the coffee

table as he lifted the cup to his lips. *Still empty.* He stood up to rinse it in the sink and brought the phone with him.

He added soap to the cup and ran the faucet. *"What's that noise?"* she asked.

"Rinsing the cocoa cup," he said. He loved Joyce. Truly he did, but not the way she wanted. He had a fling with her years ago but it was over abruptly and he was just as glad. Della made a better wife. She was solid and strong. Passive. Joyce was a hellcat when she didn't get her way, and honestly who wanted to be married to that? Not him. She was pretty, and in his day Barry did have fun with the ladies, but Joyce . . .

Hell, he thought, as he carried the phone back to the table and lowered the music, he should *still* be whipping it up. But women get funny when you can't remember their names the next day. And plus Joyce was always warning him of the dangers of opportunists taking advantage of him in his special state.

"Barry, I can't hear you. Are you still there?"

"I'm here. Hey, I was looking through the notebook from when I first got home tonight."

"And?" she asked.

"You sure you didn't see the guy in the store?"

"Very. Danny's presence is just a hiccup in your memory. Nothing else."

"I'm not hallucinating, Joyce. That's not part of the brain damage."

She sighed on the other end. *"Of course not. But confusion and misremembering is. Did you play your Memory game?"*

He nodded.

"Barry?"

"Yes. Twice. And I played music and took a lot of notes and read them out loud to myself." *Pain in the ass.*

"What about Sodoku? I read that really helps to rebuild—"

"Yes. I did two of those too." He opened the large print puzzle book she'd bought him and marked an X on two opposite blank puzzle pages. He hated Sodoku but Joyce didn't listen. It was easier to lie. "Thanks for arranging the signing tonight. It was good to get out again," he said to change the subject.

"Who's your favorite assistant?" she teased.

He grinned. "Well you've been my only assistant ever so I guess I have to say you are."

"Nice. Okay I'll let you get to your shows. What's on tonight?"

He looked down at the stack of DVDs on the table. "Nero Wolfe."

"Sounds cozy. So I'll stop by tomorrow and we'll brainstorm for a new book. How would that be?"

A wave of gloom overtook him. "We can brainstorm but I'm not going to be able to come up with any coherent plots, or follow through and finish a damn thing."

"Let's brainstorm and see what happens from there. You've still got a million stories to tell and I bet together we can pull at least one of them out." Joyce's kind voice reminded him how much he valued their friendship. She meant well.

"Okay. You win. And, and thank you, Joyce. I do appreciate you."

"Same here. Goodnight."

"Night."

As he ended the call, and leaned forward to hit the clicker to turn on the show, a loud knock rattled his wooden door. Really loud. Police raid loud.

"Just a minute," he shouted. "I'm coming!"

The visitor kept on like a woodpecker. Barry retrieved his cane and walked lamely to the door. Without looking through the side window he opened it.

The man who called himself Danny stood before him, sopping wet. Barry didn't have an awning so water pelted down on Danny's head and into his eyes. "Can I come in?" he shouted over the driving rain.

Barry stood aside and ushered him in. He shut the door and once again the house was silent and still, warm and dry. His haven.

"Let me get you a towel," Barry said.

He left for the bathroom and returned with a fluffy white cloth. He handed it to Danny.

He blotted his face and returned it. Barry looked at the image left behind. *Shroud of Turin.* He looked closer. *No, just dirty wrinkled fabric.*

The man removed his wet coat and hung it on the rack. He slid his shoes off and placed them neatly on the mat, as if he knew where they should go. "I know you don't allow shoes in the house."

Barry nodded. He didn't know how to react. Joyce should be here. She knew how to handle these types of things. He wasn't equipped—

The man walked about the room in sock feet, studying the knick-knacks, the books. Neither of them spoke.

If he was a robber he'd hit me with a pipe or shoot me, or knock me down. He's just curious.

Danny walked to a hutch and picked up a picture of Barry and Della, taken a few years ago, before her illness. "I don't understand what's going on. I really don't." He looked to Barry with woe, not anger. "I only left for a few minutes, to make things right, and now everything is different. Please help me to understand."

"Who are you? Do you need a doctor?"

"No, I don't need a doctor. I need you to fill me in, tell me what the hell is going on. Who is this? I mean, it's Della but why is she in this picture?"

"You knew Della?"

Maybe he was an acquaintance of his late wife. She'd done volunteer work at a halfway house before she got sick. Could be that he volunteered too, or was a resident. He felt bad for this young man the way you pity a hungry dog you find in an alley.

"She's my wife. *Was* my wife. I'm a widow," Barry said tentatively. He knew he couldn't outrun this man so he sat on the couch, hoping for the best. He discreetly picked up his cell phone and slid it in the pocket of his lounging pants. Even stray dogs could become mean if they were scared or provoked.

"You're only wife?"

"Yes, my first and only."

"Unbelievable. So you killed Della then instead?"

"I didn't kill her, no. She got cancer. Breast cancer. I loved her very much." Sorrow seized him as he relived the moment when Della closed her eyes for the last time.

"Della was your first wife," Danny said. "You left her when Joyce got pregnant. With me. And all those years later you knocked her down the stairs when she confronted you about—"

"No, you've got it all mixed up. I'm sorry but you've got it all mixed up. Joyce is my assistant. No children. I married Della and she died of cancer. I had a girlfriend once who fell down the stairs and died but not Della."

Danny started to fall back and caught himself on a dining room chair. He closed his eyes and managed to pull the chair out to sit. "It's rushing in. The new life. I'm getting details and emotions and, Jesus what the hell is going on?"

Barry walked to him and put a hand on his shoulder. "Are you all right, son?"

Danny looked up to him. "So you remember that I'm your son? Is that at least the same?"

Barry shook his head. "No, I don't have any children. Della and I weren't blessed."

The young man put his head in his hands. "I can't believe it. I can't fucking believe it."

"Is there anything I can do for you? To help? Coffee?"

"Your memory is all messed up too," Danny said, not acknowledging the offer. "How do *you* keep it all straight? I feel like I'm going crazy." He stood up and headed for the large white board. "What is this?"

"It helps me remember," Barry said. Anything to get the guy talking and calming down would be progress. "I have notebooks too. Dozens of them." Barry pointed to a bookcase shelf packed with wire bound notebooks. He lifted his current one from the coffee table. "I see a specialist who helps me, who gives me tricks. I write down everything I can and then read it aloud over and over and it helps to get it into my long term memory." He handed the book to Danny who opened to the recent page and read it silently.

"Did you . . . were you in a hospital before? Where did you come from?" Barry asked.

Danny looked up from the book. "You really don't remember me?"

"I'm sorry. My short term memory is impaired since my accident."

"I'm not short term. You were my father for twenty-six years. I lived in this house, with you and my mother. With Joyce."

"Joyce is my friend. Nothing else."

"She's alive?"

"Why wouldn't she be?"

Danny stood on unsteady legs and moved to the bookcases. He scanned the collection of pictures. "There really aren't any pictures of me. I never existed."

Barry was torn between feeling this man's heartbreak, and fearing him as a potentially dangerous mental patient. "I think I need to call someone for you. Is there anyone? Are you on drugs?

"You really don't know who I am, do you?"

Barry shrugged. "You say your name is Danny and you showed me an old book that belonged to a boy I knew a long time ago. Are you implying you're him?"

"No." Again he held his head and seemed to be reeling from stimuli Barry couldn't see. "I don't know."

"Listen, son," Barry said tenderly. "It's not possible. He died. Years ago, he died."

Danny sat on the fancy chair, as Joyce called it, and rested his elbows on his knees. "This is unreal. Fucking unreal."

"Who are you then?"

Danny buried his face in his hands and said nothing at first. "Unbelievable."

"What is it, son? Are you all right?"

The man clearly wasn't. He was confused and frightened and his eyes darted from one wall to the next, taking it all in and not liking what he saw.

"Please, tell me what's going on. You're frightening me. I'm not well."

"My room was down that hall," he said. "But there are these other memories and they're taking those over and all my real memories, they don't make sense anymore. They're fading away. Can you give me a notebook? I need to write it down."

Barry retrieved a new notebook from a stack in a cabinet under the television. He handed it to Danny with a pen.

He sat on the corner of the couch, inches from Danny in his spot on the chair. Danny wrote furiously for several minutes. Then he flipped the book over and wrote upside down from the other side. Neither man said a word out loud.

Barry headed to the kitchen and took out a tin of butter cookies. The Christmas blue tin cookies had arrived at CVS and he'd bought several tins. Joyce hated that he bought so many at once, resented that he could have a couple of cookies and move on and she couldn't control herself.

He brought out the tin and a couple of plates. He brewed them each a cup of hot chocolate in his Keurig. When he sat back down, Danny raised his eyes. "This helps to keep it straight." He saw the cocoa and took a sip. "Thanks."

"Can you tell me who you are now? Why you're here."

"I'm here because this is where I live. Or lived. I hoped if I came by then—" Danny's face was red, his eyes fearful. "I took a trip and now everything is all messed up and I don't know how to fix it. I'm going to die if I don't fix it. I'm not even really here."

"Did you take acid? Back in college a few of us—" Barry started.

"Jesus no. Not acid. A real trip. In your Rainbox."

Terror and excited comingled. "My Rainbox?"

"Yes. Your Rainbox. That didn't change. I traveled through time."

"But that was just something I made up. It's not real."

"It is. Real, I mean. I'm here."

Barry viewed him in a different light now. What if he really had traveled through time? What a fantastic thing that would be. What if the events in his first novel had manifested in reality? Who was to say it couldn't happen? He smiled as the idea of changing the past flooded him. *Think of the possibilities.*

"Please tell me more," Barry said. "Make me believe."

"I went back to change events and when I returned I couldn't breathe. Next thing I bounced to another time and was standing over myself as a drowning boy. I saved him. Me. And came back here. And now I was never born and your memory is gone and Joyce isn't my mother anymore. And you were the one that tried to kill me. And back here you're not my father. What if I'm dead and this is all a dream?"

Barry took it all in. A jumble of facts that made no sense. Maybe it was time travel but more likely drugs. His hopes dashed as quickly as they'd risen. He wanted to write it all down before he forgot but he needed to help this poor wet man whose brain had lost its way.

"You're not dead. I can feel you. Your pulse is racing. Do you want me to call a doctor? Or Amy. I can call my memory coach Amy. She knows about all kinds of things. She has a degree in psychology too and has helped me with so much more than memory loss. Truly during my darkest hours she's the one who helped me to get my head on straight."

"No. Not now. But thanks. You've been very kind and I can't imagine how this must look to you." He took a deep breathe to steady himself and then spoke more quietly. "Tell me about *The Rainbox*."

"It's a book. A book I made up."

"What's it about?"

"Why are you asking? You have a copy. I saw it."

"I want to know what it's about *this* time. In *this* reality." Danny said, leaning back.

In this reality, was not a term mentally well people used but he'd play along. If nothing else, his curiosity as a writer forced him to follow this where it led. He no longer felt threatened. Maybe he should, but his quest to understand this man was stronger.

"Tell me what it's about," Danny said. "Please."

"I-I- it's about a man who loses his son. To an accident."

"Go ahead."

"And the man built a time machine out of sea glass. He and

the boy used to summer in Maine and it was their ritual to collect the glass, so it had meaning you see. Beach combing for glass had comprised the boy's childhood." Barry smiled as he recalled the tale, and the magic and excitement he'd felt while writing it. "The man took all his money, and his wife thought he was crazy, but he built the Rainbox in a spare bathroom out of an old shower stall. And he wished and went back—"

"How did he go back? What was the special thing he needed?" Danny watched him now. He seemed genuinely interested in the story. *The Rainbox* started it all. He wrote it at the happiest time in his entire life.

"Red sea glass. It's hard to find that. Very hard. And this Rainbox was constructed from real ocean washed glass too, nothing manufactured. Each piece was water worn with its own bit of history. And so this man went into the box and wished and wished, and placed his son's prized piece of red sea glass in the soap dish, and next thing he was back in time and saved his son."

Danny nodded. "So it didn't change."

"From what?"

Danny dug into his pocket and pulled out a spear of red sea glass, about three inches long. He placed it on the coffee table and slid it towards Barry.

"Where did you get this?" Barry asked. "May I pick it up?"

Danny nodded.

Barry picked up the sliver, held the cool smooth piece between his fingers. He recalled the last time he'd seen a piece like this. When he was dating the love of his life, Helen Brundige. Danny's mother. He'd written the book for her little boy. Helen was going to leave her husband and Barry was going to raise Danny. *God that was a happy time.* But then Helen fell down the stairs and Danny drowned.

And Barry went home to Della with his spirit and heart broken. Good old Della. The book was a huge success but even seeing the cover always broke his heart.

Of course Della didn't know about the affair until it was over. To celebrate his number one spot on the NY Times bestseller list she'd had a full-size replica of the Rainbox built, including a mock drain since the real one was fashioned from an old shower stall. She'd installed it in a closet off their bedroom. And every single goddam day he'd had to look at it and remember what he'd lost.

"You with me, Barry?" Danny said. He stood next to Barry, clapping his hands. "You there?"

"Yes," he said quietly. "I'm here." He wiped the tears from his eyes. How dare this stranger toy with him like this? Maybe his motivation wasn't devious but the result was the same. Mentally imbalanced or not, he was not Danny. "Where did you get this?" he asked again of the glass.

"You gave it to me," Danny said. "When you were my father. No that's . . . you were my mother's . . . I'm sorry I just, it's all muddled."

"I don't know what you're pulling but Danny Brundige is dead. What do you want? Are you here to take advantage of a crippled man?"

"I want you to remember, and I want to set things right," Danny said. "There was a reason I went back. It was because of what you did. You were my father." Danny shut his eyes.

"Bullshit!" Barry said. "This is going too far. I know you now. I know why I recognize you. What does Amy call it? Misattribution. You were in a blue uniform. The plumber. You were here a couple of weeks ago and I'm getting it confused in my head because I want it to be so."

"No I wasn't. I just got here."

"You're not right in the head. You were in my house before and that's why you know your way around. You're an old fan and know a lot about me and the Rainbox and my life. That's it." Barry stood and pulled his phone from his pocket. "You posed as a plumber to get in here, to fuck with me. You've obviously taken drugs and I'm going to call an ambulance, or the police."

"I'm not a plumber. I'm not. I wasn't here two weeks ago. I just got here."

"It was you." Barry couldn't swear to it in court. Truth be told, he couldn't recall the face of the plumber at all, just the uniform with the gold stars on the lapel.

"I came through the Rainbox tonight, before your signing. I used this." Danny yanked the glass from Barry's grasp.

He walked down the hall and Barry followed. "Where are you going?"

"To the Rainbox. To show you."

"It's not possible."

Barry leaned against the wall. *No, this isn't real. He's just a con. A grifter.*

Danny opened the door to the bedroom and then the closed door to the Rainbox. He flicked on the lights and Barry gasped in admiration and amazement. He hadn't entered the Rainbox since Della died. Well, that wasn't true. Shortly after her funeral he'd spent many a drunken night in here, crying himself to sleep, wishing he could go back and prevent her death. But the box wasn't a time machine. It was just a fictional premise he dreamt up. And one night he bolted from the useless Rainbox and onto his bike and into that tree. Since then, the door had been closed.

There were lights installed behind the walls of sea glass so it provided a mystical blue-green glow.

"I came through here," Danny said. "Tonight. Came through tonight. And everything had changed. You married a different person and never had me at all."

Barry stood inside the box in wonder, having forgotten its splendor. He didn't know what to say. It was incredible and a lie, but what if? What if it was true? What if this was real the whole time and he wrote about it because on some level he remembered?

His mind swam and he felt dizzy. The overwhelming feeling of déjà vu hit him again.

"Show me that it works," Barry said. "Prove it. I want it to work. I want you to be my son or Danny Brundige but you must understand; I need to see."

"I can't sort through what's real or not and what's from before and what's from now. The notebook helped like you said but there's so much. I never thought it would be like this. Never took any of it into consideration when I went back."

"Just slow down and think. Take your time. I want to believe. Help me."

Danny looked around, took it in and concentrated. "I remember you. I remember this house and where things are and..." His face darkened. "Please give me that notebook I had."

Barry hobbled down the hall with his cane as quickly as he could. He handed the book and pen to Danny again.

Danny wrote for several minutes on one side of the book, then just as long on the flip side, almost tearing the paper with the pressure of the pen.

Barry grew excited again at the prospect. If he really could travel through time there is so much he would change. So much he would prevent.

The man set the book down and rubbed his hands. "The old life is slipping away fast and I need to record everything I can. It's not good, Dad. Barry."

Barry sat down again and awaited clarification of anything to point to this miracle, and away from Danny being insane, or worse.

"Danny, listen. Maybe you think you're making sense but you're not. Tell me what you know. Let me see the notebook."

"No!" Danny yanked it away. "I loved you. I really did and I didn't want it to be like this. But you ... you did things. Horrible things. In both lives. I don't know how but I need to fix this. I'm Danny Brundige now like it or not and—"

"He's dead. I told you."

"Do I look dead?"

Barry shook his head. Danny stood over him, suddenly looking clear headed but angry.

"I need to get out of here and think, to write it all down and figure out just how much damage I did, how much changed."

Without warning Danny shut the lights off and headed back to the living room.

Barry followed.

Danny put his shoes and wet coat back on.

"Wait!" Barry shouted, shambling with his good leg and cane and trying to keep up. "Please. Don't go." He stood eye to eye with the young man. It was hard to tell if he was that little boy all grown up. He was similar but it had been so long and he couldn't quite remember young Danny's face.

"Do you have any cash?"

So that was it then.

"If I say no will you kill me?"

"If you say no, I can't afford to eat. I didn't have a lot of cash on me when I left. I need enough for a hotel for a couple of nights."

Barry didn't react.

"Damn it, I'm your son. Don't you believe me? You wrote *The Rainbox* book for me. Danny. The main character's name. My name. I left to save Mom and it all fell apart but I'm your son even if you can't remember. And I need money to survive."

So sad, so earnest. If he was a con, he was a damn good one. And what the hell? Barry was a rich man with no heirs. If there was a one in a million chance he fathered this kid in a parallel reality, he had to help.

Barry went to his office and came out with five hundred dollars in cash. He handed it to Danny. "Are you telling the truth?"

Danny hesitated then nodded.

"And you'll be back? To tell me more." Barry sounded desperate but he couldn't help himself. He needed hope to cling to and this kid was it.

"I'll come back. Trust me. Bringing you to justice is why I'm here."

Danny walked out into the storm, leaving Barry confused by his words and tone. *Bringing me to justice?* Again, he felt afraid. He walked to his cabinet and poured himself a tall glass of single malt scotch. He emptied it down his gullet. No time to luxuriate and savor the expensive taste. This was drinking to get drunk and if there was ever a night he needed it, it was now.

TWO

- 1 -

Joyce pulled her Mini Cooper into a spot in front of Barry's brownstone, thrilled she managed to luck into a spot so close. This was going to be a great day, she thought. She breathed in the smell of warm Cinnabons and Dunkin Donuts coffee that filled her tiny car.

Barry lived on a city street lined with trees, faux gas lanterns, and cobblestone paved sidewalks. It was mid-October so it was crisp but not yet snowing. The leaves were long gone and the sky clear and bright. She smiled. *A great day indeed.*

She checked her mirror and jumped out of the car before the next one drove past. Then she walked around to the passenger side and retrieved their breakfast and her shoulder bag of brainstorming tools. Realizing she didn't have enough hands, she put the buns in her bag too. She shut and locked the car up and gazed lovingly at Barry's door, up eight stone stairs. She wondered sometimes if unrequited love is what kept her so interested in him. Maybe if she'd ended up with him, if he'd been willing, she would have tired of him by now.

Joyce ascended the stairs, using the twenty-four ounce cups, one in each hand, for balance. *One of these days,* she mused, *I'll win him over. He'll see I've been here all along.* She forced a smile and used her pinky knuckle to press the doorbell.

No one answered. Her smile dropped. "Barry!" she shouted. "Are you in there?" She rang the bell again and smiled.

Through the glass border beside the door she saw a form move closer. The bolt turned. Barry opened the door a crack. He peered through, saw her, and opened it.

"Come in. Come in. Quickly." He moved aside and shut the door behind her.

"What's going on? Why aren't you dressed?"

He was still in his pajamas, and he hadn't shaved or even combed his hair. His eyes were bloodshot. The thing about Barry, even with all that, he was damn attractive. He had thick brown hair, not a strand of gray. Joyce had been dying her Miss Clairol Chestnut Hair for over a decade. He had a deep scar on his cheek from the accident but that only made him manlier.

Barry peeked out the window and then moved from the door. "Come sit down. Something's happened and I need to talk to you."

Joyce walked into the living room and set the coffees down on the table. She pulled the buns from her bag and placed them by the beverages. She'd planned to make it known she had to go to two different places to get their breakfast just right, to celebrate a new book which she prayed he could write.

Instead she sat quietly, waiting for an explanation.

Barry plopped on the couch beside her and peeled back the cup's lid. He took a good swig of it then put it down. He picked up his notebook and stared at Joyce.

"What is it?" She didn't know to be worried or excited. Maybe he had a memory breakthrough. Maybe he—

"Don't think I'm crazy but . . . the Rainbox, I think it's real." He waited for a reaction.

Joyce flayed open the Cinnabons package and pushed it toward him.

"Did you hear what I said, Joyce? It's real." His smile stopped and became a flat line. "I don't want to eat. I want to talk about this."

She turned to him. "It's not real, Barry. I wish it were but it's not. You made it up."

"But that's just the thing. I made it up and it became viable. A time machine just like in the book." He smiled again. "Honest to God, Joyce. Honest to God."

Joyce's heart sunk. She wondered if Barry was on drugs. Or drunk. Both? A worse scenario was that his mind was deteriorating, no longer limited to memory lapses. She'd hitched her wagon to a star and now this.

"We need to call your neurologist. Have another MRI. Do you feel okay otherwise?"

"Otherwise what? This is one of the single biggest events in my life and you think I'm imagining it!"

"Just settle down. Take a deep breath. I'm willing to listen but drink your coffee and eat your breakfast." She gestured to the bun again. "Tell me why you think it's real."

Barry didn't seem to recall she was quoting a line from his novel, when he'd first told his fictional wife it was real and she had humored him.

"Danny came to see me last night. He was in the store, just like I said. You didn't believe me, remember?"

She nodded.

"He came here last night and we talked and, well, I believe it's him."

Joyce rolled her eyes. "And how is it you remember last night with such clarity and every other minute you're—"

"Because it was emotional and I made a point to remember." He held up the book. "I wrote it and then read it over and over. Even if I hadn't though, I think I'd still remember."

"Why?"

"Because it mattered to me. From the time he walked in until he left I felt , , well I *felt*. A range of emotions. So it all stayed right here." He tapped his head.

His theory implied that he didn't *feel* around her. He forgot most of their new interactions if he didn't use memory tricks to cement them. *Guess I'm just not important enough.* "Fine. Tell me what this Danny said. How did he convince you?"

He sipped his drink. "He had the red sea glass and he knew about the Rainbox. Knew right where it was and—"

"And," she interrupted. "There was a full color spread about your house and the Rainbox in the *Boston Globe* last year. Half the city could walk in here and find it, and describe it from memory."

Barry lowered his head.

"But his name is Danny, just like the real Danny."

Joyce sighed, tired of always being the voice of reason. Even before the accident, Barry was reckless and always getting himself into jams she had to rescue him from. "Did he show you any ID?"

"No," he said quietly. "No, I guess he didn't."

"It can't be him because Danny died. You know that. He died a long time ago in the lake." Barry nodded. She continued. "What did he want?"

"He said he came back . . . I can't recall now but it upset me. Goddammit! I wrote it all down as soon as he left so it's in here."

He reached for his notebook and began flipping through it. He read to himself loud and fast, a jumble of words she couldn't decipher.

"Did you give him money?" Joyce asked.

Barry peered up from his book. "He needed it. For a hotel and food. He didn't bring enough money through time and he—"

Joyce held his gaze and before her eyes he seemed to have understood how ridiculous it all sounded. "You think he played me?"

She took his hand. "How much money did he take?"

"Five hundred."

Joyce winced. "Wow. Well, think of it as a learning experience. It's all you can do."

"I guess it won't do any good to go through my notes with you then," Barry said. "How he insisted he was really my son and went back in time then became Danny Brundige?"

"It makes for good fiction," she said.

The doorbell rang. Barry began to rise.

"I'll get it," Joyce said. "If it's him, I'll run him off once and for all."

She walked to the door and opened it. The man before her had a familiar air but she couldn't recall from where she knew him. Whoever he was, it had been a long time. It was hazy, this memory of him.

He burst in, picked her up and swung her around. "Mom, thank God you're okay. It did work then. I saved you after all!" He released her and they stood eye to eye.

"What the hell is wrong with you?" she said, shoving him away. "What are you trying to pull? What's your real name?"

"I'm not trying to pull anything," he said sincerely. He shut the door.

Barry tottered over, the rubber tip of his cane thumping on the floor.

"Did you tell her? About me?" the young man asked.

Barry nodded. "She said it's not true. Can't be true. You're just a con taking money from an old man, aren't you?"

Danny walked into the living room and picked up a picture of Barry and Della.

"Where I came from, *you* were in this picture, Mom. And I was too. We were a family once." He set the picture down sadly. "Della was just his assistant."

Joyce stomped toward Danny, making sure to block Barry from making contact. "You're crazy and you're messing with an old man with an impaired memory. Don't you have any shame?"

"But you're my mother. Maybe not in the same legal way but you're still my mother. It played out the same no matter how the characters shifted around."

Barry stood next to her now. He shrugged to Danny. *Damn it, he believes this shyster.*

"I never had any children. Ever," she said. "Barry, call the cops."

He didn't move. Just watched Danny and her in their battle.

"Are you sure?"

"Of course I'm sure. What the hell kind of question is that?"

The man softened. "Did you give up a baby for adoption? You were pregnant; I know that much."

Barry glared at her shocked. "Is that true, Joyce?"

She'd never told anyone. Not her family or best friend, certainly not Barry. She'd retreated up to the mountains of New Hampshire when she couldn't hide the pregnancy anymore. Her stomach churned now and her legs refused to support her. She staggered to the couch.

She lowered her head between her knees to keep from getting sick. No one knew. No one! She'd delivered the baby and dropped him at a church. She hadn't given the nun her name.

She examined Danny when the nausea subsided. She recognized him now. He wasn't her son. He was the man she'd met in a bar all those years ago who told her that Barry would hurt her, was a cheater, would never leave his wife. "Get the hell away from him," he'd warned. Instead she got rid of the baby and ran back to Barry just in time to watch him cheat on Della with someone else.

"Who the hell are you!" she shouted in staccato words.

"I tried to save you from him and it worked. You're alive," the young man said.

"I don't know how you know anything but you need to leave. Now. I'll play along. Fine, you went back in time and saved me and now I'm here. Case closed. Go back to wherever you came from and we won't tell the police." She trembled and her words came out weak.

"You're still in Barry's life so you're in danger. I can't keep saving you," Danny said.

"What does that mean?" Barry asked, finally pulled from whatever shocked stupor he'd been in the last few minutes. "I'd never hurt Joyce."

Danny shook his head. "You really don't remember do you?"

"Remember what?" Barry asked.

Danny raised a notebook in the air. It looked like the kind in

Barry's stash. It said *NOW* on the cover. As he held it up, Joyce noticed *THEN* in all capital letters upside down on the back cover. *What the hell?*

"Maybe your accident took your memories away but that doesn't absolve you. I saved Joyce this time but what about the others you killed? You'll do it again. I'm here to stop you once and for all and I'm not leaving until you're destroyed."

Barry stood nose to nose with him. "Listen here, I am a kind man but I've about had it with you. What the hell kind of trouble are you trying to cause here? What are you accusing me of?"

Danny pulled away and walked to Joyce, who still sat on the couch feeling overwhelmed with emotions and not knowing what the hell to say or do. He knelt down in front of her and spoke quietly. "I don't care what the deal is with him in this time; people don't change. I'm begging you to get away from him while you still can."

He walked out the front door and slammed it.

Barry stepped to the couch and collapsed onto it.

"What the fuck was that all about?" Barry said. "That kid is certifiable. I'm calling the police." He reached for his phone.

"Okay but let's let this settle in a bit. I need to calm down first and so do you."

Barry leaned back. "What was he talking about? I'd never hurt you. And the others? Killing? What does that even mean?"

Joyce felt numb. Truly there was so much Barry didn't re-member. She wondered now how much was due to brain damage and how much he blocked out by choice or necessity. Joyce some-times envied Barry in his confusion. What she wouldn't give to forget some of the heartbreak and emotional pain she'd experi-enced.

If they waited long enough to call the police, Barry would forget most of this crazy man's ramblings. He wasn't Danny; that was for damn sure. Danny drowned. And he couldn't have been the man who told her to leave Barry because he'd be twenty-six years older now. Still, he knew about her baby and that was a secret she planned to keep. Barry's eyes showed pity and disappointment a few minutes ago. No, she would never admit it.

"Let's have our coffee and Cinnabons and let this all sink in. Then we'll call the police and get a restraining order," Joyce instructed.

Barry seemed relieved she was taking charge.

She opened her bag and pulled out index cards and colored pens. "Let's brainstorm. It'll make your mind stronger and if we get lucky we'll get a story out of you." She smiled at him and he grinned back. She could tell by the way his shoulders had relaxed that he was already forgetting how horrible everything was mere moments ago.

She handed him a red pen. "Go ahead. Write five items on that card that remind you of a farm."

Joyce drank and calmed down as well. Her secret was still safe.

- 2 -

Barry stared at the hourglass paperweight on the policeman's desk. The sand rested at the bottom. A symbol that meant his time was up? All he need do was to flip it and time would start again. He puzzled about its correlation to the Rainbox. He reached out and turned it over but the sand didn't move. *Time stopped.* He nervously moved his gaze to Joyce and the policeman who were still talking. *No, time moves on but this is an omen, surely.*

"Barry, tell him the story. Tell him about the man in your house," Joyce prodded.

The cop tapped the glass on the hourglass and the sand flowed, grain by grain. "Sometimes you have to help time along," he said.

Barry got the déjà vu feeling again. "Is that a quote from my book?" he asked.

"Is what a quote from your book? I didn't say anything," the cop said.

"Barry," Joyce urged, "tell him about your visitor."

They'd been here two hours already. A half hour to wait and fill out paperwork then the rest of the time with Joyce relaying a story he remembered only as random vignettes because she didn't let him write in his journal. She kept playing those damn brain games instead, filling his head with new data which saved over what he wanted to keep. She did it on purpose. He wondered why.

"Mr. Ford, we need your statement," Detective Gagnon said. He was an old grouch with a cleft pallet.

Barry began to speak but held his tongue. What to say? Should he parrot what Joyce had reported? What if Danny really was Danny and it all got mixed up somehow? What if Danny *was* his son and went back and everything had been different? He smiled as he imagined the wonder of it. What if he subconsciously wrote *The Rainbox* from a memory from his *real* life?

"Barry!" Joyce shouted, nudging his shoulder.

"I can't be sure," Barry said. He couldn't say with any certainty that Joyce's chain of events was accurate. His mind was muddy after all. And the glimmer of hope he had that this current life was just a bad copy of a real one— "I'm afraid I just don't recall."

"Do you want a protective order or not?" Detective Gagnon asked. He was understandably miffed that they'd wasted his time but Barry could live with that.

"He does," Joyce said.

"I do not," Barry asserted. He shot her a warning. He let her get away with a lot but not this time. She wasn't going to ruin his one chance. He did recall one thing Danny said. That he was here to set things right. Whatever that meant, he'd give him the chance. "We're sorry to have wasted your time."

"You can't listen to him, Detective. He's not mentally well. Everyone knows that. Barry has brain damage from the accident. For his own protection, he needs a restraining order."

Barry stood up and put his hand out for the cop to shake. "I have my faculties about me enough to know when I'm being manipulated." He nodded his chin toward Joyce. "You're going to have to trust me on that."

Detective Gagnon rose and shook his hand. "Of course."

"Again, we're sorry to have wasted your time," Barry said.

He turned to Joyce. "I'll see myself home."

She stood, shocked that he didn't bend to her will.

He grabbed his coat and cane and walked out the front door of the police station. He grinned as he made his way to the row of taxis on the next city street. *God it's cold.*

And then he utterly forgot why he was there.

A taxi driver rolled his window down. "You need a ride?" *Mr. Blue Sky* played from the inside of the car. Not blaring, just loud enough for Barry to make out.

"I don't know," he said, suddenly frightened.

"Barry?" a young voice called from the distance.

He glanced down the street toward the sound and saw a young boy standing under a streetlight.

"Danny?" he said under his breath. Couldn't be him, he thought. He'd be all grown up now, like the other Danny. He banged his fist against his head. "No, Danny drowned. He's not there and he wasn't at my house and—"

"You want a ride, Mister?" the cabbie said again. He regarded the scruffy man in the yellow car. He turned back to the streetlight. *No one there.* Still the music played from the car, reminding him of Helen Brundige

A gentle hand touched his shoulder. *Joyce.* His mind pulled back together.

"Are you all right, Barry?"

"No." He pulled away. "No, I'm not. I just saw Danny. Just like he was the last time I saw him. Little, you know." He held his hand up yay high. "But it can't be can it?"

"No, Barry I'm sorry. It can't be." She took his hand in her own, in a soft leather glove. "Let me get you home okay? And we'll talk about this tomorrow. None of it matters. Just think of today like a bad dream."

"I guess we're all set. Thank you," he said to the cabbie. The man smiled and closed his window.

They walked to Joyce's car without speaking. His boots and her loafers crunched the rock salt on the cobblestone sidewalks. Cars drove by, their tires whooshing through the partial puddles from last night's freezing rain. Other than that, there was silence. And to Barry, that was a good thing.

- 3 -

Joyce pulled up to her garage and pressed the button on her remote to open it. As she did, Linda Dingus popped her head out from behind her back door. Linda was her neighbor, a nosey senior citizen who felt obligated to say hello, each and every damn time she heard Joyce's garage door opener signal her arrival.

She waved and Joyce waved back. As she pulled into her garage assuming the daily exchange was over, Linda stepped out and approached the car. She tapped Joyce's hood so she stopped, even though she would have preferred to speed ahead and hide.

She rolled the window down. Linda was still in her pink bathrobe and blue plastic curlers. Joyce rarely saw her in street clothes. "A man came by and dropped this off." She handed a note thought the window.

"Who was he?" Joyce asked as she took the piece of folded notebook paper.

"He didn't say, but he was a tall drink of water all right. He was looking for you because he said he thought someone named Della lived here before whatever that means. Isn't Della your boss' wife?"

"Used to be," Joyce said as she thought of Danny. It must have been him. Was he that messed up and insistent on his time travel delusion that he actually thought the players merely switched places in different dimensions? *What a weirdo.*

"I told him I didn't know Della but that you had always lived here." Then I let him into my place and he wrote you that note."

"Did you read it?"

"Oh no, of course not."

A lie surely but it didn't matter.

"Well thanks. I have to go in and feed Minx."

Without waiting for a reply, Joyce rolled her window up and retreated into the garage, waiting for the door to close before emerging from her car.

Once inside her house, she set down her purse, hung her coat, and turned the lights on. Minx, her elderly black cat, ran toward her, his stomach swaying back and forth. He purred as he rubbed against her leg.

Still holding the paper in one hand, she lifted Minx with the other.

He meowed, anxious for his dinner.

The note was folded over. White lined notebook paper with dog-eared edges. The outside said only *JOYCE* in all capital letters. *MEOW.*

Joyce set the cat down, hurriedly opened a can of cat food and forked it into his dish. The cat rushed to it and began eating.

She took the note and the spare pair of reading glasses from the side table, and sat on her couch. She beheld the wonders of the room as she did nightly, admired her surroundings. There was little in the room that did not somehow portray Barry. Framed copies of book and magazine covers filled a whole wall in her living room, symmetrical and ordered, a giant grid of his accomplishments. The opposite wall was littered with photographs of the two of them together, a stark white wall and dozens of black frames that seemed to be haphazardly arranged. When she squinted her eyes and made them blurry though the placement of the pictures revealed a silhouette of Barry's face. A copy of that shadow portrait rested on her end table, the original a much smaller scale. No one knew that but her and no one ever would. She enjoyed being surrounded by him.

She slept with a sweatshirt she'd stolen from his home years ago and nobody would ever find that out either. No harm, no foul. Being enveloped by images of him completed her. That said, this interloper was trying to rattle that solace and she needed to get to the bottom of what he wanted.

She turned the switch for the side lamp and opened the paper. The ink was blue and the words printed in messy penmanship.

I know you think I'm scamming Barry but I'm not. I'm not after his money. I just need to set things right this time. Go see Fred Brundige and he'll help you. I can't do it alone and I can't keep saving you. Fred Brundige in Bradfield. I know you know who he is but you don't know the whole story. Be careful.

Fred Brundige. Little Danny's father, the boy who drowned that night after his mother fell down the stairs. She didn't know Fred well, but felt for him. Barry's affair with Fred's wife Helen surely ripped him apart. And his wife's dying the way she did, and then his son . . . *The poor man.*

Barry getting out of that mess was better for him, even if he didn't think so at the time. Della would have made his life hell if he'd asked for a divorce. She felt terrible for even thinking such thoughts, but that tragedy had saved Barry from what would have been the biggest mistake of his life. And what did Barry know about love? Joyce had worked as his assistant since she was nineteen and she'd seen him go through women like she went through Cadbury Cream Eggs in March and April.

Minx jumped up on her lap but she pushed him down.

She'd spent the better part of her life protecting Barry from himself, and if continuing to do so meant playing along with this mystery man and going to see Fred Brundige, so be it. She wished Barry had gone through with the restraining order, but hopefully Danny wouldn't show up again. If he did, she'd find a way to file it on Barry's behalf.

Barry didn't seem to remember much of Danny's performance this morning so her secret was still safe.

She dialed her phone.

"Hello?" Barry said.

"Hi. Are you all tucked in?" she asked.

"Yup, watching Nero Wolfe. I've got one more DVD to get through then I'm moving to the X-Files. I need to break open the set you got me for Christmas."

"How are you feeling?"

"I'm okay now."

"Did you complete your Sodoku puzzles?"

"Yup. Sure did. I think I'm getting better at them."

"That's great to hear. I won't keep you. Have a good night. I'll call you tomorrow."

"You too."

Joyce hung up and walked to her freezer. It was a rough day and she needed to break out the rations. She moved aside the Smart Ones meals and pulled out her second to last four pack of frozen Cadbury eggs. She pulled only one from the carton and stuffed the rest behind the diet food. She had another fifteen pounds to lose but one egg was better than a half a bottle of wine. Oh hell, she thought. This was a two-egg night. She moved the Smart Ones aside again, grabbed another egg and shut the freezer before she got herself into even more of a fix.

- 4 -

Barry stood in front of the row of taxis by the police station. He was in his pajamas and overcoat. He felt guilty lying to Joyce, saying he was home and tucked in, but she'd worry. Might try to have him committed.

He stared at the streetlight. "I know you were there, Danny. Please come back," he said.

"Mr. Ford," Jerry said, "It's been a half hour. I don't think whoever you're waiting for is coming."

"Maybe he's there and I can't see him." Barry stood glued to his spot, blinking only when his eyes grew too dry and he couldn't resist. Jerry begrudgingly drove him here and promised not to tell Joyce. Jerry was a good guy who always had his back. Even if Barry's mind slipped again, his driver would get him home safe.

"It's too cold out tonight. Come on and get in, Mr. Ford. We can try again tomorrow."

He blinked his eyes and rubbed them. "I guess you're right. It was probably just my imagination. Sometimes I can't tell the difference."

Barry opened the door and crawled into the warm car, with

the soothing blue mood lights on the doors and dome, and the thick soft fabric of the seat. "Can you play *We've Only Just Begun* for me?"

"Of course, sir."

Jerry fiddled with his iPod and set Barry's wedding song to play on repeat. As they drove back to Barry's brownstone he luxuriated in the memory of his first dance with Della as husband and wife. It was a sappy overused love song but it brought him peace. Better to set his mind to the solid memories, the acceptable and proper ones no one could fault him for.

He dozed off in the car smelling Della's perfume and feeling the stiff white lace of her gown against his fingertips.

THREE

- 1 -

Joyce maneuvered down the long wooded road to Fred Brundige's lake house. Her Mini Cooper was too low to the ground to drive faster than a crawl, and each bump in the dirt road thudded the underside of the car. She finally managed her way to the old custom log cabin. The grass was as high as the windows, and most of the panes were broken.

There were no flat marks in the grass, and the driveway proper was covered with weeds. She stopped the car and stepped out.

"No one lives here," she said. "He's left."

She walked toward the house, unafraid because the bigger danger would have been if Fred *was* there, if he brought up that day all over again. If she saw the face of the man that Barry had destroyed with his philandering.

Joyce peeked in the window. The place was empty. She tried the door. It was unlocked but a vacant house wouldn't give her any clues so there was no point in entering. Plus, was there even a mystery except for some nutty kid who told her to come here? No.

She turned toward the road from where she'd come. She re-

membered this same porch, when it was decorated with a basket
of gourds and a flag of a grimacing pumpkin. There had been
white wicker chairs with green gingham fabric. She had sat waiting for Fred to come out with her cider. It was mid-October and
cold at night but afternoons were pleasant. High 60's that day and
the fresh crisp air was a tonic. They were going to talk, he said.
He wanted to know once and for all what the hell was going on
with Helen and Barry. Was Helen really in love with him? Was
she seriously considering leaving him for Barry, and taking their
son with her? What about Barry's wife, he'd asked on the phone
that very morning. What did *she* think of all this?

Joyce had sat on this same porch mulling over the answers she
would give. Crafting replies that would portray Barry as a good
stand up man, who had done nothing wrong except fall in love
with a married woman. Barry and Helen approached, the car tires
swooshing over the pine-needled carpet of the dirt road. As Joyce
sat, watching them arrive on cue for what was to be a grand con-
frontation of lover to husband, she knew Barry wasn't in love. He
was using Helen like he used all women, and if this played out
his career as a much-loved science fiction writer with his block-
buster first novel would be over. Sure he'd still sell books but his
loving family man reputation, which was much of the appeal of
his image so said his agent, would be out the window.

And so she sat in the wicker chair on the warm fall day
dreading the next few hours . . .

Later, Helen lay sprawled at the base of the stairs. A tragic accident. All the king's men and all the king's horsemen couldn't . . .

Then Danny Brundige drowned in the lake off to the right.

She never had to have the talk with Fred.

Barry returned to Della with his tail between his legs. She
forgave him and they never spoke of it again, so said Della. Barry
never admitted it to Joyce, but she knew he was relieved.

Fred didn't fare so well from what she heard, but Barry walked
away unblamed and unscathed and that's all that really mattered.

She shook off the memory as she stood now on the sagging
neglected porch. She peeked to the lake. Still and placid, as if a

little boy hadn't lost his life just below the surface.

Whoever this adult Danny character really was, his asking her to see Fred Brundige was suspect. He was obviously trying to blackmail Barry about the long-dead affair, using Joyce to do his dirty work. Rubbing her face in the crime scene. Using her to dig up the dirt of the past and then smooth it all back out again. She didn't like it, one bit, but she'd track down Fred's new address. She assumed he was the one behind all this, that he'd sent "Danny" to them to cause trouble. Fine, Joyce had always been Barry's clean up crew.

Tomorrow she would see Fred, wherever he lived now, and they'd have a little talk. She'd write a check, and then life would go back to normal.

- 2 -

Barry stood in the mirror of his master bathroom. He opened his lips wide to check for spinach between his teeth. He combed his thick brown hair and felt his chin to make sure he'd not missed a spot shaving. He traced his finger along the scar that ran down his right cheek. The original gash spread from his scalp to under his chin but the plastic surgeons did a good job minimizing the monstrous effects of the crash. Now when he smiled he resembled Harrison Ford after a street fight. He laughed. Right. He was a book geek who only knew how to *write* about adventure. Still, the ladies didn't exactly turn away when they saw him. He'd not acted on any flirtations since the accident, except for that one time with Amy, but he did appreciate their letting him know he was a still a commodity in the 40's singles scene. He reflected for a moment. *50's scene.* He'd turned fifty last month.

The doorbell rang. He straightened his tie and walked from the room to the foyer.

He opened it to find Joyce before him. "You're beautiful," he exclaimed. He hadn't viewed Joyce in a sexual light since that affair when she was barely out of high school. But tonight she'd really done herself up, in high black heels, black nylons, a short leather skirt. He glanced up and saw the face of his old buddy Joyce. His attraction waned.

"Thank you. It's nice to see you all dressed up too." She entered his home. "You want to know the surprise now or later?"

"You can tell me when we get to Foxwoods. I like surprises. Any show is a good show."

"Seeing a show after your first signing of a new book is tradition but you're really going to love this one. I just got the tickets today. The plans I had for us initially wouldn't have been nearly as memorable."

"Fine, tell me." She'd taken him and Della to fantastic performances in the past and he was curious.

"Ian Rushmore, Master of Illusion." She pulled gold tickets from her purse and held them out for him to see.

"What are these, Wonka tickets?" he said, trying not to react to the sledgehammer of shock he felt.

"It's supposed to be terrific. He was from Maine. A local magician from way back."

"Was he?" Barry asked. Joyce could be a real bitch when it came to his indiscretions. It's not like he cheated on *her* but she seemed to find it amusing to keep throwing his past back in his face, in an oh-so-innocent way. Joyce knew there was no proof he'd even *met* Monica Rushmore much less—

"He had a little shop by the arcade in Old Orchard Beach. And a daughter too, but she died young."

"Huh. I'm sorry. My mind is, you know, cloudy. I don't remember anything about Maine. About being there. No, wait. Funnel cake. I remember funnel cake with powdered sugar."

Joyce's face dropped as if he'd ruined her night.

"But I love magic shows and this will be a fun night out." He grinned.

"Right," she said, placing the tickets back in her purse.

"I'll be right back."

Barry walked into his bedroom and shut the door. He sat on the bed and tried to stave off the flashback of Monica from Maine, the girl who'd flirted with him even while Della stood beside him in line for funnel cake. Joyce had been with them too and had commented about *that little tramp*. Della had laughed it off. Good old Della.

Later he'd pretended to go out for beer and had instead met the girl in her father's closed and darkened magic shop. She unlocked the door and took his hand, mischief in her eyes. He was in his twenties and she said she was eighteen. He didn't ask for ID. The only light in the store was a flashing blue neon sign from the tattoo parlor across the street. She was short with green eyes, red hair, and fresh young tits that with only a little coaxing poured out of her powder blue V-neck t-shirt. Her nipples were so light he couldn't see where they started and stopped until he ran his eager fingers over them and felt the texture and the hardness of their outline.

She had soft shiny lips that tasted like her clear cherry lip gloss. She lured him into the backroom of her father's shop, to a set prop called the Time Travel Box. It was a plywood box with sea glass and seaweed painted on the out and inside, done by an amateur surely. It screamed junior high school stage set. "It's a trick where Dad pretends people travel to another time and back again," she said through staggered breaths as he slipped up her skirt, ripped her underwear away, and propped her up against the inside of the box.

Monica was so little and skinny, not like Della who was 5' 10" with man hands. As he fucked her he wished he could have this every day. A pliable firm little body with skinny legs that wrapped around his waist. "God, you're so tight," he said, caught up in the feel and smell of her, of her delicate cherry flavored tongue darting into his mouth.

"Wrap this around my throat," she said.

"What?" The request caught him off guard, pulled him from his passion. "What did you say?"

She held up a white scarf, the kind a magician used to distract his audience, to drape over a hat or bird cage. He took it from her. It was smooth and cold. "Tie it around my neck. It's okay, it just makes it better." She smiled in a way that showed him she was not the innocent girl he thought.

He had no experience with whatever this was she wanted but he was willing to try. He draped it around her neck, bunched it up in back. Just a little. He didn't want to hurt her. She writhed with excitement. "Tighter," she said. "Make the scarf tighter!"

"Ssh," he whispered. He clenched his fist around the bunched fabric and twisted. She smiled and her eyes fluttered in ecstasy.

He closed his eyes entirely, and thrust deep and fast, blocked out all sights and sounds except his own pleasure.

After he came, he focused on her again, and gasped. Her face was dark pink. She wasn't breathing. *Oh my God!* He loosened the scarf and let it fall to the floor. "Monica, wake up. Come on, wake up!" He shook her, slapped her face. Nothing. He tried to take her pulse but his own heart was beating so hard he couldn't tell if the beat in her wrist was his own or hers. Drool ran down her slack cherry-flavored mouth.

"Fuck," he said. He watched her, sure any second she would take a breath. She didn't. Finally he lowered her skirt, and set her down gently into the corner of the Time Travel Box. He pulled up his pants, zipped them, and shoved the scarf in his pocket.

"I wish this box was real. That I could return to a time before this ever happened." He kissed her forehead and bolted out of the dark store and back to the cottage he'd rented.

He waited for the police to come to arrest him, assuming someone had seen them together. But no one did. The story of her rape and murder was all over the news the next day. She'd been eighteen, thank God, as if that softened the level of his crime. Found dead in her father's magic shop.

"Barry, there's that slut that was flirting with you," Della said on seeing the newscast. "I guess she must have flirted with the wrong man after you and he took her up on it. Poor little girl. Can you imagine? Her family must be crushed."

Joyce was silent on the subject then. She couldn't have suspected, but seeing her gloating with these show tickets now, who knew?

Barry reached to his bedside stand, and popped out the drawer. He retrieved the scarf that hid on the floor under the drawer.

Guilt flooded him, just as strong as the night it happened. He hated himself for what happened that night, hated Joyce more for torturing him with it. He wished sometimes his long term memories had been damaged in the accident but this one held fast, down to every detail.

"I just need a few more minutes," he called down to Joyce.

He folded the scarf, caressed it with love. "I'm so sorry, Monica." Carefully he placed it back under his drawer. Barry wiped his eyes and headed out to begin an evening of denial.

- 3 -

Danny watched Joyce and Barry leave the brownstone in her Mini Cooper. They were dressed up which gave him at least two hours by his estimation. No one dressed like that hallo for a trip to the mall or a quick dinner at Chili's. He stepped from behind the bus stop and walked across the street to Barry's place. He marched up the steps and opened the door with the spare key he'd pilfered Sunday night from the basket in the kitchen. He knew Barry's habits, and if nothing else there was something refreshing in the predictability of humans. No matter how you shook things up, with memory loss or death, people retreated to what they knew, repeated patterns ingrained in them without ever realizing the danger that put them in.

Once in, he shut the door behind him and slid the deadbolt. The lights had been left on. He removed his shoes. Barry was a neat freak and any outside prints on his clean floor would be suspect.

Danny opened the cabinet by the couch. Barry's camera was in a case with the cords and charger. More predictability.

He didn't have a specific plan, just wanted to explore. Wanted to find something that proved Barry was responsible for the deaths of at least three women over the years. Not including Helen's death and his drowning.

From his reading on the topic, he knew serial killers kept trophies. But they could be anywhere in this house. And who was to say Barry fit that profile? Maybe he only killed to get out of a jam. Maybe for him it wasn't about the thrill of murder but about avoiding the repercussions of screwing around. Joyce would contact Fred, and together they could handle this investigation from the police end. But Danny needed to get started, find irrefutable proof for the police and for himself.

He walked to Barry's bedroom and through the door that held the Rainbox. He turned the lights and couldn't help but smile at the craftsmanship. Magical. No doubt about that. In his first life he'd spent hours in here at a time, wishing away the present.

For every minute he was in this time, his regretful wish was granted a little more. His old life fell away from him. These new memories devoured his own no matter how hard he tried to hold on.

His first life was now represented by little more than the notes in his journal, scribblings that could as easily have been fiction penned by a lunatic.

I am Danny Brundige. Always was.

As he ran his fingers on the cool smooth lighted stones, he reminisced about being Danny Brundige, raised by Helen and Fred. Barry had taken him here, to this exact house to see the Rainbox. The book had been out a several months, and Della went to visit her sister in Cleveland. Barry drove Helen and Danny to his place.

The Brundiges lived on the rural side of Bradfield, a town with areas so remote your neighbors couldn't hear you if you screamed. He'd learned that the hard way. Being in the city was a lot more exciting, he'd thought at the time. With the subways and street performers, and Barry's house that was in a row of connected houses. When Barry revealed the replica of the book-inspired Rainbox, Danny was blown away. He touched all the smooth stones and asked Barry if it worked.

"Well, son, what do you think?"

Danny nodded. "I think if we wish hard enough, it'll work. Just like in the book."

Danny was about the proudest kid in sixth grade that fall. He couldn't tell anyone his mom was banging Barry Ford. Mom forbade it, said it would paint her as sleazy. Dad was a cop with a temper and Mom said it wouldn't bode well for anyone to find out until the time was right. But they'd had a thing going for a long time and Barry told Danny that eventually they'd be together, a family. He'd named the main character in his book Danny to prove he meant business.

The kids in school thought it was pretty awesome that Danny was famous.

Yeah, it was a really great year until it all tuned to shit.

He studied the glowing stones in the Rainbox now. "What am I supposed to do?" He took pictures with Barry's camera. He'd need these to brief his partner.

Danny walked through the rest of Barry's bedroom but found nothing of interest. All of Della's clothes were still in her closet, and half of the bureau drawers contained her items. It had been two years since her death and Danny had to give Barry credit for keeping her alive the best he could.

In Barry's office he found a wooden box containing a large pile of cash. He pocketed all of it. Digging through drawers yielded nothing incriminating. He found a stack of medical records that explained Barry's motorcycle accident had nearly killed him but he'd survived with a bum leg and short-term memory issues.

Under a pile of writing contracts Danny found a framed photo resting face down. He flipped it over and was shocked to find it was of Barry and him together. He was holding a fishing pole. Barry had his arm around him. Danny pulled the picture from the frame and read the back. "My little buddy and I fishing. Helen took the photo."

Danny stared at the picture. It was taken when the affair had first started. Dad was working a lot of hours on the force. He was undercover so he'd be gone weeks and sometimes months at a time. He'd sneak a call home when he could but told Danny it was really important that he did his work so he could stop the bad guys. That picture was taken on Father's Day, when Dad couldn't get away or call. He was undercover pretending to be a drug dealer named Angel.

Dad lived to work undercover and become someone else. His whole life was his job.

Barry liked hanging with Danny and his mom more than anything, so Danny with his simple child's logic liked him better.

It wasn't until later he learned that Barry didn't love them at all.

He snapped a picture of the photo and then put it back in the frame. He left the room and placed it on the mantle in the living room.

"There, that ought to fuck with your head," he said.

A shelf in the living room housed copies of all the books Barry had written, including magazines and anthologies in which his stories appeared. Danny knew *The Rainbox* story by heart but was curious to see if things had changed in the book. If there had been a rewrite since he'd last seen it.

He opened the copy from Barry's shelf and moved to the end pages. He clenched his fingers in anger when he read the last few paragraphs.

And so for all of Donald's trying, dashing through time again and again, to save his stepson from drowning, he had succeeded. But to what end? Donald wondered for the millionth time if he had been wrong to tamper with God's plan, to change fate and to save Danny.

"All Rise," the bailiff said. Donald wore his expensive court suit; Danny wore the prison issued orange jumpsuit, and shackles on his hands and feet. They rose along with the attorneys, the families of the victims, and the press. All waiting for the verdict.

"On the first count of murder in the first degree, and on the kidnapping of Alison Olsen what say you?" the pigeon-faced old judge asked.

"Guilty," the foreman said.

And on went the readings of the verdicts, all told convicting Danny of the kidnapping and murder of five women. Donald looked at his son. "I'm sorry," he said. But it would change nothing.

Donald could not go back again and make things right. He had smashed the Rainbox to keep Danny alive this time, keep him from his repeated fate of drowning in childhood. He had succeeded where God had failed but there was no usurping God. Donald knew that now, and cursed the day he had first stumbled upon a piece of sea glass and a little boy who'd dreamt of magic.

Danny closed the book. "I was your *son* in the first draft.

None of this happened in the real book!" There was no one to hear him, but it didn't matter.

He sat down hard on the closest chair. Memories of his two pasts mingled and separated and merged again. He flipped open his notebook to the THEN side. "Rainbox was a book about a man who saves his son. He died in a sledding accident, not drowning."

Danny suddenly grew dizzy and his vision blurred. When he regained his composure he read the top of the page in his journal. "What the fuck is this? No, it was always his stepson. He wrote the book for me. We were going to be a family. The character died by drowning." He rubbed his eyes and looked again but still the writing showed mysterious untrue arguments about the book's contents. "The book is the same as it's always been and I'm losing my fucking mind."

He pulled the piece of red sea glass from his pocket and held it tightly.

God help me. Please.

He flipped back to some of the earlier writings, when he'd first arrived.

Barry killed Joyce-Mom because she found out about the murders. I told her. Then I ran back in time to convince her to run away from him before it was too late, before I was born. And when I came back he was alive, and I was dead.

He shook his head. *No. Joyce isn't dead and I'm here. If I died, I wouldn't be here now. What the hell is wrong with me?*

He looked up to the ceiling. "There must have been truth to this or I wouldn't have written it. God, help me stop him. Why do you keep punishing the wrong people?"

God didn't answer.

"I have to trust my notes, there's a reason I wrote them and a purpose for my being here, alive."

He took a pen from his pocket and opened *The Rainbox* book again. At the end of the last page he wrote *–This is NOT how it ends.* He circled the section several times, and then took a picture of it.

He checked his watch, one he'd stolen from Barry's desk. Gold with an inscription that said, *So you always know what time you're in.* Another quote from the book.

Barry and Joyce could return any minute. He left the book on the coffee table with the TV remote as a bookmark. He popped the memory card from the camera then put it back under the cabinet.

Danny let himself out and ventured into the night.

- 4 -

"You were here the other night right?" Bonnie said. "I saw you. At Barry Ford's signing."

Danny glanced from the book he was reading to see the skinny girl. He didn't recognize her but he'd had tunnel vision that night, was focused only on one person. "Yeah, I was a little upset huh?" he said.

"You come here a lot?" she asked.

"This is only the second time," he said.

"It used to be a bank," she said. "Went under a bunch of years ago and finally a guy bought it. Quirky old guy but really nice."

She remained a good six feet away from him, friendly but tentative like an abused dog. "Do I know you?" He knew he couldn't possibly, yet there was a familiarity about her.

"I don't think so. I just felt bad for you, coming into the store that night right before closing time, dripping wet and angry."

"Disappointed and frustrated was more like it. I'd come a long way and hoped—I don't know, long story. I'm Danny."

"Bonnie." They nodded to each other. "So, you new in town?"

He laughed. "You might say that."

"Acting books, huh?" She moved closer. "You an actor?"

He shook his head. "No, buying these books for a kid. My nephew. He's working on landing a part, sort of, and needs some practice."

She pointed to a bulging bag from the Gap. "You getting him some clothes too? For his audition?"

He hesitated and then, "Yeah. He needed some stuff."

She studied the book titles he'd placed on the shelf sideways. "Think you can learn how to be somebody else from a book?"

"I don't know, but I won't be a very good teacher. This one

talks about emotions, and making yourself cry, or making yourself smile. Might be helpful."

Bonnie leaned against the bookshelf and twirled her hair.
Her coat was buttoned almost up to the top, to where a couple of
buttons were missing. Her lower half revealed high heels, torn
purple tights, and a cheap silver sequin skirt. He assumed that
she was a prostitute. Lost hope and emotional destruction decorated her as much as the costume she wore.

She sidled up closer. "You want to go somewhere?"

Sex was the last thing on his mind, the last thing he could
afford to get tangled up in. Honestly, the last thing he could afford
financially either. Though her services probably wouldn't fetch
a high price tag as those things went, all he needed was an STD
or to find out the hard way she was a cop.

"I'm good," he smiled at her. No need to be a jerk about it.

There were two chairs at the end of the acting section. She
walked to one and sat down, then stared off into space. Her eyes
welled up with tears. Danny faced away, tried to go back to his
interest in the book he'd pulled from the choices.

But he could feel her sadness from here.

He selected two books on childhood acting and walked to
the chair beside hers. "Mind if I sit here?"

She smiled, wiped her eyes. "No, go ahead."

"You okay?" he asked.

"Never learned much from books. Got my experience hands on.
Interning. I'm really good at pretending to be happy. I've got it down pat."
She tried to sound enthusiastic but her words were draped in pain.

"And pretending to cry?" he asked with cynicism.

"No." Bonnie sighed. "That's just how it is when I'm caught
off guard. Sad is easy. Happy took practice."

Their eyes met and held, and her sorrow coursed through
him like acid in his veins.

"You do brave pretty well too," he said.

"I'm a fucking warrior." She laughed. "No pun intended."

"You hungry?" he asked. "I mean if you're on a break, maybe we could get some food."

"I'm on a break till my boss says I'm not."

"Come on. I know a place."

He paid for the books and walked her across the street to a 50's diner called Joe's. She shivered during the short stroll. It was especially cold for mid-October.

When they arrived and she removed her coat, he gasped. She was skeletal, and what he could see of her arms showed track marks or cutting scars or failed suicide razor drags. The fabric moved up her arm for only a second before she slid it back down, covering whatever she'd done to herself.

Her collarbones were like coat hangers under the flimsy black mesh top she wore. A tattoo across her chest read HOPE in large black letters just above the line of her black lace bra.

"A fucking joke, right?" she said when she saw him staring at the mocking message across her front. "Got that once when I was strung out on crack. Got the tattoo then jumped in the harbor. In December."

"You drowned?" What were the chances?

"Well no. I'm here. Some fucking Good Samaritan—literally, he was part of the group, the Samaritans, saw me and jumped and fished me out. He dragged me to a rock then *he* drowned. So I have *that* to deal with. His death hanging over my head."

Jesus.

"Why did you do it?"

"Why do you think? Why does anyone ever do it? I was tired of life. Tired of *acting.*"

A waitress came by, probably the same age as Bonnie but round, healthy. Trendy eye glasses, a genuine smile. "What can I get ya?"

Danny and Bonnie both picked up their menus.

"I'll have the meatloaf with mashed potatoes and a chocolate malt. And can I get an order to go too?" Danny asked.

"Sure," the waitress said, her pencil poised above the green lined pad.

"A cheeseburger, no onions, no tomatoes, and fries. Large. And a chocolate malt to go too," he continued.

"You're really hungry," Bonnie said.

He gestured to the books and the bag of clothes. "For my nephew. He's back at the hotel."

"Oh." She scanned the menu items. She twirled her hair, a nervous tic. "Can I have the chicken pie? No peas though. Hate peas. Hate, hate, hate peas."

Danny knew then who she was.

"And can I get a vanilla shake?" she asked, as if for permission.

"Sure thing," the waitress said.

"You'll want to squirt a little cherry syrup in there for her too," Danny said. The waitress scribbled that and walked off.

"How did you know I like cherry syrup in my vanilla shakes?"

He didn't answer, only smiled.

Her face fell then and tears flooded down her cheeks. "No, you're not my Danny. He died."

He held her trembling dry little bird hand. "Did I?"

Her cell phone chimed. She read a text. "I'm sorry, I have to go."

"Bonnie, please. Stay."

She stood and donned her long worn coat. "You're not real. This is just the drugs. I've seen you before, Danny Brundige. Not this real and solid but I've seen you. That don't mean you're back from the dead."

"Please. Stay. Call me whatever you want. Call me Ed. Bobby. Whatever you want. I'm just a nice guy buying you dinner, no strings."

"There are always strings. Don't you know that? Whatever you do, something else gets undone. It's how it's always been."

She stood at the foot of the wooden booth. "It sure was good seeing you again even if you are just a made up guardian angel."

Bonnie ran outside to a waiting car and an impatient pimp.

He signaled the waiter to cancel Bonnie's order. *Whatever you do, something else gets undone.* Another line from Barry's book. She'd read it too. Of course she had. She'd been his neighbor and best friend in the world when they were young. Her parents and his used to hang out, come by for drinks. One summer they shared the cost of a stand up pool but it collapsed and broke halfway through the summer. They had some wonderful times together. She was a sweet, bright, damn pretty little girl. A year younger than he was.

When Mom started seeing Barry, the Blakes pulled away. Bonnie said her mother said Danny's mom was a slut. It hurt him, deeply. There was more to the story, he wanted to say. Dad was never around, and he drank a lot, and Barry was really nice. And he was going to marry Mom. But instead of saying all that, the last time he saw Bonnie, he'd shoved her down and told her to go to hell.

And she had.

Shit.

- 5 -

Danny walked into the hotel room and found his young charge sitting on the bed reading a script handwritten on notebook paper. "Sorry I was gone so long. Ran into someone."

"That's okay," the boy said. "Did you bring food?"

"Yeah, come over to the table."

The boy joined Danny and began to devour his dinner.

"Thanks for this."

"I got you some acting books. You think you can act out the script I wrote for you?"

The boy nodded. "And if I do what it says I can go home, right?"

"You got it."

"In movies sometimes kidnappers promise that, but then they say 'You've seen my face, now I'll have to kill you.' Are you gonna do that?" He stopped chewing as he awaited the answer.

"Of course not. I haven't hurt you or tied you up or anything right?"

"Right."

"You can leave whenever you want," Danny said gesturing toward the door. "You can walk right out and scream for the police."

"No," the boy said, both startled and resolved to his fate. "I don't have anywhere safe to go. I *have* to stay with you," he said.

"Just a little longer."

"Once we hurt Barry enough?"

Danny sat on the adjoining bed. "It's not about hurting Barry, it's about justice. I wish none of this had happened and you were home with your parents. But Barry did things and he can't go on doing them. We're the only ones who can break the cycle."

The boy shrugged. "I just want to go home so I'll say and do whatever you want."

"Listen, I mean it. I'm really not going to hurt you, but I can't pull this off without you."

"Cuz I look like you?"

"Yeah, cuz you look like me," Danny said.

He rifled through the Rainbox pictures he'd printed at CVS on the way home, and then spread them out on the boy's bed. "You need to memorize all these, down to the tiniest detail."

The boy sat on his bed and studied them. "Okay."

"If someone quizzes you, you'll have to be able to describe the Rainbox and anything else in these pictures."

"I know. I will." The boy spoke in monotone. Danny grasped that the boy was in emotional shock. It sucked he was putting the kid through this but without his help there was no other way to see this through to fruition.

"It's gonna be okay. Oh, got you some clothes too, and shoes, in the bag over there."

"Thanks," he said quietly, always on the verge of tears. Danny couldn't blame him.

He felt like shit for nabbing the kid the way he did and keeping him here, but they had to bring Barry down.

- 6 -

Joyce pulled up in front of Barry's house. "There're no spots so jump out here and I'll park down the street."

"I'm a little tired. I'll just go in and call it a night. Thanks so much for the evening out. It was a great show," Barry said.

"Oh. Okay," Joyce said. "Is something wrong?" It was but

he'd yet to admit it. She knew damn well his memories prior to the accident were intact even if he was pleading disability. She'd gone to most of his doctors' and therapists' appointments with him for God's sake.

"No of course not but it's late. It's almost two. We're not as young as we used to be."

"Right. The show? You liked it? Didn't stir anything up for you?"

"I said I liked it, Joyce. What did you expect it to stir up?"

She put her car in park but kept it running. "You know damn well, Barry. You fucked that girl in Maine and killed her. I never told anyone but I'm on your side here. You need to be honest with me."

He shook his head. "She flirted with me at the funnel cake stand. That was it. You were there. I went home with you and Della. And then she was dead, on the TV."

"I followed you out when you said you were getting a beer. That girl lured you to her father's shop." Barry didn't respond, didn't even blink. "She didn't lock the door behind her and I walked in too. I heard what you did."

"Joyce, I don't remember anything about a magic shop or that girl except that she flirted with me at the funnel cake stand and then she was dead, just like I said. If you've questioned my innocence all these years, why didn't you ask me? Why wait and then buy me tickets to a show hoping for a big reveal and a confession for a crime I didn't commit?"

Joyce stared at him, incredulous. She knew he had fucked her. She'd been hiding behind the cabinet where the card tricks and flower dusters were stored, sobbing with every erotic moan that carried from the Time Travel Box. Until suddenly it was dead silent and Barry unknowingly ran past her, and to the safety of his foolish wife.

She'd never told a soul, had never brought Monica's death up to Barry, not once. But when this Danny guy showed up asking questions and sending her to Fred, she wanted Barry to know she'd kept his secret. She'd kept lots of secrets and covered for him and it was time he thanked her for it. *But it's not going to happen tonight.*

"Ok. I guess I was wrong," she said.

"I guess you were," he barked.

He stepped from the car, leaving Joyce alone. He'd never been so cruel to her. He'd been close, using her and tossing her away at nineteen, pregnant and in love, but he hadn't known about the baby. And since then she'd been his right hand. His confidant. A friend he said he valued far above Della even if she was the one he married. A horn beeped behind her so she sped away.

First thing tomorrow she'd find Fred Brundige and they'd have a little chat. Whatever Danny was up to—hell, maybe he was a cop trying to trick her into a collusion charge—she was not about to be blamed for Barry's sins.

- 7 -

Barry stood in his brownstone and watched Joyce's taillights in the distance.

Bitch. No sooner had the insult come to him though, he regretted it. Joyce had been his friend for years. Longer than anyone else. And hell, he *did* kill Monica. It was an accident but he was at fault, more so because he never confessed. He should have gone to the police, told them what happened. He probably could've gotten involuntary manslaughter if he had a good lawyer. A suspended sentence. Sure his marriage would have been over and probably his career before it even started, but he wouldn't have had to live with this guilt, this worry that one day the police would show up . . .

The way Joyce went about it? What did Joyce hope to gain by bringing him to the show? A confession? If she thought he did it anyway and had never turned him in—

He grabbed his notebook from the table by the door. Tonight would likely stick in his memory without writing it down or repeating it, or using his visual cues. The memory of Monica dead at his hands was omnipresent in his mind. But he did want to record what Joyce said, and why, and how she kept leaning into him at the theater, too close for comfort. He wanted to make sure all of *that bullshit behavior* made it to his long term memory, and at the very least, became a topic of discussion for Amy at their appointment next week.

"Chilly in here," he said as he moved into the living room. He flicked the gas fireplace on. "What the hell?"

The picture of Danny and him sat in the dead center of the mantle. He picked it up and held it close.

"Oh my Lord. It is you isn't it, Danny? It is you. You found a way."

He set the picture down and peered around the room. "Are you still here? Are you in the Rainbox?"

He shuffled to the room and opened the door to the Rainbox. The lights were already on. He entered "Are you in here, Danny? Are you in here? Can you hear me?"

No reply.

He shambled back to the living room to get his phone. Wait till Joyce heard this. She'd have to eat her words.

It was then he saw the copy of *The Rainbox*. He glanced to his shelf and saw a space where his copy had been. He opened it to the marked page and read the text.

He had succeeded where God had failed but there was no usurping God. Donald knew that now, and cursed the day he had first stumbled upon a piece of sea glass and a little boy who'd dreamt of magic.

The handwritten message next to it was the most disturbing. "This is NOT how it ends."

"How does it end then, Danny?"

He suddenly felt very afraid and alone. He'd killed Monica and told no one but what if there *were* others, as Danny implied. What if he was a killer and didn't remember? He needed to consult with Amy. She'd be able to explain it to him. Tell him if his old memories were becoming cloudy or if somehow chunks of his past were erased. Or if he was innocent and Danny's suggestions would eventually implant false memories.

He checked his watch. *Two-thirty in the morning. Too late to call Amy.* With no other option, he swallowed his anger and dialed Joyce.

"Hello?"

"Can you come over? Please? I'm going to call the police but can you please come over?"

"Of course. What happened?"

"Just come over."

He hung up.

He could be pissed later about her taking him to that performance and trying to force his hand. It would keep. Or maybe it wouldn't and that might be for the best.

He grabbed his notebook and pen and wrote down as much as he could remember about the evening, about what he'd found back at the house. Amy instructed him to write down the memories in the order of most recent. By the time he did, usually everything else from the few hours before was gone but sometimes, if he wrote quickly, he could remember a whole evening. At least long enough to write it, even if the next morning it seemed like a stranger had recorded the night.

As he scrawled the notes, the doorbell rang. He checked his watch. Twenty minutes had passed. He wrote, "Joyce arrived at 2:50 a.m."

He rose to answer it. "Joyce, thank you for coming." He walked her back to the living room. "Have a seat."

She sat in the chair she favored and he went to the couch. "What is it, Barry? What did you want? Are you all right?"

He glanced down at his notes. "Check the mantle. What do you see?"

She did, and flinched. "You took out the old picture of Danny."

He shook his head. "No, I don't think I did. There are no notes about it in here." He held up the notebook. "I would have written it down."

She walked to the picture, frowned, and set it face down.

"What'd you do that for?"

"You don't need to dredge up those memories, Barry. It's not healthy. Are you positive you're not the one who put the picture up there? A hundred percent? Because if you call the police and they find out you did it, it may show up in the papers and we'll be dealing with the tabloids all over again. You do remember what a hassle that was right?"

"Not really but I trust you on that."

She sat next to him on the couch.

"If you can't be sure—"

He consulted his notebook again, and then looked her square in the eye. "You know my handwriting."

"Yes. I've been deciphering your chicken scratch for years."

He opened *The Rainbox* to the last page and slid it toward her. "I didn't write that, did I? The handwritten part."

She read it and winced. "No. No you didn't."

He held his fingertips up. "It's fresh ink." The edges of his fingers were smudged black. Just a bit, but enough to prove it was not an old inscription.

"He was in the house tonight, Joyce. We need to call the police and get a restraining order. And if I forget, you show them the book and these notes."

"Are you going to back out again and insist he's Danny come back from death to reunite with you, popped from another dimension?"

"I don't know where he came from or who he is, only that he's angry with me and wants revenge. Or money. Or both. Part of me wants to see him and find out more, just in case it's real—but he wants to ruin me. You heard what he said about my killing people. *He* was the one in the book that was the serial killer, not me. Not me."

"None of this is real, Barry. He's spewing a lot of crazy talk and he's confusing your novel with his life. The man should be in a mental hospital. Maybe he escaped from one. But he's not Danny and that's all you need to know."

"It's crazy talk all right but he can cause trouble for me. A lot of trouble. I need him to stay away from me." He grabbed her arm. "Will you call for me? Please?"

Joyce nodded. "I'll take care of it."

Music to his ears. Those were the words she said time and time again that saved him, allowed him to move on with his life and his work.

She rose to call the police.

"I'm going to close my eyes for a few minutes. It's awfully late."

He reclined on the couch and put his feet up on a throw pillow. He shut his eyes and saw Helen, broken at the base of the stairs.

And Danny's sneaker by a still and cruel lake.

And Joyce telling him she would take care of it.

She'd driven him home to Della. He'd lost the love of his life and the son he always wanted, but no one ever pointed a finger at him.

"The police are here, Barry," Joyce said, shaking his shoulder. "Wake up."

Two uniformed men stood before him.

Shit, it's about the magic show, about Monica. Joyce told them. He offered his hands for cuffs to be slapped on his wrists. Joyce pulled his arm to straighten him out.

He readjusted on the couch.

"Do you recall what you found this evening?" the first cop asked. He was short and young.

"He keeps a notebook, and he showed me," Joyce said. She handed over the book.

"He came into my house when I wasn't home," Barry began. Dread ran through him, borne of panic of everyone finding out—

"Who came into your house?" the cop asked.

Barry deferred to Joyce. She spoke. "A man who has been hounding Barry. We first saw him at his book signing, Sunday night, then he came here that night."

"And the next morning," Barry said. "Monday morning he came and Joyce saw him that time." *I remember!* "He said he was a boy I used to know. A boy named Danny."

The policeman asked, "But it's not him?"

Barry shrugged. "I don't think it can be," he said.

"He died. Fifteen years ago that little boy died," Joyce said. "He's a con man tricking Barry. He gave the guy money. Five hundred dollars. Write that down. Five hundred dollars is a felony correct?"

The second policeman spoke, the one who until that point had done nothing but walk around and run his gloved fingers over surfaces in the house, as if that would help.

"It's not a felony unless he steals something. There's no law against accepting money. What was your relationship with this boy?" he asked Barry.

"The *boy* is dead!" Joyce slammed Barry's notebook on the table. "It can't be *that boy*. This man is a scammer." When she got angry she bunched her fists up. Barry used to think it was cute, spunky, but now he wished she'd just calm down. Not be so insistent on everything, all the fucking time.

The older man, Martinez, per his shiny nameplate, observed Barry for a moment before he spoke. "Before he died, what was your relationship to the boy?"

"My son. He said he was my son." Barry smiled, remembered Danny as his little boy. He recalled him as a toddler, and riding his first bicycle, and even as an infant when Della... No, that wasn't right. This is what Amy called suggestive memories. Things his mind invented based on what he thought had happened, or was supposed to remember. Della never *had* children. Danny wasn't his son despite what he'd alleged about time travel and the Rainbox and—

He corrected himself. "I dated his mother when he was a child and we were going to run off. I loved her very much. Very much." A tear came to his eye and he wiped it with the back of his hand. His fingers scratched against the coarse scar on his cheek.

Joyce walked from the room. "I'm making coffee. Anyone want any?" she called as she exited. No one answered her.

"And you didn't run off with her because?" The young cop asked. His tag was continually out of focus so Barry didn't know his name.

"We told her husband. That very afternoon. He already knew though. Seemed everyone did. I was going to take little Danny in as my own. He was a great kid. I swear to God he was the nicest kid you could ever know."

His voice failed him and he wished the memories weren't so sharp and painful. It had been years but talking about it brought it all back.

"It was like a scene from *The Great Gatsby*. We drove up in her new car. Wasn't a yellow convertible or anything but—"

The blank stare on both their faces told him they didn't know the Gatsby tragedy so he moved along.

"And well, time went by and I went into the kitchen with her husband and we were shouting and he threatened me. He shoved me and I pushed back. He stormed out of the room threatening to kill me. I stayed behind, trying to hatch a plan."

Barry stopped. The crack of Helen's skull smashing that bottom step still deafened him. He didn't know then what it was. "I heard this, this terrible noise. A sound I'll never forget no matter how many trees I drive my motorcycle into. I ran into the foyer the same time as Fred, who came from the other direction. We saw her. Helen, the woman I loved, had fallen face first down the stairs. Her feet were still up on the fourth step. Blood pooled out from under her beautiful soft hair. I ran to her, pulled her down the stairs to make her more comfortable." He stared at the police. "I didn't know she was dead. Just didn't want her hanging with her feet all crooked and up like that, her dress flipped up, her underwear showing. I just wanted her to be comfortable. I put her head on my lap and held her.

"Then Danny ran in from outside. 'Mommy!' he screamed. He glared at me with this, this hatred. The blood seeped out from her head, onto his new backpack. She'd packed it for him, because we were going to all run away together, like I said. Danny stared at me, terrified. Called me a bastard.

"I reached for him. 'No, I didn't do this, Danny. I swear to God, I didn't.' I told him it was an accident. He didn't believe me.

"Fred stood in the corner and called an ambulance." Barry wiped at his eyes again.

"Danny grabbed the backpack, shook it to get the blood off, spraying drops onto my shirt but I didn't care. I had her blood all over me.

" 'I thought you loved us,' Danny said."

Barry was haunted to this day by Danny's reaction.

"Before I could reply, he ran out of the house with his backpack. I followed him, and Joyce and I drove into the woods then split up to find him." The memory was so sharp. "And I never saw him alive again."

The cops' eyes met and they both shrugged. The young one had stopped taking notes a while ago. None of it was germane to the present.

"So this man who came into your house, he claims to be that boy?" Martinez asked.

Barry nodded. Joyce walked into the room with a silver platter, replete with a carafe of coffee, mugs, and his CVS butter cookies. "What the hell are you doing, Joyce? This isn't a tea party for God's sake."

She ignored his comment and instead replied to Martinez. "Claiming is the key word. Little Danny drowned in the lake beside his house."

"Any reason this man, assuming he's not Danny, would do this?"

"To get money, clearly," Joyce said, pouring a cup of coffee into her mug. She added sugar cubes with a little tool he didn't know he owned. *Princess fucking Diana.*

"Are you sure you didn't invite the man in this evening?" Martinez asked.

"I wasn't home. I was out all night. With her," Barry pointed to Joyce. "I don't know what this guy wants. I don't want him to get in trouble or anything but it's just—I don't want to see him. He's not who he says he is and it—it brings it all back and it's a devastating day I never got over. I never got over losing Helen or Danny and I can't handle—"

"We can get you a protective order," the young man said. "Do you want to press breaking and entering charges, assuming we can catch the guy?"

"Yes," Joyce shouted.

"No," Barry said at the same time, louder. "I do not. I just want him to leave me alone."

No good would come of telling them about the Rainbox, or time travel. It wasn't real and it would portray him as crazy, or weak. He was both, he figured, but he still had a fan base and needed to put on a strong front for them.

Eventually the police left. He promised to go to the courthouse later in the morning to fill out the formal order.

Tonight he'd had no mental lapses since he awoke on the couch. Maybe the Memory game and Sodoku really were helping.

He turned to Joyce. "Can you go home now? I appreciate your help but I'm really tired. It's almost four in the morning."

"Let me just clean up."

"No. Please, I need to sleep."

"You're not cross with me are you?" She shot him her cat expression. He never mentioned it but her face was unreadable like a cat's. Her eyes and mouth were the same if she was going to scratch his eyes out, or cuddle, or bring him a fledgling robin with its head torn off.

"No, of course not. I know it's just as hard for you, reliving that day. You were right there too, had to deal with all of it same as me."

She walked to him and gave him a hug. "I've always been right there with you, Barry."

Before he could say much more she grabbed her coat and purse and walked out the door. "Lock this behind me."

"Will do."

A few minutes later he was dressed in his PJs and in bed. He waited for the evening to slip away and finally it did. His drowsiness gave way to a dreamy state and the magic show appeared as snapshots in an old photo album, instead of a live action true memory. Pictures of the old store in Maine appeared, Monica from the funnel cake stand. More dog-eared photos floated by in his mind: Danny and him, and Helen from back then when they were a family. Of Danny's lone wet sneaker found by the edge of the pond that next morning.

He clicked his white noise machine as high as it would go and finally all the pictures fell away from his mind, and he welcomed the loud *whoosh whoosh,* that carried him off to a place where memories didn't haunt or hurt, and there were no regrets.

FOUR

Danny didn't have a hell of a lot of time to plan his mission. He had but one goal, to set things right. That meant a lot of things. First and foremost, play with Barry's fragile mind and screw with him, terrify the man the way Barry had terrified him. Shake Barry's sense of reality so hard he didn't know which way was up.

Barry holding Helen's bloody head on his lap was an image he'd never forget. Same damn image from his other reality, when it had been Joyce's head on his lap. An accident Barry had said, both times. An accident. *Stupid fool should know that the same stories play out over and over, no matter how many times you jump though time.* Barry was always going to kill Danny's mother and he couldn't stop it. And he was always going to rip his heart out, be it emotionally, or by holding him under water.

What Danny could try and change was the aftermath.

Second, Barry needed to understand what he'd done. Needed to accept and repent. Not in the Biblical way where he would say he was sorry. No, he needed to go to jail.

A boy about seven or eight years old stood on the corner next to the coffee shop by the hotel. "Wanna buy some candy bars for our troop?"

Danny smiled at the uniformed child. Fate had a way of helping out. A trail of breadcrumbs that fate laid out to help him in his quest. It confirmed he was on the right path.

"Sure, I'll take some." He pulled out his wallet, stuffed with Barry's cash. A stack of photos in clear plastic bulged from inside and he pulled them out, curious which past and which set of players they'd display. They were blank. Yellowed rectangles of photo paper with no faces. He managed to hide his fear as he spoke. "How much for the whole box?"

"Really?" the boy said. He nudged the older gentleman next to him, probably his grandfather.

"Yeah, how much?"

"Forty dollars," the man said.

"I'll take the Hershey Bars. No nuts." He handed over the money. "Where did you get your uniform?" he asked the boy, and the man, figuring one would answer.

The boy handed him the box of bars. "Thanks."

"What do you need a uniform for?" the man asked. He knew what the guy was thinking, that he was a pervert.

"I have a foster kid. A little boy. He's eleven and been through a lot. Saw his mother die. I figured I would set him up with a scout troop. If I start with a uniform, even if it's not the right level or whatever, it might get him out of his slump."

The man smiled. "That's very nice of you. Scouts can really help a boy find his way." The man stared at Danny until he had a rare and precious flashback of his first life. *He was my scoutmaster. What are the chances?*

Chances were actually good, he knew. He'd read *The Rainbox* and experienced it himself first hand. Coincidences and parallels were sometimes so strong Danny worried he might just be an escapee from a mental hospital who had kidnapped a little boy to fuel his delusion. *I fucking hope not.*

"There's a store on Highland Ave. by the police station. Do you know where that is?"

Danny nodded. "Still there huh? That's where I got my uniforms when I was a kid."

"Some things don't ever change, no matter when you are."

Danny eyed at him curiously. "No matter *where* you are, you mean."

The man nodded. "That's what I said."

"Well, thanks for the bars and the information. Maybe I'll see you at a troop meeting once of these days." Danny scurried away.

- 2 -

This was a tough day for Joyce. There was the fight with Barry about Monica Rushmore and her death, then the second meeting with the police where Barry went on ad nauseam about how damn much he'd loved Helen.

The biggest emotional struggle today though was due to the fact that twenty-seven years ago today, she gave birth to a little boy she'd never seen again. That boy was her chance to link herself to Barry forever, have a stronger bond than Della or any of the others. And she blew it. He never would have committed to her, sure, but that was no reason to give the kid away. Not a day went by she didn't regret it. And not a day went by she didn't curse the privacy laws that prevented her from tracking the boy down.

As she did every year, she pulled a cupcake from a bakery bag and set it on her kitchen table. She drank a glass of red wine slowly, as she allowed herself a good long bout of mourning for the road not taken. She picked one blue candle from a small box and pushed it into the chocolate frosting.

A knock at the door interrupted her from lighting the candle. Must be Barry. There was no one else. She rose and walked to the front door, and opened it to find little Danny Brundige standing before her, in his old boy scout uniform, holding an open tray of Hershey Bars. She couldn't speak. *No, this isn't possible. He'd dead and—and even if he weren't, he wouldn't be a boy. He'd be a man.*

"Hello, Joyce."

She couldn't speak.

"I'm selling candy bars for my troop and wondered if you'd be interested in buying some. The money is going toward our camping trip in New Hampshire this summer."

He even has Danny's voice. What the fuck?

She backed away slightly. *He's an actor, has to be. Anyone with time to spare could track down pictures of the real boy and hire someone who resembled him.*

He stepped into the house at the same slow pace as she did. "Would you like to buy any," he asked. "They're two dollars each which is pretty cheap for a king size."

"What's your name?" she asked finally. His answer would set her at ease, surely, prove she was overtired and her imagination was in overdrive.

"You know my name, Joyce," he said. "You remember me." He'd stopped smiling now and glared at her with a *Children of the Corn* malevolence.

"What do you want from me?" she asked. "Who sent you?"

"I'm selling bars for my troop." He saw the cupcake then. "Is it your birthday?"

"No, no it's not." She felt sick.

He appeared sad suddenly, as if he'd just remembered something.

"What's the date today?"

"October twenty-first."

"It's my birthday," he said in little more than a whisper. "I didn't even know. Didn't know what day it was."

"Happy birthday," she said slowly. *Lots of people have this birthday. There's no correlation between this boy and my son, or the real Danny Brundige. It doesn't mean anything!*

"I wish I could go back where I came from and see my dad." His lip trembled as he spoke. His eyes clouded with tears.

"Where is your father? Is he outside?" She leaned toward the door but the angle was wrong and seeing outside to the stoop wasn't possible.

"Not where, Joyce. When," he said firmly.

When?

"Are you going to buy a bar?" His distress pained her.

She hastily pulled a ten dollar bill from her purse. "Give me five of them."

He handed them to her. "There's a secret message for you in the wrapper. Don't forget to check." With that he ran out. She heard his feet scrabble down the walk until there was silence. She locked the door and picked up one of the bars. Her hands shook as she carefully opened the taped wrapper. "Go see Fred Brundige. He will help you do the right thing." All the bars yielded the same note, in the same handwriting as on her garage door note.

She never bothered lighting the candle for her lost son. This boy pretending to be Danny, pretending it was *his* birthday too. No, Danny Brundige could not be the same one she left at the convent. It would be too cruel a trick for even a vengeful God to play.

The man who'd been hounding Barry surely hired this kid to manipulate her as well as to set her on edge. She held a wrapper in her hand. She had planned to find Fred's new address and see him anyway based on the first message, but now felt an urgent need.

She stuffed half a chocolate bar in her mouth, and headed to her computer to do some research on Fred, both to get his address and to see what he'd been up to for the last fifteen years.

- 3 -

Danny sat in a wooden cubicle in the public library just down the road from Barry's place. He had an hour of online access to find everything he needed, and then would have to relinquish the computer to the pimply teen next on the list. He'd known the details by heart in his old life and when he first arrived: the names of the women, the dates, the places, their manners of death. But now, like everything else from before, specifics were murky. As current events filled his mind the old ones vanished entirely, According to his notebook, he'd been at this library before. He vaguely recalled his surroundings. He'd sat in this same chair, the one with Karma carved into the wooden arm, and printed out the articles.

His notes from when he first arrived were so angry. He raged about Barry's killing Joyce and all the others. So much venom, and unwavering conviction that Barry was a murderer. But when Danny reread the notes now it was hard to fathom that Barry was capable of these horrific crimes. It didn't seem possible and yet…All Danny could be sure of were the words on the page. He couldn't trust any of his memories or feelings. *Last time*, the journal said, *this backfired on me, but this time I'll handle it differently. This time Barry will go to jail for his crimes. All of them.*

He closed his eyes and tried to remember writing in the journal, tried to recapture the past, but all that came to mind was the last day at the lake house.

Seeing his mother's dead eyes. Barry holding her in his lap, as blood puddled under her. Crushing grief and hopelessness giving way to fear. Running for his life. Then later the fingers digging into his shoulders, holding him under the water. Fighting hard to escape but only breathing in more and more water until he wished he was dead too. He pulled at his collar now, struggling to breathe.

"Are you all right?" He jolted up, free from the memory, to find an elderly librarian staring down at him, her hand on his shoulder.

"Yes, sorry. I just—asthma attack I guess. I'm all right."

Danny hoped the rest of his past life changed, and that somehow in this time Barry hadn't killed all those poor young girls. He took a deep breath and began to check facts online.

Danny typed a series of keys and watched as a news article appeared on the screen. It was a picture of him as a child, smiling in his scout uniform. *Missing Boy Assumed Drowned.* The story chronicled the family tragedy of the Brundiges. In essence it was true. Helen Brundige fell down the stairs. Young Danny entered the room, found her dead, and ran out in terror. He was never seen again though one sneaker was found by the edge of the lake.

He reached out to the screen, seeing his own face, in the picture taken at such a happy time. Drowned. He knew damn well it wasn't accidental, or by his own hand, but the reports never once hinted at foul play.

He scrolled through articles, from that next day to a year later, to two years. Never an investigation into his death or Helen's. Both unfortunate accidents. Emotion welled up in him, disgust at how everything had gone to shit for Fred and he hadn't done anything wrong. Yeah, he drank and worked too much but at least he never killed anyone. And he loved Danny. Taught him how to ride a bike and throw a ball. He wasn't all bad, not like Helen had pushed him to believe.

He typed in *Fred Brundige* next. The first item that popped up was an ad for *Fred Brundige, Investigations*. The address was in the city part of Bradfield. He checked the listing for the old lake house and saw that it has been foreclosed upon years before. A little more digging revealed that Fred had left the police force and started a business that specialized in insurance cases. His career ended shortly after Danny disappeared. He pulled up the website for Fred's business again and printed the page with the contact information.

"Hey, that's my dad," Young Danny said, still in his scout uniform. He appeared behind Danny's shoulder. He smiled broadly. "He's older but that's him. He's an investigator? I thought he was a cop. Is that the same thing?"

Danny turned, "A lot changed since you left, but we're going to make it all okay. Just go back over there and read. I'll explain once I check a few more things."

The boy shrugged and left the area.

Danny typed in a name, hoping to God it didn't have any hits; that something good had come out of this trip.

He viewed the screen, at the smiling face of Claudia Daley, a petite twenty-four year old, found poisoned in her apartment on April 12, 2006. She had a small gap in her front teeth but otherwise was damn near perfect. She lived in New Haven CT and worked as a nursery school teacher at Little Sprouts. And, Danny knew, had the unfortunate luck to be a fan of Barry Ford and attended the debut signing of *The Shadow Box* in her town. Her parents offered a ten thousand dollar reward for any clues to her death but they never got to pay it. No leads. Still an unsolved case. Danny printed the article and all the photos he could find online of Claudia Daley. He made a note in the THEN side of his book. *Still dead. Same circumstances.*

Maybe it was just this one girl, Danny thought. *Maybe the others were spared. Something might have stopped the cycle.*

But in 2008, it happened again. This time, it was Barry's first signing of *The Other Lives,* his newest sci-fi novel. Manchester, New Hampshire. A cool Sunday night in late September. Mallory Dennis was twenty. A nursing student at UNH. He'd signed the book to her, *My prettiest fan, - Barry.*

Late that night, about one in the morning, she was hit by a truck and killed instantly. The driver of the truck said he saw hands push her from behind a tree but it happened too quickly for him to hit his brakes or see the rest of the person. By the time ambulances and police arrived, she was long dead. Her friends said she'd attended Barry's signing with them and then had walked home alone. No one could account for the missing three hours. Her parents were poor so there was no reward offered. The case remained open. Danny printed two different articles about her as well as an enlarged picture of her face. With angst he jotted a note next to her name in his journal. *#2 also dead. All facts the same.*

The final girl was Alice Johnson, in 2013. *Boxes of Life* had its debut signing in Worcester, Massachusetts on June 10, 2013. Alice was on welfare and had twin toddler boys at home. She'd left them with her sister to attend the signing. Her friend took a picture, cozying up to Barry, whispering something in his ear. That was not entered as evidence, only on a social media page to celebrate her life. She was strangled and murdered and left in a Motel 6 room she rented with cash. The motel clerk said that she was a regular hour-to-hour renter and he was sorry it came to this but wasn't surprised. Her murderer was not identified. He printed her information too. The final note in his book read, *#3 Still dead. How can I make this okay?*

The pimply teen looked at Danny and then at his watch. "Time's up, Mister."

"Just one more minute. This is really important."

Danny accessed Barry's website and found a list of all his signings, year by year. Three of the dates lined up with those of the crime scenes. He printed them and gestured to the kid in line. "All yours."

Whatever I altered in time didn't stop the murders. Barry did it. Facts don't lie.

He took his stack of printouts to the copier and added quarters to the machine.

- 4 -

"Now when you see Barry you know what to say, right?" Danny asked the boy.

Young Danny nodded. He was still in uniform and carried a tray of candy bars. He stood under the street lantern and shivered. Danny had bought him a coat but it was important that he show up with his uniform fully visible.

"I can't go with you. I need to hide around the corner but I'll be watching you. Whatever you do, don't go into his house."

"Okay," he said, clearly afraid. For him, everything horrible had just happened. Danny was a lifetime and fifteen years removed so for him the emotional and physical pain had diffused over time. He hated putting the boy through this but he had to believe it would make a difference.

He struggled to comprehend the physics of it all. When he thought now of Helen's death and his drowning, it felt so long ago; though on one plane it just happened. Times like this he questioned his own sanity. Prayed for himself and the boy that they were on the right path. The only proof he had was a notebook filled with scribblings of events he no longer remembered.

And the printouts of the murders and signing dates. *Right. That's proof. It will have to be enough. We need to follow through, for all our sakes.*

"Remember what he did to your mother, and to you. That will give you the strength you need." He patted Young Danny's head and pointed him toward the stairs of the brownstone. He walked across the street and stood behind the post at the bus stop. Young Danny slowly walked up the stone steps.

- 5 -

Barry sat on his couch. He was reading through his journal from the last week, and taking notes with a red pen on a yellow legal pad. The colored paper and pens was another trick Amy had given him to help his memories take root. So much had happened and only small pieces stayed fresh in his memory even with the constant reading and writing. He closed his eyes and thought of the man, Danny, who had come to his house, and then of Danny Brundige as a young boy. "No, Joyce is right. It can't be him. I made up the idea of the Rainbox. It's just a replica of the fictional box, nothing else."

A soft quiet knock at the door interrupted his thoughts. He rose from the couch and placed his pad and pen down.

He peeked out the side window and saw a boy scout on the steps. The boy held a tray of items, probably for sale. Barry smiled. Finally some normalcy in his life. He'd never felt so relieved to see a solicitor.

He turned the knob and gasped. Little Danny Brundige peered up at him. The boy was wide eyed and afraid too.

"Danny?" Barry said. He knelt down before him. "Oh my God, Danny is it you?"

The boy smiled broadly, but at the same time there were tears in his eyes. Barry hugged him, knocking the tray of candy bars onto the ground and down the stairs. He let go and leaned back. "Don't worry about those. I'll buy them all. Is it—is it really you?"

"It's me," the boy said quietly. "But . . . you're different."

"How can it be you? You haven't aged." He prayed the boy would give him the right answer.

"I came through the Rainbox," he said.

"So you didn't die?" Barry asked. Tears of relief streamed down his cheeks. "Oh my God you didn't die. I'm so glad. So damn glad."

The boy stared at him. "You tried to kill me," he said.

"Me? No, you can't believe that. You can't. I'd never have hurt you. Ever. I loved you, Danny. Still do. Come in. Come in, please," he said as he stood up with some effort.

"I can't. I need to stay out here."

"Why?"

"I can't come in. Not today. I need to go back home soon but wanted to see you. So you'd believe in the Rainbox." The boy had tears on his cheeks too. Barry wiped them away.

"I believe. My hand to God I believe. What can I do to help?"

"Nothing. I just came back to set things right."

The exact words the adult Danny had said. Barry didn't understand but then he didn't know how it really worked. It was only supposed to be a book, not a user's guide to time travel.

"Let me know what I can do to help. If there's anything you need, anything at all," Barry said, "please tell me."

"I have to go," the child said. "I have to leave now." He turned and began to descend the steps.

"I love you, Danny. Wherever you're going, you need to know that. I loved your mother and you more than I loved myself or anyone in my whole life. You two were the only ones I ever really loved. I never would have hurt either one of you."

The boy turned around and said quietly, "I love you too, Barry. And I'm sorry. For whatever has to happen, I'm sorry."

He ran away, leaving the candy bars scattered on the steps. Barry watched him run down the street and disappear around a corner. He went inside and shut the door.

Barry opened his journal and recorded every second of the conversation they'd had. He smiled as he described Danny, his voice, how it was all the same as fifteen years ago.

He came through the Rainbox and that's all I need to know.

If he told Joyce, she wouldn't believe him. For now, this would have to be his secret.

- 6 -

Fred stood over his kitchen table and smiled as he lit a birthday candle on a small Carvel Ice Cream Cake. Danny's favorite. *Maybe he'll come back again. He's alive and can come back anytime.* The apartment was clean and no longer cluttered. Fred was stone sober and his mind raced.

He sat in the chair and stared at the flame. "Happy birthday, Danny," he said. "Please come home." He held a framed picture of Danny when he turned four years old. The small boy was dressed in a pirate costume. Helen had made him an elaborate pirate ship cake and had given gold chocolate coins as party favors to all his friends. Danny was such a sweet happy little boy, he reflected.

He heard footsteps outside his door. "Danny?" The steps retreated. He ripped the door open but there was no one. A manila envelope sat on his welcome mat.

Fred retrieved it then ran inside. He blew the candle out and spread the contents of the envelope onto the table. "Holy shit. What is this?" Articles of girls murdered in various states over the course of several years. It meant nothing to him. They all died of different causes. The last page answered his question. It was a printout of book signings by Barry Ford. Three of the dates were circled.

He crisscrossed the articles against the dates. "No, this can't be."

He checked the page for the dates again and found a note stuck to the back, crooked, as if it was attached to the wrong page. In Danny's handwriting it said, *He killed me too.*

The man thought back to the day that had destroyed them all.

Barry and Helen pulled up to the house late that afternoon. They blustered in and laid out their plan. Fred was fucked. They were going to get her things and Danny's things and leave. That night.

He was drunk and it was still hazy what happened except that at one point he went to the kitchen to get another drink. Barry followed, trying to reason with him, explained that he loved Helen and Danny, as if that was supposed to make him feel better. "No," Fred had replied, "*I* love them. They're mine and you're never taking them away!"

He shoved Barry and Barry shoved back, knocked him down and into the counter. "I'm gonna fucking kill you!" Fred yelled. He meant it too. He ran out of that kitchen in a blind rage to get his gun. It was in his drawer and he planned to blow Barry's head off. He made it to his office, his hand on the drawer, when he heard the crash.

He ran into the foyer to find Helen at the bottom of the stairs. Barry ran from the kitchen, then without pause pulled Helen up and held her. Cried and held her. Fred just stood, stunned. He picked up the phone to call the police but didn't dial, just watched in terror.

Danny ran in and stared at them both in horror. He said some things Fred couldn't hear, grabbed his backpack, and then bolted out the door. Fred called 9-1-1 and watched as Barry ran after the boy.

Fred took Barry's place next to Helen on the floor. For all the good that would do, he sat next to his wife. He held her hand and stroked her hair until the paramedics and police arrived.

She was dead as soon as she hit the bottom step, they said. Freak accident.

They took her body away and he stood there, helpless.

And it wasn't until then he remembered Danny. He took the final swig of his warm beer and ran outside. "Danny!" he'd called. It had gotten dark in the time that had passed. He ran back in and grabbed his flashlight. "Danny! Where are you? Come back!" He called the boy's name for a while before he noticed that Joyce's car was gone and she and Barry were nowhere to be found.

"You bastard! You took him!" He spied his Jeep in the driveway then squeezed his right pocket and felt his keys. He knew he was shitfaced but that bastard was not getting his kid. Danny needed to be with *him* now, more than ever.

He threw the flashlight on the passenger seat, revved the Jeep, and headed for the city side of Bradfield where Barry lived.

Fred made it just a few miles when his Jeep skidded on black ice and careened into a ditch. He woke up at dawn, unharmed.

His car was fine. He backed it up and drove the short distance home to regroup. Maybe Barry had returned Danny by now. They could have a good long talk. Things were going to change from here on out, he vowed. No more drinking, no more undercover work.

When he pulled toward his house, he saw flashing lights. His heart sped up and he felt his blood pressure rise. Police cars and ambulances, two fire trucks.

What the hell?

He jumped from the Jeep and ran straight for the center of the crowd, right into his captain.

"Where the hell have you been?" Charlie asked. He sniffed. "Jesus, you're drunk!"

"I'm trying to find my Danny. Barry Ford took him. I know he did. My car skidded—"

"Barry and Joyce were out here the whole time searching for Danny while *you* took off."

"No they were gone. The car was gone. I called for Danny and then figured they must've—" Fred tried to push past Charlie to see what everyone was looking at but the man held him in place.

"Listen, Fred. I don't want to hear any more of your bullshit excuses of why you weren't around for your son. None of that matters now." Charlie's voice softened. "We think Danny drowned in the lake. There are guys in boats out there trolling." Charlie pointed to boats only mildly visible as silhouettes against the pink sky.

"Barry called us a couple of hours after we left, after we took Helen away. Said they found Danny's body, but then it was gone. We've been probing the waters ever since. All of us, all night. Where the hell were you?"

Fred had nothing to say.

In the distance he saw Barry talking to the police. Fred hated himself. Barry clearly was the better father, the better husband. Fred was a no good jealous selfish drunk. Danny and Helen had deserved him, would have been better off.

"I saw him," Joyce said, as she approached. "I saw Danny in

the water. Dead." She paused as Fred absorbed her words. "I can't swim," she continued, "so I ran to get Barry and when we got back, his body was gone. He's out there somewhere."

Fifteen years later, Danny was still out there somewhere. They never found a body. The assumption was that he got spooked seeing his mother fall down the stairs and ran to get away. He was a great swimmer but maybe it was too dark and he got confused.

All these years, Fred lived with the guilt of his actions: that of being an absent father, an absent husband, a drunk. Of driving away in a jealous rage instead of trying to find Danny when it may have made a difference.

He regarded Danny's note now though. "He killed me too."

Relief and an incredible sense of purpose filled him. He hadn't felt this since his days on the force, when he'd stopped at nothing to apprehend the criminals. "You had us all fooled but it's over now, Barry Ford. I'm gonna bring you down."

- 7 -

It wasn't difficult for Joyce to find Fred's new home address. She waited an hour before driving because she'd been drinking wine and didn't want a DUI. She drove by his office first. It was wedged between a laundromat, and a liquor store whose L and I were burnt out so QUOR flashed in erratic red letters. Fred's office didn't have a fancy sign, just sun-faded text in his window that stated his name, Private Investigator, and his phone number and hours.

His apartment was a few streets over, in a section just as run down. It was a far cry from his once beautiful lake house. She pulled into a long driveway, boxing in what she assumed was Fred's car. The house was a blue tenement with a sagging front porch. She checked the address and cast her eyes up. Fred was on the second floor, up the outside stairs.

"Well, here goes nothing," Joyce said as she stepped from her car and locked it. She hoped this would be a short visit where he'd admit to blackmail, she'd write him a check, and he'd crawl back into his sad little hole of a life. He was crafty, she'd give him that. She'd underestimated him. Hiring actors to screw with her, finding out about her baby . . .

Joyce ascended the bowed stairs and held the chipped railing. "What a dump," she said under her breath. She reached the door and knocked.

Fred ripped open the door, a huge grin on his face. "Danny!" When he saw her, his face dropped. "Oh, hello. Sorry, I thought you were—"

He moved closer and stared at her under the light. "Joyce Tuttle?"

She nodded. "Hi Fred. You were expecting Danny?" *Of course you were. The actor called Danny. Actors. Man and boy versions.*

"Want to come in? I've got to show you something. Right away. Come in please." He took her wrist and pulled her into his tiny apartment.

She smelled sulfur, the scent of a candle blown out. "What's that smell?"

He ran to his table to show her something, only half listening. "What?"

She saw then a Carvel ice cream box on the counter and a melted blob with a candle sticking out of the top. She pointed. "Oh Jesus," he said, carefully carrying the mess to the sink.

"Listen, Joyce, it's a huge coincidence you should show up here now, after all this time but I have to show—"

"Is it your birthday?" she asked, shaken by all of this. It's not what she anticipated at all. She'd expected him to be cool and calculated, to be awaiting her arrival. But he was all over the place.

"No, it's Danny's. Listen you won't believe this but I think he's alive."

She plopped on the couch as her stomach clenched and her legs weakened. "Danny's birthday?"

"Yes, he would have been twenty-seven today." The same age as the boy she gave up for adoption. "But that has nothing to do with anything. I got a note from him. He said he's alive. I'm sorry; this is a lot at once. Let me take your coat."

Joyce sat in shock. Danny had visited her and Barry and Fred. What the fuck was going on? And was he really *her* son? They had DNA tests now so it would be easy enough to find out. But that didn't explain about the boy at her door.

"Joyce, let me take your coat. I've got the heat cranked and you'll get hot."

Robotically she removed her wool coat and handed it to him. "I was told to come here to see you. I thought you knew. That you put him up to it."

"Who? Put who up to it?" he asked as he sat next to her on the tattered couch.

She didn't want to fuel his delusions but there was no other way to say it. "Danny."

"Hot damn, I knew it! I knew it was true. Did you see him? I got notes but haven't—"

She took his hands. "You need to calm down. You're freaking me out and scaring me."

"Sorry."

"Let's take it slow, okay? A man has been coming by to see Barry and me. He says he's Danny come through the Rainbox. A time traveler." She waited for the insane story to settle in, for Fred to roll his eyes. He didn't. She continued. "He saw Barry first, then we both saw him. Then he left a note for me to contact you. I went to the Lake house first. Didn't know you moved."

He nodded. "Left there a long time ago. I couldn't stand to live where I lost them both; see that house and the lake. It was too much. The look on Danny's face when he saw Helen. He begged me to do something but I was useless then. Sure I called the police but that was—God I did everything wrong back then. I wish I could go back and—"

He sat for a moment, moved his hands over hers. She felt warmth. A connection. Strange for her, a cold-hearted bitch by her own admission, who'd carried a torch for Barry, and only Barry, her whole adult life. But here was this middle aged chubby guy whose life had fallen apart and there was a feeling. She didn't move her hands. It felt good to hold someone, even like this.

"Can I ask you a question?" Joyce said.

"I'm sure we have to ask each other a lot of questions."

"Was Danny adopted?" She prayed he'd say no, and then bore her with gory details about Helen's labor or morning sickness.

"What does that have to do with anything?"

"Just please answer me. Was he?"

He nodded. "Hardly anyone knew. We got him from a convent in New Hampshire. Helen's sister was a nun."

"I didn't know."

"Why would you? You were my wife's lover's friend. I met you once. The day Danny disappeared."

"Right. I don't know anything about your life."

"Well, Helen's sister called us in the middle of night and we just went and picked him up. Didn't give it any thought just went and brought him home and filled out paperwork a few days later."

"I didn't know," she said again, not able to form a more intelligent answer.

"Not sure if Helen told Barry. Maybe. Danny knew. We were gonna wait until he was eighteen but Helen thought it was better to—"

"He's mine," she said. It was the first time she had ever spoken those words. "Danny was my son."

Joyce couldn't hold it in anymore and cried in the arms of a man who'd lost the same son. The only one who would understand, even if he didn't know the big picture.

He held her, let her cry it out, and eventually she calmed down enough to relay all she could remember about Danny's visits.

Fred made her coffee and gave her a box of tissues.

"I'm so sorry, Joyce."

"There were so many times I saw him back then. Barry would meet Helen and the boy and sometimes I'd come along. Probably spent five or six afternoons with him and . . . he was a stranger to me, the son of a woman Barry loved and nothing else." Her sadness was deep. An unfamiliar ache. "But the whole time he was *my* little boy. My flesh and blood. I didn't know."

Fred held her, rocked her like a child. "Irony is a bitch."

His words made her feel worse but they were true.

"I know this grown man who came by can't be Danny, still alive after all this time, and the young boy scout can't be him either. But who is doing this, and why?"

Fred took her hand and led her to the kitchen table and pile of papers that were fanned out on the surface. "Come here. I need to show you something. It's hard to swallow but you need to see it."

First he showed the note from before. *I'm still alive*, it said. But she wasn't falling for it. When she sat and saw the articles and photos though, her perspective changed.

"I spent years thinking Barry was a standup guy, and I was the shit heel because I was never around," Fred said. "And then Danny dropped this package of evidence off. Three murders. Different women, but notice when they died, and where. All on nights of Barry's debut book signings. There's a connection."

He moved the three articles in front of her, faster than she could read or process what she was seeing. "Barry was there every time," he explained. "Must have seen them all before they died. And I bet that if we exhumed the bodies and checked it against Barry's DNA—"

"Stop. Just stop," Joyce said. "I need a minute." She rose from the table and walked aimlessly around the room to clear her head. "This is compelling but Barry wouldn't kill anyone. He may have liked the ladies but he was never violent. Ever." Barry's night with Monica Rushmore flashed in her head and she pushed it away.

"Joyce, come back here and read this note from our son. *He killed me too*. That's what it says."

"I can read it," she said.

"Our son, Joyce. He killed our son but somehow he's really been alive this whole time or through some miracle he's back. But whatever it is, we have evidence now. I still have friends on the force."

Joyce didn't know what to say. She couldn't protect Barry. He *had* been with these women. She knew that. Had kept many of his secrets all these years. She didn't know if Barry had used a condom. For his sake, she hoped so.

"This is our chance to set things right, Joyce. You need to be on my side here. I know Barry is your boss, your friend, but grasp what he did to these women. I need to stop him and I need your help. You can confirm he was there."

He held her hand again. She saw in Fred a chance to start things over. Change everything from how it had always been. A break from Barry and his selfish needs, from the love he dangled in front of her but kept just out of her reach. Fred offered her an escape from that life. A fresh start.

"I love Barry but if he's really done all this," she gestured to the articles, "Then he's not the man I thought he was."

- 8 -

Danny and Young Danny sat at a booth in the diner. Young Danny had changed out of his uniform. He was shaken and his eyes were red from crying.

"I just want to go home," the boy said. "I don't like it here. I don't want to hurt people." His burger plate sat before him, untouched. "Barry said he didn't kill my mom or try to drown me. He said it wasn't him and I believe him."

Danny felt the boy's doubt, his fear, and his conflict.

"What if he didn't do it? What if Mom really did just fall down the stairs?" the boy pleaded.

Danny reached across the table and pulled aside the boy's shirt. "Someone held you down under the water and left these bruises. Someone tried to kill you and made you breathe in water until they thought you were dead. That wasn't an accident."

"But Barry loved us," the boy said.

Danny welled up with emotion. He didn't want to have to show the boy the articles about the murders, or even tell him, but it was the only way to prove Barry's evil. The connections between the girls' deaths and Barry's proximity to them was circumstantial but his notes implied there was no doubt.

The bell on the door of the diner clanged and Bonnie entered. Her eyes were hollow and he knew she was stoned. He didn't blame her. No one could tolerate her life without drugs.

She walked toward the counter. "Bonnie!" he called out. The girl turned toward him. "Come sit with us. I never got to buy you dinner," he said.

Bonnie considered, and then walked to the table. She sat down next to Young Danny.

"I know you're not real," she said.

Danny shrugged. There was no point in convincing her otherwise. It wouldn't change anything. "Maybe not, but are you hungry?"

"I'm always hungry."

As she sat in a fog of comfortable numbness and stared at her hands, Danny moved to the counter and ordered a meal for her.

He returned and spoke to Young Danny. "This is what happened to your friend Bonnie. When Barry drowned you, Bonnie was never the same again. He didn't hurt only you."

"Bonnie?" the boy said.

Slowly she turned toward the voice. She gasped but not in horror. It was more of wonder, of relief. "You're not dead," she said quietly, as she smiled. "You're exactly the same."

She cast her eyes to Danny. "How is that possible? How is he here?"

Danny took her hands. "For tonight, your life is just a bad dream okay? None of this is real. You're a little girl and Danny is your best friend and everything is different. None of it ever happened."

She lit up and smiled. She removed her coat revealing only a thin white lingerie top. No bra. The dark HOPE letters shouted from her skinny birdlike chest. New track marks bruised her thin pale arms.

Danny held her hand firm. "Tonight, pretend none of the bad stuff that happened to you was real. It's just us again, having dinner."

The waitress brought a shake to start.

"Vanilla with cherry syrup." With a shaking hand she held the straw and took a sip.

Young Danny watched her with tears in his eyes. "Are you really Bonnie?"

She glanced his way, for a moment transported to the last time she was happy. "As sure as you're Danny Brundige." She touched his face with her long fake-fingernail hands. Black claws tenderly caressing a frightened boy's cheek.

"Do I look the same to you?" She meant it sincerely but the delusion was only in *her* mind. She was able to pretend but Young Danny could not.

"Sure," he said. "You haven't changed. Still my best friend." He was a hell of a good kid for saying it.

"Hey, isn't it your birthday today?" she said. "Both of you, right? You're both Danny." Her eyes closed and she slumped back in her seat for a moment, and then woke up again. "I like it here. This place, being with you. I wish it could stay like this." She closed her eyes again. Danny didn't know what she took but hoped it eased her sorrow.

"Are you okay, Bonnie?" Young Danny asked. He nudged her shoulder. She opened her eyes slowly, like a lizard. "I'm okay. It's your birthday." The waitress brought Bonnie's meal.

"Can you bring them both a piece of birthday cake?" she slurred to the waitress. "It's his birthday. Both of them. But they're one person." She swayed now. Whatever drug it was it hit her hard now.

The waitress glared at Danny. "Is she all right? We can't have any trouble in here."

"She's fine. Can you bring us two pieces of cake though? She's right. It's our birthday today. Both of us," Danny said.

The waitress nodded. "Happy birthday," she offered without enthusiasm or sincerity.

Bonnie's cell phone buzzed. She read a text. "I have to go. Work." She began to stand but fell back into her seat. "Whoa, that was crazy." She stood again and this time it took.

"But what about your dinner, and our birthday cake," Young Danny said. "You have to stay."

"I can't, buddy. Max doesn't give me time off. But I'll see you again real soon. Real, real soon, don't worry." She began to leave.

She's overdosed. She's going to die tonight if she has her way.

Danny rose and took her in her arms. "Forget your boss. Forget work. Let's get you to a hospital."

Young Danny's eyes showed terror. This poor kid was going through hell but it was a reality he needed to face. This was life now unless he helped Danny to change it.

A scrawny blonde guy with bad teeth and gold chains opened the door of the diner. "Come on, sweetheart, we have to go."

He tried to pull Bonnie from Danny's arms but he held fast. "I'm taking her to a hospital."

"Not tonight. Call and make an appointment and I'll see if she can squeeze you in." The man winked at Danny. Bonnie grew more lethargic.

Danny released her.

None of this mattered. Death would be kind for her if that's what she wanted. If he fought with the pimp and got shot or stabbed or arrested, Young Danny would never get home and this reality would be set in stone.

Danny returned to the booth and watched as the pimp guided Bonnie to a waiting car.

"Where is he taking her?" Young Danny asked, alarmed at what he'd seen.

"He's taking her to the doctor. She'll be okay. If you work with me, I promise it will all be okay."

"Then I'll do whatever I have to do. I don't want my Bonnie to end up like that."

"Me either."

FIVE

- 1 -

Joyce awoke to the sound of car horn blaring outside, and a trashy woman screaming, "I'll be out in a minute!" She found herself in Fred's bed. He wasn't there but she smelled coffee and heard him typing on his computer in the living room. She smiled. What a difference her life had taken so quickly. Fred was a good guy and she could make him love her. She knew how much he loved Helen so he was capable of commitment. It had been long enough for him to love again. Sure he wasn't handsome like Barry, or famous, or rich, but that wouldn't matter a damn bit when Barry was in jail. She was sick of being overlooked anyway. *I matter,* she thought. *I deserve someone who really cares about me. Fred Brundige may very well be that person.*

She slid on yesterday's clothes and walked into the living room.

Fred looked up from the computer. He smiled at her. "Good morning."

"Good morning."

"Have a seat. I'll bring you a coffee."

She hesitated. "I can get it."

"No please. Sit. You're my guest. I'll get it."

This was a first. Barry, God love him, never waited on her. Sure, she was his assistant but after so many years you think he'd grasp that she was also a human being, and a woman.

Fred brought her a mug with the Patriots logo. "I added cream and sugar. Hope that's okay." He also handed her a small plate with some Oreos on it. "Not used to overnight guests. This is the best I can do for a fancy breakfast."

She laughed. "It's perfect." Truly it was. Coffee with sugar and a plate of cookies . . . this guy warmed her heart. "What are you working on?"

He went back to his desk. "Trying to come up with a complete, good file to bring to the police. I have a few friends on the force but I didn't leave under the best of circumstances. I was obsessed for a long time with finding Danny. Ruined my life and my career over it. I was drunk all the time and depressed and they had no choice but to get rid of me by the end. I'll need solid data or they're going to boot me right out of there."

It was partially her fault Fred's life had deteriorated the way it had. She could fix it and her own life at the same time. It would mean betraying Barry but this was her chance to remove herself from his misfortunes and fly out on her own with a decent guy and, if she could suspend her disbelief, her son.

She sipped her coffee and ate two cookies while she pondered her next move. It would be irrevocable and she had to be damn sure this was a route she could commit to. "I'm sorry you went through all that."

He stood and walked to her, kissed her on the lips and hugged her. "I'm so glad you came into my life. I don't know when I've felt like this," he said. "Maybe it's the excitement that Danny could still be alive, or knowing I've got information on a case, a bunch of cases, that might gain me respect from the department. But I don't know. I think a big part of it is just you. I've got a good feeling about you." Her heart and ego swelled. She made up her mind.

"Search for Monica Rushmore," she said. "Old Orchard Beach, Maine. It's an unsolved murder. Or it was. I just solved it for you."

She kissed him then grinned. "Go on. That should be a huge help. Barry did it. I'm sure of it."

Fred darted to the computer and began to search.

Joyce sat on the couch, watching him, wishing Barry didn't have to be her lamb to slaughter. There really was no other way.

- 2 -

"Freakin' cold out here," Barry said under his breath as the sea breeze blew through him.

"What's that sir?" Jerry called from a few feet away. The two of them were dressed for beach combing. Sneakers, jeans, parkas. Not sandals and shorts, not in October. The beach was empty except for the two of them. It was cloudy and cold and the wind snapped at them as if to deter them from its shore.

"Just said it's goddamned cold out here!"

Jerry walked closer and held out a red Solo cup. "I've got three blue pieces and two green."

Barry studied the sea glass pieces his driver had collected, then his own take. One brown, one green, and one blue. All small. "We can't leave until we find a red piece. I told you. I need to get back in that goddamned Rainbox and fix this mess."

Jerry nodded, didn't say a word, and walked in the other direction toward the water.

Barry glanced down the shore and thought he saw a young boy running toward his mother. *Danny?* There was no one. He ran up to the spot just in case but there were no foot prints. It was just a memory. He sat on the cold sand and gazed again down the shore, allowing the good memories in.

Danny was nine or ten. Fred was undercover and had been away for weeks. Barry took Helen and the boy out here to hunt for sea glass. The boy had never heard of it, had never seen it. So Barry had walked with him for hours on end, gathering every piece they could find. It was Danny who found the rare treasure of a piece of red sea glass. "Well that one is magic, Danny," he told the boy. "That's the piece that unlocks all the secrets."

"What kind of secrets?" Danny asked, always immensely interested in what Barry had to say. Such a trusting and good child. It was then that the Rainbox story had begun. The magic of a young boy's wonder, crossed with the sickening nightmare of Monica Rushmore's death, years past but only a few blocks away.

"Well," Barry began. "There was a man who had a little boy, just like you. His name was Danny."

"Just like me!" he said excitedly.

"Yes, just like you. And, well it's a long story but something happened to the boy. Something terrible. And this man was so very sad that he couldn't accept fate, had to find a way to change it. So this man took all the sea glass he could find from that beach where they owned a summer house, and he built a secret time travel box. But he um, he called it a Rainbox, because rain can wash away everything bad and uncover new life beneath. And the man went into this box and wished as hard as he could that he could go back in time and save his little boy."

"And could he?" Danny asked, his eyes wide.

Barry nodded. "He could, but only with the magical red piece that the boy himself had found."

Danny held up his red piece proudly.

"And they lived happily ever after?" Danny asked.

Barry felt the wind whip across his scarred face and deformed leg. He thought of Young Danny then. Thought of the man who appeared recently claiming to be a version returning from another time. If that *was* him, neither of their lives had ended happily ever after. He could fix it. He knew he could. He just needed the key.

He leaned on his cane as he trudged through the sand. He knew as he drew closer to the pier he would encounter the old Rushmore shop. The owners were long gone by then. The father had moved away, closed his business to start his tour on the casino circuit. Now it was one of many t-shirt shops. The memory haunted him but he wondered if facing it was part of the process. Questioned if heading toward the store would balance the scales.

On unsteady legs, he slowly walked closer to the bridge and

then under it. When he emerged on the other side and walked up the sand hill he saw the location for the old store. "I'm sorry, Monica," he said.

He closed his eyes and bowed his head in shame. When he opened them, there sat a piece of red sea glass peeking from the golden sand. *This can't be coincidence. This is part of someone's plan. A path that involves my making amends.* He picked up the glass and turned to signal to Jerry. "We can go home now! I've got it!"

- 3 -

Fred walked Joyce to her car and kissed her goodbye.

"Be careful."

"I will." She smiled, but was eager to get inside her car.

"Listen, Joyce. I have to say this. You must have suspected about the Rushmore girl all this time and yet you stayed by Barry's his side anyway. Obviously you didn't know of the other murders but—"

"What are you implying?" She crossed her arms and scrunched her face up like a child ready for a tantrum. Surely her emotions were all mixed up right now and he couldn't blame her. He gently touched her arm.

"Only that Barry is a good liar to fool the woman who knew him better than anyone. I know what he's capable of and if he gets wind of what we suspect, you may not be safe."

She relaxed her face; let her arms fall to her side. "Of course. You're right. I'm lucky I'm still alive I suppose."

"I've been alone a long time and with you I feel . . . Well, it doesn't matter now. I need to dial back my overprotective instincts. Just promise me you'll be careful."

"I will." She pecked him on the cheek and got into her car.

He watched as she drove away. He'd been alone too long, had practically become asexual. For years his only interests had been finding Danny, and drinking. Then it was just drinking. And now, he'd flicked a switch and was awake again.

He was cautious to buy too much into the Danny story. Anyone could be screwing with him and the chances of Danny still being alive were slim to none. The chances of him being whisked into a time machine, not possible at all. But Fred was never wholly without hope when it came to Danny. Until he saw a body he'd never believe his son was gone.

Fred had a busy work day ahead of him. If his work wasn't time sensitive, if there weren't clients on the other end whose lives hung in the balance of what he found, he'd blow it off and work on Barry's case. He was a PI, not a brain surgeon, but sometimes secrets saved a life, or at least a bank account, and that was something. He was a mere cog in the wheel but he needed to honor his commitments.

He checked his phone for an address and drove to the Lucky Star Motel. It was early in the day to meet a lover for an extramarital affair but he had to follow the clues his client fed him. He was on the downslide of life. Forty-nine and not the sprite young man he once was. A few days ago he would have scoffed at the idea of being up this early for a quickie in a hotel but now, with Joyce . . . Affairs didn't follow rules or convention. Love and lust didn't watch the clock.

Anyway, the wife who hired him was thirty and her husband thirty-five. That was another ball of wax entirely. He pulled up to the hotel where the wife swore her husband would be meeting a woman.

A half hour later and Fred was still sitting, waiting for her client's husband. He'd give it another half hour then call it quits. Wouldn't be the first time a husband was innocent of adultery.

"Well I'll be damned," he said. A handsome young man, the one in his photos, pulled up in his black Lexus. He stepped out of the car, with a noticeable spring in his step, and ran up the stairs toward a room. Fred adjusted his camera and zoomed in. The door opened even before his client's husband knocked, revealing another attractive young man, in a towel. Shaggy blond hair, trimmed beard, washboard stomach. Fred took several pictures. The two kissed and then Fred's client's husband walked inside. The door closed behind them. He had enough evidence to prove his client was correct, which would likely signal an end to his client's marriage.

Whenever he discovered affairs, he was torn. He felt vindicated, proving his clients' cases so to speak, but also repulsed at humanity and the endless secrets, the lack of integrity in the population.

He shut off the camera and set it on the seat, then checked the calendar on his phone. For the next few hours he was scheduled to sit outside the home of Cathy Leroy. She was suing her employer because she stood on a chair in their lunchroom to hang holiday decorations and slipped and fell. The corporation didn't flinch at paying her medical bills and short term disability payments, but when she asked for half a million dollars the insurance company called Fred. He'd been to her home twice this week already and the most movement he witnessed involved Mrs. Leroy walking to check her mail. The trial was in two days so the insurance company was growing desperate for evidence she was faking. He agreed to one more day of watching. Just in case she forgot herself and did something that would weaken her case.

More than anything he wanted to go to the police station and get an investigation started on Barry, but he'd made a commitment to his client and needed to honor it.

He parked in front of a brick Tudor with a wrought iron fence. *It's gonna be a long morning.*

- 4 -

Danny watched Joyce kiss Fred goodbye. "Huh, didn't expect that," he said under his breath. Luckily, Young Danny was looking out the other window, lost in thought.

Danny kept an eye on Fred as he drove away.

"You gettin' out?" the taxi driver asked.

"Yeah. Yeah sure." He nudged Young Danny's shoulder. "Come on, kid, let's go."

"Where are we?" They exited the car and it sped off.

Danny checked his notes against the street address. "This is where your dad lives now."

"Why? What about our house? We don't have our house anymore?" The tears started. Danny threw his arm around him.

"Nothing is the same but we're going to change that. It's part of why we're here. Whatever you see, it doesn't matter, okay? It doesn't matter because everything is going to go back to just how it was before."

The boy stood firm. "No it's not because Mom will still be dead."

Danny had no consoling words to offer except, "Yes, but *you're* not and that's the best I can do. Come on."

He led the boy up the stairs. "Do you have a key?"

Danny shook his head. "No, and we need to pray he doesn't have an alarm system." From what Danny could remember about his dad, from his mixed memory, Fred was proud. He was the type to booby trap the house for burglars, to leave a piece of tape in the door to check. Old school noir methods. Danny broke a small pane in the window beside the door, and reached up to unlock the latch. He waited. No high-pitched beeps. He didn't see an alarm system. Taking a gamble, he opened the window and climbed in. Young Danny followed.

"I remember this chair and couch. He bought them for us a couple of weeks ago. He wanted to treat us better he said." The fabric was worn and old, sun faded and beer stained. The boy sat in the recliner, staring off into space as tears rolled down his eyes. Danny wished the kid could get a handle on his emotions. He didn't remember being so damn sad all the time. Then again, he didn't have this life, and his mother hadn't just died in front of him. There was no way anyone could grasp all the shit Danny was throwing at him. No kid should ever have to see what he did.

"It smells like him," Young Danny said. "He must still wear Old Spice."

Danny couldn't help but lean in and sniff the chair. "It does smell like him. See, everything didn't change."

"Hey, it's me!" Young Danny jumped from the chair. There

were several framed pictures of him on Fred's desk and the bookcase. "He really loves me huh?"

"He does. He always did, just got caught up in some grown up stuff. But yeah, he loves you. No question."

Thank God that seemed to alleviate a fraction of the boy's torment.

He wandered around the apartment while Danny walked to Fred's desk, curious if the ex-cop had acted on the contents of the folder. He had. Each murder was now separated into its own file, with the name and date of death in Fred's writing on the tabs. He flipped through them and found a fourth folder.

He sat down and reviewed the newest addition. "Who's Monica Rushmore?" He read the file. *The Rainbox* wasn't written yet so the debut signing connection was absent. *How does she tie into any of this?* He consulted his notebook. *Maybe I forgot about her, or I never knew.* He flipped through the pages of the THEN part of his journal. *Nothing. Only the three girls. He's even more of a sociopath than I than I thought.*

Young Danny walked out of Fred's bedroom wearing a Bruins jersey. "This smells like him too. Can I keep it?"

"Of course you can. He'd want you to have it."

"It's his favorite shirt. Or was. Guess it's old now. He never let me wear it before."

"Trust me, kid, he'd love to see you in it."

"Cool." The boy stretched his arms out. They barely reached the end of the sleeves. "Can I dig through his other stuff?" He smiled. A rare sight.

"Knock yourself out."

The boy walked back into the bedroom and Danny proceeded to rifle through the notes in Monica's file. She was a very young girl, raped and murdered. In Fred's writing it said, *Joyce said Barry did it.*

Danny sighed. "I wonder how many more there were." He felt sick when he thought of Barry. *Such a wonderful man in public, but a monster in private.*

Fred's folder contained an article about Monica's father, Ian

Rushmore. He was a well-renowned magician with a permanent spot at Foxwoods. This story talked about his early days in his shop at Old Orchard Beach, and his daughter's tragic murder in the Time Travel Box, a disappearing box trick painted to give the appearance of being covered inside and out with sea glass.

He closed his eyes and immersed himself in memories of Old Orchard Beach. They were different from his own, but now *were* his own. Barry and him on the beach, finding the red glass in Old Orchard Beach. Barry telling him . . . he strained, telling him about a magic box. As a child he didn't have a good grasp of where the store was in relation to where they sat on that beach that day, but it was a tiny downtown. At most, they were a mile from where Barry had killed Monica.

And then you had the gall to write a book about The Rainbox, you bastard. He read the graphic details about the investigation in Fred's pile. Monica was only eighteen and found dead of strangulation. Danny shivered at the thought as he used Fred's scanner to copy and print everything in her file.

He quickly flipped his notebook upside down and scribbled the memories as they came to him. He'd listed several before but this had a different connotation. His notebook had both sets of memories in as much detail as he could recall, both of them scattered and different but overlapping, both sets expanding and reaching toward the center of the notebook where they would meet and he would finally expose the truth. Or so he hoped.

Young Danny entered the room again. "Can we go now? I'm trying not to be sad but I can't help it. Can I leave a note for my dad, tell him I'm okay?"

Danny smiled. Time to go all in, he thought. "Come here. Sit in his chair."

He sat Young Danny on the chair facing the monitor. "See that circle up there? That's a camera."

"Really? Like a super high tech spy camera?"

"No, everyone has them now."

Danny clicked a few keys and Young Danny's face appeared on the large monitor. "Wow, that's so cool!"

"Here, take this pen and write him a note."

The boy wrote on the paper and went over the letters so they were thick and dark. "Okay, I'm ready."

He held the note and faced the camera. Danny clicked a key and took the photo.

"Are you gonna print it out for him?"

"Even better." He tapped a series of keys and Young Danny's smiling face appeared as the computer's wallpaper. He wore Fred's old Bruins' jersey and held a note. *I love you dad. I'm coming home soon.*

- 5 -

Joyce called Barry twice from her house and he didn't pick up. She didn't bother leaving a message. She dug through her freezer but there were no snacks left. *Nothing in this goddamned house to eat but protein and salad!* She slammed the freezer doors as well as every cabinet door and drawer that yielded similar results.

She stood on a chair to reach the top shelf and on it a very old container of Hershey's unsweetened cocoa. She took two heaping spoons full and dumped them into a mug with a little milk. She stirred up the clumpy mess with a spoon then poured sugar from her dispenser until a tiny glistening mountain rose from the pile of brown muck. She stirred that too and popped it in the microwave for forty seconds. While she was waited, she dialed Barry's house again.

The microwave beeped at the same time as Barry's answering machine. She hung up, took a mouthful of her creation and spit it out. *This tastes like shit!*

Joyce moved to her living room chair, unaware of the fudge smudge on her lower lip. She groaned when she viewed her Barry walls with fresh eyes. That man had been her center, her motivation for all she did and believed. A twinge of guilt struck her. She'd thrown him under the bus, given Fred Monica's name. She couldn't take it back but was worried about Barry. It wasn't like him to not answer his phone.

Plus she had to get her hands on sugar or she was going to kill someone or herself. She grabbed her keys and jacket and fled the townhouse.

Fifteen minutes and a Friendly's Jim Dandy later, all five scoops of ice cream chocolate, all three toppings chocolate, Joyce felt buoyant and unstoppable and happy. But Barry still hadn't picked up. She circled his street three times before settling on a spot a block away. She ran the last few feet there, and up his stairs. "Barry, are you there?" She was shaking but that was just the sugar, she knew. It would wane soon. She knocked again.

No answer. He could be out. Surely that's it. Maybe out for a walk. No, he hates walking with his cane, especially on the cobblestone. Her mind ran a hundred miles an hour as she dialed Jerry's number.

"*Hello?*" he said.

"Jerry, it's Joyce. Is Barry with you? I'm at his house and he's not answering and didn't pick up his phone."

There was a delay, a suspicious pause, and then he replied with, "*No, I haven't seen him all day.*"

"Should I call the police?" It's the last thing she wanted to do. It was better to keep cool about everything until Fred could plan it out.

"*He's probably taking a nap. I wouldn't worry. Try again later. I can stop by if you want.*"

"No, it's fine. I'm overreacting."

She hung up without wasting time on small talk. "What the hell, Barry?"

Joyce opened her purse and dug out the key for Barry's front door. "Barry, are you here?"

His loafers and dress shoes were beside the door. Next to them rested his old pair of sneakers. They were encrusted in sand. "What the hell?"

She ran down the hall. "Barry!"

In the distance she heard mumbling. *Oh my God, he's had a stroke!* She rushed to his room—and found him in the Rainbox. He was crouched in a corner with his eyes closed, talking to himself.

"Barry, what's going on?"

He popped his eyes open and gasped. "Joyce, what are you doing here?"

"I was worried. I called and you didn't pick up."

He stood and glared at her and she suddenly regretted coming. "So you came to my house? Let yourself in?"

"I was worried. With Danny and all that. Thought maybe something happened to you."

He softened, thank God. "I'm fine; I just wanted a little time alone. I think he's real, Joyce. I think it's all real. The Rainbox is a time travel machine." He reached to the soap dish and withdrew a piece of red sea glass. "I went to the beach today and found this. Was there all morning with Jerry, beachcombing. It hasn't worked yet but I think it will."

She shook her head. "It's not real. And even if it were, what could you possibly want to change?"

"Seriously? I'd change everything. All of it. I'd go back to before Danny was born and meet Helen. She's the one I loved most of all. Then Danny would be my real son. And I never would have cheated on *her*. My hand to God I never would have cheated on her; and all these murders Danny talks about, they never would have happened. I don't remember them but I believe him. I believe what he says. You know I can't trust my own mind."

He was too stupid and self-absorbed to realize how he'd hurt Joyce, that those words devastated her. He'd always dismissed her; never once acknowledged that she'd given up everything for him. Her own son, a chance—lots of chances— to marry other people. She had done nothing but sacrifice for him yet all he talked about was that two-bit adulteress Helen Brundige.

She steeled herself. Fine, she could draw blood too, just by telling the truth. "There is no reality where Danny would ever be your son, except this one, where you threw him away."

"What are you talking about? I never threw him away. Never!"

"Danny was my son. Our son. Together."

He fell back against the wall. "What?"

"Yeah, that's a real kick in the teeth right? He was our son. I was going to tell you, was going to keep him. Figured you'd leave Della for me because when you fucked me all those times in your office you told me how important I was to you."

Barry stared at her, more sad and horrified than she'd ever seen him.

"But a man came up to me in a bar, told me you'd hurt me, that I needed to run away from you. A stranger in a bar." Whose face, goddammit, burst into her mind with crystal clarity. It was Danny, their mysterious stranger who was ruining everything. "So what did I do? I had the baby in secret and gave him away. I thought maybe that's what it would take to win you over. And by the time I came back you were already cheating on Della with a new woman."

He reached out to her, tried to touch her face but she moved. "Get away from me. You made me give away my son and he died. Because of you. All because of you. You wouldn't love him if he was mine but if he was Helen's well, of course. Helen was everything!"

Barry slumped back down into the corner of the Rainbox. "She *was* everything. But Joyce, if I had known about the baby, everything would have been different. Don't you get it? All the times I screwed around I never used a condom. I hoped one of them would show up one day and tell me I'd fathered a child. My whole adult life I waited for a knock on the door from one of those book signing hookups but nothing. If I knew about our baby I would have left Della. Hell, you and I would have made a great team." He reached out his hand. "We did make a great team, didn't we?"

Guilt, stupidity, and foolishness flooded through her and she didn't know how to react or what to do. "How dare you say this now? How dare you tell me now that the boy I gave up, who is dead, would have changed everything?"

"But he did change everything didn't he? He's back and trying to get justice. I think he wants me to admit what I did, but if I can go back and change it all now, then we could do what we should have."

"What about Helen?"

His face dropped and tears sprang to his eyes. "I guess I'd never meet her at all."

Barry's big emotional dream was bullshit. She'd never be *the one*. It was always going to be Helen no matter what he promised. Now or in the past or future, Joyce was destined to be second choice, his big compromise.

"Fuck you, Barry Ford. Fuck you!"

She ran from the house, crying so hard she had a hard time seeing the path to the exit. She slammed the door, jumped into her car and took off.

- 6 -

Fred finished his last job, just barely. Being stuck in front of a woman's house, waiting endlessly for her to emerge and make a mistake and violate her insurance claim, was mind numbing and a waste of his time. Especially when he wanted more than anything to focus on Barry and Danny and Joyce right now, all for different reasons.

Three hours of sitting on his ass in his car, spying from across the street, and then finally, the woman walked out. He grabbed his camera assuming she was just checking the mail. Instead she scouted out her surroundings for spies, miraculously didn't notice him, and proceeded to toss a Frisbee for her very large dog. She used her right arm, the one supposedly destroyed by nerve damage from her fall. Again and again she heartily threw that Frisbee, with no ill effects. Then she climbed a small ladder to fill her bird feeders, lugging a twenty pound bag of feed with that same useless arm. Fred snapped enough pictures to thrill the insurance company.

He raced to his office. Forty minutes later he had delivered great news to the insurance company and devastating news to his first client, the one with the gay cheating husband. He figured the news about cancelled each other out in terms of karma for the day.

It was early afternoon by the time he told his secretary he

was going to be out the rest of the day. His stomach growled so he stopped at a McDonald's drive through on the way home. A quarter pounder and a large fries would give him the energy he needed. He had a full day left and couldn't do it on an empty stomach. He rested the food on the passenger seat.

At two-thirty, with his paper bag of warm food and a thick chocolate shake, he arrived home and ran up his stairs, eager to grab his reports and take them to the police. Then he saw the broken window. He set his food down and pulled out his gun. He tried the door which was unlocked. That likely meant whoever it was went in the window and out the door. He pulled out his phone to call the police but stopped. What if it was Danny?

He opened the door slowly, aiming his gun and letting it lead the way. "Anybody in here? I've got a gun."

No answer.

He checked the bedroom and bathroom, the closets. Whoever was here had left. In his room his closet door was open, his things moved.

The papers on his desk in the living room had been rearranged. He was sure of it. He'd fastened the paperclips to the stacks on the left then right in alternating piles. Someone had removed the clips and set them *all* to the left. He checked his scanner and saw it was powered on.

He sat at the desk and inspected every inch but didn't see anything missing, just moved. Banging his fist on the desk clicked his monitor awake.

Danny's smiling face stared at him from the nineteen inch monitor. He wore Fred's 1999 Bruins' Jersey and held up a note that read, *I love you dad. I'm coming home soon.*

"Oh my God," Fred said.

He jumped from the desk and dashed to his bedroom closet. He swung the clothes, banged the hangers together. He smiled. "The shirt is gone. Holy shit, the shirt is gone. You're back, Danny!"

He took a deep breath. *Need to focus.*

The address book in his desk had the names and numbers of all his friends on the force from the old days. He didn't know how many of them were still there but he knew where to start.

He opened the book and dialed a number.

"Can I have Cindy Looper please?"

"Cindy MacAfee you mean?" the receptionist asked.

He felt a twinge of jealousy but caught himself. *Good for her, she married old Mac.* "Yes that's her."

"Cindy McAfee, speaking," said a familiar voice after a moment.

"Hey, it's Fred. Brundige."

"Wow, it's great to hear from you."

"Thanks."

"How have you been?" she asked.

"Congratulations on your marriage," he said, ignoring her question. A pause and then, "I need your help."

"Are you all right?"

"I don't know. It's about Danny."

"Fred, you know you need to move on." Her voice grew sad.

"Please, this is different. I swear to God it's different."

"You've said that before. I want to believe you. You know that but—"

"Listen, I have proof. I think he's alive."

Cindy had been his high school sweetheart, his prom date, his first love. She broke up with him when she went away to college in Vermont. He was crushed and drank his misery away for a good long time until he met Helen. Helen kept him on the straight and narrow for years but even she couldn't keep his demons away.

When Cindy joined the department after college in the forensics lab they were able to maintain a friendship. Not close, but it wasn't awkward either. At that time Fred was happily married and Danny was a toddler. Cindy was still single, still beautiful. But Fred was a faithful husband even if he was lacking in other areas.

When he lost Helen and Danny years later, Cindy stuck by him. Just friends, but she was by his side night and day. Through the worst of it. She got him a good therapist but he only visited twice. She led him to AA but that didn't stick either. After his DUI and losing his job, after a year of his spinning into a downward spiral, she told him she had to let him go, let him work through it on his own. He was obsessed with finding Danny and it was "killing us both" she said. Until he accepted Danny's death—

"Please," he said now on the phone. "He contacted me. He was in my house. He took a picture of himself with my computer and left it for me to find. Today. This all happened today. There's a lot more but—"

She sighed. *"It's not possible."*

"I said I had proof. You can't tell anyone yet but I swear to you it's him. They never found a body. He could have been kidnapped. You see that all the time on the news."

He didn't tell her that the picture was of Danny as he looked fifteen years ago, or that he suspected he had traveled back in time. It didn't matter. His son was here and he could prove it.

She didn't speak but she didn't hang up either.

"Do you still work in the crime lab?"

"I run it now." He knew she must be smiling. She was a hard worker and deserved that position.

"Could you possibly come and sweep for fingerprints? A tech might question the picture he left. He could have Photoshopped it. But fingerprints don't lie." No answer. "Please Cindy. For old times' sake."

She waited before answering. *"Are you still at the house by the lake?"*

"No. I'm at 343 Bay Road. Bradfield."

"Against my better judgement, because we were so close once, okay I'll help you. But only to help you to accept the truth."

"You have no idea how much this means to me." At a time in his life when all his old friends and coworkers had written him off, this act of kindness gave him hope.

"I'll come out in a few minutes. I'll bring my intern along. She won't ask any questions and she's really good with technique. She has a degree in forensics too and will do anything to land a permanent job here. She knows a lot more about all the new stuff than I do but don't tell her I said that."

"Thanks so much, Cindy."

"Fred, I hope it's him. Really I do."

"Thanks."

They hung up and Fred sat on his couch, away from the evidence. He called Joyce but got her voicemail. He didn't leave a message. His stomach growled but he was in no mood to eat now. His lunch was still in the bag out on the stoop but he didn't want to move. Wanted to sit and relish the picture of his boy on the computer monitor a few feet away. He'd be counting the seconds until Cindy showed up and proved Danny was alive.

▲▲▲

Cindy knocked at his door about a half hour later. Using a dishtowel, he carefully turned the knob and let her and the intern in. He'd been around enough crime scenes to know that he needed to stay out of the way.

He hugged Cindy when she walked in. "You haven't aged at all," he said, truly meaning it.

"That's sweet of you to say but trust me, I have. It's great to see you." She sounded worried, not excited. She agreed to come but he knew she didn't believe. Yet. She would.

"This is Connie."

Thanks for coming by. Nice to meet you." The intern was short, thin, Asian, and she smiled a lot. Oh to be young and eager about a career again. He remembered those days.

"Nice to meet you too," she said pumping his hand heartily.

He let go and pointed to his office area. "I appreciate you both coming by and don't want to waste a lot of your time so I'll get right to it. He was over here, by the computer. My things were moved, and check this out." He clicked his mouse with the end of a pen and Danny's face burst onto the monitor.

Cindy jumped back. "Is that Danny?"

"Yeah, from today. He wrote that note today." He pointed to the notebook. "I didn't touch it but see the grooves underneath? He sat here and wrote this note on that pad. And he went through my closet. Found that shirt. My old shirt. See he's wearing it in that picture."

The intern seemed confused but he doubted Cindy would have given her the history. "Can she keep a secret?" he asked Cindy of Connie.

"I can. I swear I won't say a word. What's going on?" the young girl asked, excited to be included in a mystery.

"His son disappeared, what was it, fifteen years ago give or take?" Fred nodded. "They never recovered his body and he was assumed drowned."

"They just found a shoe," Fred said. "But that doesn't prove he's dead." He smiled.

Cindy shook her head. "*If* he's not dead, *if* he was kidnapped and returned after all this time, this isn't how he would look. He'd be an adult. This is a cruel trick someone is playing on you." She turned to Connie. "We shouldn't have come. We're just giving him false hope."

"Listen," he said, grabbing Cindy's arm. "Please wait. I know it's incredible and you're going say this picture was altered or that boy is an actor who resembles Danny but Jesus, Cindy. You know that face. That's him." He grabbed a photo from the nearby table to compare. "It's my boy."

She gave the photos a cursory glance. "The picture means nothing. I'm sorry." Cindy then reached for the notepad with her gloved hands and studied it. "But you said fingerprints don't lie. I know we're not going to find what you want, but I'm willing to get prints to prove to you once and for all that you need to let him go. Maybe the prints will yield a match in our database and we can track down the person who's messing with you. I can do that much."

"Fair enough." Fred had to know either way. He hoped he proved her wrong but if not, at least he'd know.

"Connie, start dusting the surfaces. Get this pad, the mouse, everything on this desk. Get the closet door," Cindy instructed.

"Check the doorknob too," Fred suggested. "He came in the window but left through the door. It was unlocked and the window was broken."

He moved to the corner of the room, out of the way.

"You can't get your hopes up, Fred," Cindy said. "There's no way this little boy in the picture is the one who was here. Damn straight it's Danny from before but it's got to be doctored. Someone is messing with you. Probably the ex-husband of one of your divorce clients."

"I know his writing. It's him," he insisted. "And there's more to the story, things I can't say right now." Because he knew he'd lose all credibility if he did.

The intern held a paper out to Cindy. She frowned and nodded, gestured for her to keep going.

"Just so you know, I cut my left thumb on a boning knife a few years ago." He showed the two women the scar. "So if you find any left thumbs with a jagged line, it's mine."

"You don't happen to have Danny's prints do you?" Cindy asked.

A happy memory flashed in his mind. "I do. I totally forgot. Can I get into that drawer, or can you do it, with the gloves?"

When Danny was seven he'd invited Fred to school for parent career day. Danny was so proud of him. What a kid. After school, Fred took him on a tour of the police station. He saw the holding cells, the booking area, and the interrogation rooms. Fred had fingerprinted Danny for fun and had put them in a file.

Cindy opened the drawer and pulled out a thick folder. She handed Fred a pair of latex gloves. It took only a minute to find the fingerprint card. Seeing it tore Fred up. These prints would tell him conclusively. Now being faced with it, he knew there was no chance in hell Danny was magically still a little boy come home through the Rainbox like nothing had ever happened.

He handed Cindy the fingerprint card. "Don't lose this. It's all I have left if it's not really him."

"I'll return them once I'm done," she said kindly.

The rest of the sweep only made him sad. He'd been so enthusiastic when he'd called her and when she'd arrived with her helper. But her tone and the way she and the intern frowned added to the reality of the situation and cut him down to nothing.

They finished without a word to him about the results. At best it would be a guess at this point. He felt like those X-ray techs that scanned and viewed your insides then told you they couldn't divulge what they saw, like it was a goddamned state secret.

He spent a few awkward minutes sharing small talk with Cindy and the intern, the whole time wanting them to expose what they found. I can handle it, he wanted to say. The truth was, the longer he could hope before they totally crushed him, the better.

Cindy hugged him goodbye, promised to call him as soon as they had results. She said they should get together with Mac. He agreed the way people do in those situations.

And then they left and he watched out the window until day turned to dusk, and the prospect of another long lonely night taunted him like a cruel parent.

- 7 -

Jerry insisted on walking Barry into his book signing. Joyce wasn't answering her phone and he was relieved. He was a fiction writer, didn't know how the science worked, but despite what he promised he would never relive his life to end up with Joyce if Helen was out there. He would instead plan to approach her earlier and more directly, keep her away from stairs and Danny away from water. He smiled with hope as he walked into the already crowded bookstore.

"Mr. Ford," Jerry said, nudging his shoulder. "We're here."

"I know, Jerry. I know where we are and why we're here." He tapped his head. "I think I'm getting better," he whispered. "Fingers crossed."

Since Danny had approached him the first time, his memory seemed stronger. Maybe it was the adrenaline, the hope. Stress generally made his memory worse but this was happy stress. He had an appointment the end of next week with Amy. She'd said all along that his memory may begin to repair itself, or at least find new ways to compensate to allow him to start to take his life back. He still had his black outs of course, and if he misplaced his notebook, he'd be a wreck. He patted his coat pocket now to be sure it was there. It was.

He remembered every bit of Danny's meeting yesterday. The boy *was* Danny and Joyce wasn't going to trick him into thinking otherwise. He was sorry now he'd filed a protective order. Didn't matter. He wouldn't stop Danny, the adult or child version, from coming to him.

One thing he did need to do though was convince Danny that he did not kill Helen and certainly did not in any way shape or form drown him. If nothing else came of this before he went back into the Rainbox and changed the clock back, he had to make sure Danny believed him.

Danny was his son. *His* son. Of all the women he chose to have an affair with, it was the adoptive mother of his biological child. It couldn't be a mere coincidence.

"Mr. Ford," the store clerk said. "Are you all right?"

"Yes, just lost in thought. Let me take a seat and start signing books." He moved behind his table, set his cane down, took off his coat.

"Hey, you can't cut the line!" a woman shouted.

Barry saw a line of people, including an angry fat woman with bright pink lipstick. She growled at a man who was trying to make his way through.

"Danny!" Barry said. The adult one. Screw the restraining order. This was his son. *His* son. He smiled and leaned on the table to stand.

The young man did not smile back. Instead he thrust down a stack of papers. "Where did you get the idea for *The Rainbox*, Barry?"

"Collecting sea glass with you. I know it's you. I believe you. Please, let's talk when I'm done. What you think happened, that's not how it went." He studied him closely, could see a resemblance to the boy he knew and to himself. *My son.*

Danny gestured to the article. "The Rainbox. Was it called the Time Travel Box when you raped and killed Monica Rushmore in Maine?"

The crowd gasped. Barry fell back as if he'd been slapped. How could he know? No one knew. *Except Joyce.*

His hands began to shake and his mind turned to mush again. He beheld the crowd and wondered why they were all staring at him, muttering amongst themselves. He saw a stack of books in front of him and did not recognize the cover. He knew his name but the book jacket was unfamiliar. He opened it. Copyright. 2015.

The young man in front of him shook with anger and his face was contorted in a snarl. He was the man who came to his house and took money, the one who—no it was his son. He wrung his hands. He viewed him again and saw a child in a boy scout uniform. Little Danny Brundige.

"No," he cried. "No, you're not dead. You're not really dead. You came back through the Rainbox!"

The man backed away. "You know what you did, Barry. You know what you did and you have to turn yourself in." He walked out.

Barry heard the hum of the crowd talking, unintelligibly, increasing in volume. He refused to look up from his hands. He concentrated on the grooves in his nail beds. In his mind, he played *Mr. Blue Sky* and thought of Helen. He danced with her effortlessly and she was so lovely. He closed his eyes to drown out the unpleasant roar of noise around him.

"I'm sorry, everyone," Joyce called out. He felt her warm hand on his shoulder. She'd saved him, as always. He covered her hand with his. *Good old Joyce.*

"Please don't listen to anything that man said. He has been stalking Barry and there is a restraining order against him. Just give us a few minutes to collect ourselves and then Barry will sign your books. You can see how that man upset him but Mr. Ford be all right in just a few minutes."

She signaled to the clerk. "Can you take Barry in the back for a few minutes?" Joyce dug through Barry's pocket and retrieved his iPhone. She scrolled until she found a song then hit play and handed it to him.

"Listen to this song. It'll put you in a happy place and I'll be right back." He just sat, didn't know what to think or do. He was all mixed up and needed to focus but—

Hazy Shade of Winter by the Bangles played. He contemplated Joyce as she'd been when she'd first joined him as an intern, then as his lover. This was their song, even if it was a silly one. They used to sing it together in his home office, when he was editing a magazine, so many years before any of his books were written. He smiled as he recalled how cute she was, how bubbly and helpful.

"Come on, Barry," she said now. "Go with Betsy and I'll be along in a few minutes."

He stared at her glassy eyed, but happy. He followed the clerk and remembered a happy time in his life.

- 8 -

Joyce ran out the front door expecting Danny to be long gone. He was just down the street. He stood next to a young boy. As she approached them two streetlights away they didn't run. Instead they faced her.

Danny and the boy looked at her. Their faces were the same but one was an adult and one a child. Little Danny. The boy from her house, from Helen, from the lake.

"What do you want? Why are you coming after Barry?"

"He needs to confess his crimes," Danny said. "He needs to own up to what he did."

"And then what?" she asked. She was trying to rationalize with blackmailers or time travelers and both choices were insane. "What will you get from this? Do you want money?"

Both of them shook their heads in synchronicity. Had they rehearsed that or were they that much alike, she wondered.

She stared at the boy again, could see Barry in him, could see herself. "This is impossible and I'm not falling for it, got it? Sure this kid looks a lot like Danny Brundige and so do you but you're not him. I am not your mother. Barry is not your father."

The boy tugged Danny's sleeve. "What is she talking about?"

"Were you adopted?" she asked.

"Yes."

He mouthed "Shut up" to Joyce.

"Danny," she said to the boy. He wiped his nose with his sleeve. "What year is it?"

Without pause he said, "2000."

"What's going on?" she asked Danny tenderly. "Please just tell me what I can do to—to make it all okay again."

"Help us to bring Barry down for all his crimes," Adult Danny said.

The boy looked up as well, his eyes wet from crying, voice quivering. "As soon as we get Barry I can go home. I really miss my dad. Please help us. Do whatever he says and help us. My dad needs me."

She reached out and hugged the boy then bowed down. She wiped his tears. "I'll help you. I promise. I won't let you down."

▲▲▲

"What do you say we do something fun?" Danny asked the boy when they left Joyce. The kid had been through the wringer and his work wasn't done yet.

"Like what?" His eyes had dried but he was far from feeling okay, and a world away from happy. Until he could get back home, a distraction would lessen his sadness.

"They have a dinosaur movie at the Bradfield Museum. I saw a flyer. They're showing it on the huge IMAX dome surround screen."

"I don't know what that means but I really like dinosaurs," the boy conceded.

"You'll love it. Let's go."

Not long after, they were seated in the dark theater. The movie began and Danny was relieved to see Young Danny smiling at the special effects and giant dinosaurs on the screen surrounding him. "This is so cool," he said.

"Yeah," Danny agreed.

Tonight there would be another job for them to do, and maybe one more after that. Then it would be over. Danny had no idea what would happen to *him*. Sure, putting Barry in jail in this reality would stop him from future murders and punish him for prior ones, but what if they went back and he tried to kill Danny again? He cursed himself for bringing Danny back to this time but staying in the past wasn't an option because they were alone in the woods and not safe. Staying here wasn't a choice either. They couldn't coexist. And yet they did. It was science he didn't understand any more than Barry did when he wrote the book. The novel was only about wishes and hope and justice.

He pondered bringing Young Danny to Fred, letting him live in the here and now. It couldn't work though. One of them would have to perish and it could be Young Danny. He couldn't break Fred's heart again.

"Did you see that?" Young Danny asked, pointing to a T-rex tearing apart a smaller dinosaur.

"Yeah that was great," he said. At any time, this could all change, and the laws of physics and time would catch up with them. He needed to do as much as he could, and make every minute count.

He settled into his chair and focused on the movie, on the moment. The smell and taste of the popcorn, the smile on Young Danny's face, the knowledge that if nothing else, he tried to make a difference.

▲▲▲

"Do you remember me?"

Barry heard a young voice as he slept. It was Danny. Another dream of the boy. It's all he could think of these days.

"Barry, wake up!"

He opened his eyes and saw little Danny standing next to him beside his bed. Barry sat up, reached for his light. It took his eyes a minute to adjust.

"What are you doing in here? How did you get in?"

The boy pointed to the door. "I came in through the Rainbox."

Barry shook his head. "But you were already here, I thought. I saw you the yesterday."

"Did you?" The boy eyed him curiously. "I just got here."

"No, you came here. First as an adult and then as a child. You tried to sell me candy bars." Light reflected off tears in the boy's eyes. "It's okay son, it's okay. I'm not mad. I'm always happy to see you."

"You killed me," the boy said.

"No, I didn't. I did not, at all. I told you the other day. I didn't kill your mother or you. You have to believe me."

The boy stood just out of reach. "I want to go home but I can't because you'll try to kill me again. And it's your fault my dad is so sad and you don't even care."

In a way yes it was Barry's fault and he knew that. If he had never met Helen she may still be alive.

"I was in your kitchen when your mother fell down the stairs. I heard a crash and ran in and she was already gone. It happened that quickly. I held her in my arms because I loved her but I didn't do it. No one did. She must've fallen. A badly timed accident courtesy of God."

Danny's tears overflowed.

"On my soul I promise you it wasn't me."

Barry reached for the boy and hugged him. He cried and Barry hugged him. "I swear to God and to you that I didn't do any of it. Please believe me."

The boy nodded and then pulled back. "I believe you." He smiled. Just a little one but it was enough. "I have to go. I was supposed to give you this." He handed Barry a large brown envelope and then the power went out.

He heard the child run from the room and then the light went back on. By the time Barry grabbed his cane and tottered down the hall, flicking lights on as he went, there was no sign of Danny. The door was locked.

"Are you here? Danny, come to me if you're here. We can talk. I can help you get home. I'll go back with you and you'll see."

The house was silent except for Barry's loud heartbeat. He sat on the couch and didn't move. Surely the boy was still in the house and would turn up. He waited a few minutes then tried the Rainbox.

Danny was not in there either, but of course he wouldn't be. He must have just popped into this time and back again. "Fantastic," he said. If only he could get the damn thing to work. He smiled as he recalled the conversation though. Danny believed him now. Knew he hadn't caused Helen's death or his drowning. Maybe now things could go back to normal. Maybe now the boy would stay back in his time and in the morning life would be different.

He was too tired to write this all down. He'd do it at sunrise. Barry walked to his bed and sat down, moved his feet under the covers. And then he saw the envelope. Danny had given it to him and he'd forgotten. "Wonder what this is." He pulled the papers out and flipped through them. "Oh my God. Oh dear lord."

- 11 -

Danny grabbed the boy as he ran from the brownstone and rushed him down the street. "Did you do it?" The boy nodded. "What did he say about the envelope?"

"He didn't open it. But he insisted he didn't kill Mom just like he said before. Said he was in the kitchen when it happened. He ran out when she fell and was holding her when I walked in. And he said he didn't hurt me either."

Danny felt a burst of emotion and sadness pass from the boy into his own heart. *Could that be true?* "You believe him?"

"I told you I believed him before when I brought him the candy bars, and this time he swore on his soul and to God. It's my fault. I shouldn't have run out that day. I shouldn't have run out and then I wouldn't have fallen into the lake."

"You didn't fall into the lake. Someone tried to kill you, kill me." He touched the child's shoulders. "You've still got bruises from where he held you down."

"It wasn't him."

Danny nodded. The boy's feelings were his now and he couldn't argue what they both felt, but that didn't change Barry's other crimes. The notebook didn't lie, nor did the police reports of murdered women. He pulled up basic articles online but Fred's addition to his files contained graphic details and photos. Private investigators had a lot more access to that level of information, he assumed.

"What was in the envelope I gave him?"

"It doesn't matter. You've been through enough."

"But what was it?"

Danny shook his head. "He did other things. Things I know really happened. Maybe he didn't kill Mom. If she fell down the stairs then I feel really bad for hating him for it but it doesn't change what happened to the others."

"What others?" the boy asked. "Please, I need to know. If I'm going to hate a person, ruin his life, I need to know why."

"Let's get back to the hotel. I don't want to talk about it here."

"But you'll tell me?"

"I don't want to but you deserve to have all the facts. Once I tell you though, it's going to change everything. You need to understand that."

"I get it. But it's not fair for me to punish him if I don't even know why."

Danny hailed a taxi. As they sat in the back on the short drive to their hotel they didn't speak. He needed time to think. He was conflicted on so many levels. Presenting his case to Young Danny would be a bitch if he wasn't a hundred percent committed to his findings. Suddenly he questioned all of it. What if it was a mistake? A series of coincidences that painted Barry to be a serial murderer? He clenched his fists and fogged up the window on his side as he started to breathe too fast. He felt his lungs fill with water and groaned as strong fingers dug into his shoulders and neck and held him under water.

"Come on, we're here. Are you okay?" the boy asked him. Danny gasped and was able to get a good breath as the flashback passed.

"Yeah, I'm okay." He handed the cabbie cash. He and Young Danny stepped onto the curb and into the lobby.

He pressed the elevator button and hoped he was doing the right thing.

- 12 -

"Is this the boy you saw?" Fred asked Joyce.

She sat in his desk chair and stared at the computer monitor. "It's him. He told me it was his birthday and tonight he told me it was the year 2000."

Fred moved to the couch and sat. "How could it be possible though?"

"I don't know," Joyce said, joining him. "But does it matter? What if it is him and the Rainbox is real? We could be together, the three of us."

He nodded. "It would be wonderful but it can't be. He'd end up in a lab. The government, whatever branch controls that stuff, they'd want to know how my son appeared fifteen years later at the same age. Our life would be a circus."

"So we'll run away. Move to a town where no one knows who we are. Surely you could get paperwork that could bend the truth a little, show a later birthdate. No one would have to know."

Fred smiled at her dedication, her desire to commit to him and Danny. He was her son after all, so she said, and he got that, but he needed to think clearly. "We need to assume it's not him. He's got to be an actor."

His phone rang. "Hello?"

"It's Cindy."

Dread filled him as he awaited her next words that would surely prove he'd been conned. "Hi, Cindy."

"I can't believe I'm saying this and I know this is impossible but the prints match."

He set the phone to speaker so Joyce could hear. "The prints match?" He smiled at Joyce.

"Yes but the thing is there are two almost identical sets of prints besides yours."

"Almost identical? What does that mean?"

"It doesn't make any sense but there are two sets of prints that match your son's card. One is from an adult and one from a child. It's almost as if Danny was there at two different ages."

Neither Fred nor Joyce spoke. This would fit Danny's Rainbox story. His impossible and wonderful and life-changing story.

"Are you there?"

"I'm here," he said. "Cindy, I'm going to come in to see the captain in the morning. Can you make sure he gets the fingerprint results? Tell him I'll explain everything when I arrive."

"Of course, but can you explain it to me? We don't know what to think in the lab."

"Let's just say that there's been a miracle and I'm not questioning it and neither should you."

"My job is to question everything," she replied.

"Meet me at nine in Charlie's office and you can listen in while I tell the whole story. He's going to think I'm nuts but you and your evidence can be there to back me up."

"Does this mean Danny is alive?" Cindy asked.

"I think it does but please don't say a word to anyone. Promise me."

"I promise," she said. *"See you tomorrow."*

Cindy hung up. Fred squeezed Joyce's hand. "Our son is alive after all." He hugged and kissed her. "Our son is alive! You might just get your chance to raise him after all," he said. He wasn't a religious man but was going to donate money to the church first chance he got.

Joyce held his hand tight. "What do we need to do? I can't wait to start this new life with you. It seems it's all fate."

"Fate and help from a cryptic visitor. I want you with me at the station tomorrow. It's going to be hard for the captain to swallow but when we present all the evidence we have on Barry and these cold cases he might not think I'm such a nut."

Joyce's smile faded. "For a moment I'd forgotten about Barry. About the women."

"I didn't. He's going to pay for what he did. I hope Barry is getting a good rest because tomorrow night he'll be sleeping in a jail cell."

▲▲▲

- 13 -

Barry squatted in the corner of the Rainbox. The door was closed and the soft blue and green lights seemed to pulse. Next to him rested his notebook, an empty bottle of scotch, and an empty snifter. Copies of articles of murdered women were spread along the floor.

He had placed photos of three of the women in a row. Monica's was set aside. For her he had only apologies and regret. But these three . . .

"I didn't kill you. I swear, I didn't hurt you," he said to the smiling faces in the newspaper articles. The crime scene photos terrified him. Not because he was afraid of seeing violence but because he could not accept he had caused it.

Barry leaned against the wall and dialed Joyce for the fifth time. The machine went straight to voicemail. "Please call me, Joyce. Danny was here and he accused me of horrible things. Horrible. I need you to come help me. You can tell him it wasn't me. You know me. You're my only friend, Joyce, please I need you."

It was a similar message to the last four but this one featured more slurring, more desperation.

"I didn't do it." As he said the words he realized that had become his new mantra since Danny showed up on the scene.

But what if he had? He hated entertaining the thought but why would Danny go through all this and frame him? He thought his past memories were intact but what if they weren't? He thought to the ending of *The Rainbox* novel. He had saved his son only to have him become a serial killer.

"What if I wrote that because I was the killer and I wanted people to know? Hoped my readers would make a connection?"

Without Joyce to tell him what to do, he was stuck. Jerry couldn't help. He knew Barry only as his boss, not as his friend. He didn't know his past. Amy only knew him post-motorcycle accident so she couldn't help either.

He reached up to the soap dish where his new piece of red

sea glass lay. His fingertips touched it to make sure it was still there. Barry closed his eyes tight, jammed the balls of his hands into his eyes until he saw clouds. "Please take me back. Please, please, please take me back. I'll do anything. Please."

He opened his eyes. It took a few minutes for them to adjust to the dim colored lights in the box.

"Shit." The floor was still littered with articles about dead women. The empty glass and liquor bottle sat beside hm. Nothing had changed. There was no fucking magic. Or if there was, he was not the magician.

SIX

- 1 -

"What do you want me to say?" Joyce asked. All told, Barry had called fourteen times last night, and left messages each time. The last one was unintelligible. She played them all for Fred who instructed her to keep them as evidence.

She wasn't afraid of Barry, as she faced him now at his house, but was nervous about how all this would shake out. Her whole adult life had been about being by Barry's side. "Why did you call me so many times?" she asked the pathetic man.

"Why didn't you pick up? I was worried."

He'd brewed coffee and fixed her a cup. Even set a spoon beside it. First time in history. She peered into the mug. It was black. She hated black coffee.

"You weren't worried for my welfare. You were upset I wasn't here for you. So what was the emergency?"

He looked at her like she had two heads. "Why are you being so mean?" His skin was pale and his eyes shadowed from lack of sleep. "I called because you've always been the person I call. If it's good news or bad news, you're the one."

She softened a little as she sat back in the fancy chair. That was true. She was his rock but what did *she* ever get out of it? She'd spent the night with Fred again. He'd run out before she awoke and picked up bagels and Dunkin Donuts coffee with cream and sugar. He wanted to be with her. Only *her*. And besides, they were going to be a family with Danny. It's like none of the unpleasantness ever happened.

It could be that easy, she thought, smiling. And she didn't have to go back in time to fix a damn thing. All she need do was betray Barry and her life would be perfect. That thought made her feel guilty, especially when she saw his anguish. But when she thought of what he'd done, with no repercussions.

"What was so important that you had to call me that many times? I'm here now."

He was dressed and showered which was a good sign, but based on his squinty eyes today and emotional, desperate messages the night before, he was also hungover. He pulled contents from an envelope and laid them on the coffee table. They were the same articles she'd seen at Fred's. She acted surprised. Had to. He laid them out like cards in poker game.

"What the hell are these?" she said, poking at them with her finger.

"Little Danny showed up the other night. I know you're going to say it wasn't him but it was. He showed up selling candy bars in his scout uniform. He hugged me, said he loved me."

She didn't expect *that*. Danny certainly hadn't been warm to her when he'd sold her bars, or after. Of course he didn't know she was his *real* mother. It would happen though; she just had to be patient.

"Then last night I went to bed. I thought I was dreaming he was there but then he said, 'Barry wake up.' I opened my eyes and he was there. Right there. I finally got him to believe that I didn't kill Helen, that she fell when I wasn't in the room. And that nonsense about my killing him, he knows now. I thought that's all he wanted and he'd go home back to his own time."

"And did he?" Joyce felt a stab of panic.

"I don't know. But when I went back to bed after he disappeared I saw this and opened it. Joyce what if I did kill these women? I'd swear in court I didn't do it but what if I don't remember?"

"Do you know any of them?" She knew damn well he did, had slept with every one of them.

He scrutinized them. "They have familiar faces, I think. But we already talked about Monica. I wasn't with her."

Joyce fumed. He'd bedded all four of them, and others too not shown in this stack. Girls who died as well as those who were clever enough to run away in time.

"Look at me, Barry. Look at those faces and look at me. You slept with those girls. All of them."

He shook his head. "I fooled around behind Della's back occasionally. You know that. But killing? I don't have it in me." He sighed. "Do I? Jesus. I don't know what to do. Should I call a lawyer?"

"No one has charged you with anything have they? Apart from a mysterious time traveling little boy no one can see but you? And an adult man who stalks you and spouts nonsense?"

"No. No they haven't. But what if the police do? I was with those women." He studied Monica's picture again, turned it sideways. "Not her but the others. I sort of remember."

"It's probably someone trying to blackmail you and black-mailers won't go to the police."

She knew it was just a matter of hours before Fred would convince the police he had a case and Barry would be arrested, but her loyalty was with Fred now.

"Danny is no blackmailer. My hand to God it's really him. That boy was almost my son so I should know."

"*Was* your son. We talked about this. He *was* your son."

"Yes. He was my son after all, but whatever he was by blood, I knew and loved that little boy and this new incarnation of him we're seeing. He's no actor. I need to get back into that box and make it all okay."

"Why are you still denying you slept with and killed Monica Rushmore?"

Joyce prayed at least about her he would be honest. It was a mistake maybe, but Joyce had put her life on the line for years. The least he could do—

"I told you, I was never with Monica. I swear it."

The evidence was there in front of him and he had the gall to deny it.

"What about last night? What Danny accused you of in the bookstore? What about the fact you wrote *The Rainbox* based on a time travel prop in Monica's shop? Where she was murdered."

Barry cast his eyes down.

Come on, Barry, admit it. Just to me. I was there for god's sake!

He faced her, so trusting. Still believing she was his best and only friend in the world. "Okay, I fucked Monica too. Are you happy?"

"Of course not. But thank you for admitting it."

"What should I do?" he asked. "I can't just sit here and wait to see what happens next."

"That's all you can do," she said. Joyce needed him to sit tight while Fred built his case.

"I'm going in the Rainbox and try to go back. I can do that at least. I have to try."

"Let me ask you this. Are you a hundred percent sure you didn't kill Helen? Didn't knock her down the stairs that day?" She watched him, coolly.

"What? Of course not. I wasn't even in the room. I loved her." His voice cracked. "You know I loved her."

"But what if you killed her, and these women? What if all those years you were conscious of it and planned and killed them all, and after the accident just forgot?"

Barry didn't answer. Joyce knew he had never considered *that*. He grabbed his notebook and flipped through it. "You didn't keep a journal before the motorcycle accident, only after. All I'm saying is that even if you didn't do anything wrong in your eyes, if the police wanted to come after you, they could piece together enough circumstantial evidence against you to make all of it stick."

"Joyce what should I do? When I think about it, it's all fuzzy now. I knew the past. Knew it sharp and clear as anything. But now when I think about those girls and see these pictures—What if you're right? What if Danny is right? What if I am a monster?"

Joyce's phone buzzed in her pocket. It would be Fred. No need to check in front of Barry.

"I have to go. I hope Danny is wrong. I hope I'm wrong. But there's nothing we can do about it now either way."

She rose and left him on the couch, utterly confused and guilty as hell. As he should be, she thought.

- 2 -

"It's just around this bend," Danny told the taxi driver. When they moved around the corner, Danny gasped. The lake house was derelict, the grass overgrown, windows boarded up. Of course he hadn't thought it would be the same but this was startling. Disturbing.

He spoke to the driver. "Can you come back in two hours? Exactly two hours? I don't have a phone so can't call you."

The man nodded. He was young and foreign. Quiet for a cabbie. Hardly any talk all the way here and Danny sure could have used a bit of friendly conversation.

It was all coming to a head now, he thought as he stepped from the car onto the cold hard ground. He'd brought his evidence to Fred who would take it to the police. Young Danny dropped the pictures with Barry. Wheels were set in motion. Later today or tomorrow the police would question Barry. Young Danny told him Barry didn't kill Helen or try to drown him. And if he believed that, then all the rest came into question. He had to remember what happened that last day he was here, alive in the past. Bringing Young Danny here would have confused and saddened him. There was no point in upsetting him further. His work was done and he would go home soon, hopefully. He'd changed things enough to keep him from death that one time and with Helen gone Barry wouldn't come back and kill him. There would be no point.

So here he was, reconstructing the details.

The cab pulled away, leaving Danny alone on the abandoned lot of the broken down lake house. It was mid-afternoon. He had an hour of light left. Maybe two. With trepidation, he approached the house, walked onto the porch. It creaked under his weight but held. He tried the knob. Unlocked.

He went inside the old house. It was empty. Cobwebs, mouse droppings, and a couple dozen empty beer cans littered the floor. The smells of mildew, dust, and cigarettes filled the main room.

Danny saw graffiti on the far wall by the kitchen. Purple spray paint formed a whimsical three-foot mushroom. Under it, the words Trippy Time revealed the kinds of activity this house saw since it had been abandoned. *Partying teenagers.* He was plagued by what had become of their family home but wasn't here to lament or dwell in self-pity for all he'd lost. His only goal was to remember.

He faced the staircase. Danny closed his eyes and tried to recall exactly what had happened. It was difficult at first. Static vignettes popped into his head, photographs of the day flashing furiously, too fast to comprehend.

I was outside when it happened. Not here.

Despite the cold weather today, he headed out to the porch and stood by the steps. He tried his best to recreate the scene.

Mom opened the front door. "I'm going upstairs with Joyce to pack your bag. You be a good boy and stay right on this porch. No matter what you hear you stay right here, okay?"

He nodded both then and now.

Mom was flustered. Her face was red and she'd been crying. She turned and walked inside.

He knelt to peer in the window as he had that day.

Danny watched Mom walk up the stairs. Joyce emerged from the bathroom and walked up the stairs too.

Danny had forgotten Joyce was there with Mom until now.

Come on. Remember it. Remember what happened, damn it.

Dad and Barry shouted at each other. He saw them both enter the kitchen. The yelling was muffled once they went in there and he was glad for it.

Dad ran from the room and toward his office. "I'm gonna fucking kill you!" he yelled to Barry. Danny tensed up. He knew Dad's gun was in his office and that's where he was headed.

He remembered standing, running to the door. He held the doorknob to burst in and take action. But fear stopped him. Fear of his father, a gun, a bad temper. He held his hand around the doorknob, but didn't touch. He waited. Began to walk down the porch stairs toward his mother's car.

Then there was a scream and a crash.

He burst inside and saw Barry holding his mother's bloody head. At first he thought Dad had shot her but his hands hung slack by his side, empty. No gun. Pure terror on his face.

So he'd transferred the blame to Barry because he was there. He was holding Mom's broken body, her oozing skill. Her blood pooled under him, as if he were sitting in a big red spotlight that grew in diameter each second. A spotlight that shined on him to reveal what he'd done. *Killer.*

That how it went, but his perspective was different this time as he looked in Barry's eyes, at the despair, the agony was felt, the utter heartbreak. In the present Barry swore he didn't do it and now when he remembered, it was different. He didn't feel anger toward Barry. It truly could have been an accident. *Shit.*

Danny rose from the kneeling position now and walked numbly, and full of anguish, toward the woods as he had that day. Even if Barry didn't kill Mom, surely he had been *his* executioner. He had trouble breathing now. His lungs were heavy and sore. Whatever he thought he was doing to do to stop the chain of events wasn't working. Jailing Barry wasn't enough. He had to remember. He'd been spared his life to change a horrific outcome. To make it right.

A powerful kick to his back collapsed him. A rock smashed his skull. A branch slammed into his side.

When he opened his eyes he was under the freezing water of the lake. The moon was behind . . . her. *Joyce.* He saw her now, as she held him under. Her fingernails dug into his sweatshirt and he remembered it all. Her face was evil-clown white and menacing in the glow of the moon, smudged but magnified by the water between them.

She pulled him up and he gagged and tried to breathe. "I know you saw me push Helen, you little bastard. No one is taking Barry from me. No one!" She shoved him back under.

Suddenly the hands were gone and the figure disappeared. He was back in the present and still underwater but no one held him down. He raised his head then his body. *Joyce. The whole time it was Joyce. Not Barry.*

Danny staggered out of the shallow water, frozen and sopping wet. The farther he got from the lake, the more his lungs cleared. He took a deep breath.

He walked to the house and back inside where the walls would shield him from the wind. It would still be ninety minutes before the cab returned.

He sat on the bottom step in the foyer. He thought of Barry, how sad he had appeared. "You did love me. And my mother." He wiped a tear from his eye.

He needed to get to Fred and tell him never mind. Tell him it was Joyce. "Shit!" he said as he recalled that she'd spent the night with Fred. "He'll never believe it was her." He considered a solution. "But he'll believe Young Danny."

All the book signings, all the murders. Joyce had been right by his side, killing every woman who slept with him. "*She* is the one I came back to stop."

He would have to wait it out until his ride came back. It was growing dark and he was drenched. Alive and relieved about Barry, but soaking wet. A few hours wouldn't make a difference. He had a plan.

Until then, he gathered wood from outside and lit a fire in the hearth. He thought fondly of the times Mom and Dad and him sat by the fire, before Dad's undercover days. They'd had a nice family. Dad was a good guy. So was Barry. He grimaced now when he thought of the notes from his first life, the ones he couldn't remember anymore. Joyce had been the villain in both dimensions, always jealous, always the murderer.

- 3 -

"Good to see you again, Fred," Charlie said. He was old now, and he hadn't aged well. He'd been a chain smoker back in the day and his voice now was deep as a toad's. His skin was as wrinkled as a man twenty years older.

He held out his hand and saw the wedding ring which reminded him to ask, "How's Marge?"

"Died of a heart attack last year," Charlie said without emotion. Fred should have known. This wasn't starting off well.

"This is my friend Joyce Tuttle."

She shook Charlie's hand.

"Have a seat," Charlie said. They were in his office. It was sloppy like him.

"Cindy should be here in a second," Fred said.

Charlie picked up a file. "She said she had fingerprints."

"You didn't read the results yet?" Fred asked.

Charlie shook his head. "No disrespect, but how many times did you come in here telling me you had a hunch?"

"I know." Fred felt defeated but only for a moment. This was different. This time there was evidence.

Cindy walked in. He introduced her to Joyce who looked her up and down and rolled her eyes. That was catty, he thought, but found it endearing that Joyce was jealous. Fred shrugged to Cindy in apology.

"Okay, I've got two different things going on but they're connected." He stopped for a minute, wondering if Danny's prints were even relevant. Why not just present the Barry information and leave Danny out of it? He had his prints and his proof. What good would it do to tell the captain? If he didn't have him committed, the Danny return would be splashed all over the tabloids and they'd never have a normal life. He liked Joyce's idea. They'd just run off and start fresh, maybe with new identities.

"What do you have?" Charlie asked.

Fred handed him the envelope. "Four murders over the course of twenty plus years. Different states. No connection, so we thought."

Charlie glanced the photos and articles. "I'm listening."

"Barry Ford. He was there for all of them. He killed those girls."

"The writer?" Charlie asked. "Not to dig up old wounds but isn't he the guy who Helen was gonna to run off with?"

"Yes but these are unrelated. He didn't kill Helen. That was an accident. But he did kill Danny. He drowned him. Tried to."

"How do you know? And what does *tried to* mean? Did he do it or not?"

Damn, so much for keeping that out.

"He's not dead. He came back, left me this folder. Left me a couple of notes. Even took a picture with my computer and left it as my wallpaper."

Charlie motioned to Cindy. "And that's where your evidence comes in?"

She walked to his desk and opened the folder. "Connie and I dusted for prints and came up with . . . well we got two sets that weren't Fred's. The sets matched."

"What does that mean? So it's one set? Not following," Charlie said. He scratched his comb-over.

"There were two identical sets of prints, one from a child and one from a man. Both matched the prints Fred had on file of Danny before he died."

"He's not dead," Fred asserted.

"The evidence seems to show that Danny was recently in Fred's apartment. I don't have an explanation for the prints being identical but different sizes," Cindy said.

"I'm sorry I still don't get it. How are you involved in all this?" he asked to Joyce.

"I'm Barry's assistant. Have been for many, many years. I was with him when the murders happened," she explained.

"There in the room?" he asked her. Then to Fred, "Is she an accessory? Is she under arrest?"

"Jesus no. Nothing like that at all," Fred said. "It's a long story."

"I got time," Charlie said, putting his feet on his desk.

Fred began to relay it all from the beginning.

By the end, Charlie had become both interested and befuddled.

"Let me get this straight here. A guy comes through a time travel machine and he's an adult and a child at the same time. Then he gives you all these murder clues, and he says he's your son, Fred, and also your son, Joyce?"

"When you put it like that it sounds crazy," Fred said.

"Forget all that, Charlie," Cindy said. "All that matters is that there may well be a connection in all these cold cases. Fred is handing it to you to investigate."

"Even so, what do we have to go on except Barry was in all those towns and states at the same time? Even if the girls went to his signings it's circumstantial. Can't do much with it."

Joyce spoke for the first time in an hour. "He never used a condom. He told me never used protection when he cheated because he wanted a child. If these women were raped—he said it was consensual but since that's what you're calling it—you should have DNA right? On file? Do you save that sort of thing?"

"Depending when the murders happened and what state and what lab, but it's easy enough to check if the labs kept samples. Otherwise we'd have to exhume their bodies." To Fred, "Tell you what; I'll humor you. We'll go talk to Barry, get his DNA, and see what happens. Can't guarantee anything."

He moved his legs from the desk top. "We'll need your DNA too, Joyce."

Her face dropped. "Mine? Why the fuck do you need mine? I didn't kill anyone!"

It was a hell of an overreaction that caused Fred and Charlie to flinch. "Just to rule you out. Also, if we can swab Danny we can prove he's your son. Wait, which one do you think is yours? The little one or the big one?"

Joyce didn't answer. She was suddenly quiet.

"I can run down the hall and get a swab kit," Cindy said.

She left the room. Joyce fidgeted. "I'd like to go home after this. Barry was my best friend for a long time and it's had been very hard on me, betraying him this way."

"I'll take you home," Fred said.

"I'll go to Barry's myself with a couple of the guys," Charlie said. "Just to ask questions. See if this thing has legs. Need to eat dinner first though. Meeting MaryAnn from Dispatch for fish and chips."

"Really appreciate it, Charlie." Fred shook his hand. "Let me know how it goes."

Cindy returned quickly and swabbed Joyce's cheek. She went along with it but a change had come over her since they arrived. He supposed turning in her long time boss and friend for murder took a bit out of a woman so he cut her some slack.

"Let me take you home," he said to Joyce when Cindy finished.

Joyce nodded but didn't say two words, which was not like her at all. *She's holding something back.* He took her arm and led her away.

4 -

"You sure you want to do this?" Fred asked Joyce as they pulled up in front of Barry's house.

"I'm sure," Joyce said. She felt sick. On some level she always knew it could come up, but after Barry's accident things had changed. He had settled down now, was putty in her hands, counted on her for everything. And no one had ever made a connection to his signings and the murders. She wanted to run off with Fred, and would damn it, but this part would be hard. She wanted to jump forward six months from now when Barry was in jail. Fred and she would be living off in a faraway town raising Danny, all of them with new names. She wanted that *now*. Wanted to forego all the immediate unpleasantness.

"Joyce listen to me," Fred said as he parked the car. "I saw how you reacted when Cindy asked about the DNA. Level with me. Do you really think Danny is yours? You didn't make that up right? Is that what you're afraid of? That if we can get his DNA it won't match yours?"

She sighed with relief. Fred wasn't so smart after all. Fine, she could work with that.

"He looks like me and the dates match up but I—I've wanted to find him for so long and I guess I am afraid that it's not him. I want us to all be together, a family. And if he's not really my son—"

Fred nodded. "It won't make a difference to me either way. We'll still be a family." He squeezed her hand. "Let's go in if you think it will help."

He stepped from the car. She waited on her side until he came around. Barry didn't open doors for her but she'd just sit until Fred did. This time she was going to do everything right, demand to be treated well right from the get go. He did open her door and held out his hand to help her from the car. Yes, she'd found her future and sanctuary in this man.

They knocked on Barry's door. He opened it and greeted them.

"Fred, come in. You too, Joyce, come in." He waved them into the house and shut the door against the cold wind that was picking up speed as the last of the daylight left and evening descended.

"Been a long time, Fred. I'm still so sorry about Helen. You have to know that."

"I know. Mind if we sit down?" Fred asked.

"No, go ahead." They settled onto the furniture. "Why are you here together? I don't understand."

"We've all seen Danny. Young Danny," Joyce began. "He told me to seek out Fred."

"Are you still a cop?" Barry asked.

"No. I'm a Private Investigator now. Barry, we want to talk to you about the murders—"

"It wasn't me," he defended.

Joyce shot Fred a let-me-handle-this glance she hoped he understood. He leaned back into the couch.

"Barry, here's the thing," Joyce said. "I've known you a long time. A damn long time, right?"

"Yes."

"Well there's a lot I saw, that I witnessed more or less over the years. I kept quiet about it, for our sake. I didn't know how bad it was of course, not until you showed me those articles Young Danny left you. But I wondered. After Monica—"

Barry put his face in his hands. "Monica was an accident okay? I was there. I slept with her. My only crime was cheating on my wife. Monica was young, kinky. She wanted me to wrap a scarf around her throat. Said that it would, that it would give her more pleasure."

He looked at them. "I was so damn young myself. I didn't know what new sex things were going on, what the younger people were up to. I did it like she asked. Like she begged. Honest to God she begged for it." He shook his head. "Then she said it needed to be tighter. Tighter!" He wiped his eyes and then continued. "I don't know if the scarf was on too tight or I held it on too long but it was an accident."

He wrung his hands. He'd aged ten years. "I looked down when I . . . finished. And she was dead. I ran. I didn't know what to do and I was stupid and I ran and never told a soul. I admit that. I will admit to that in court and take whatever punishment there is because I owe that to her family and to her. But the others you're talking about. I didn't kill them, I swear to God."

Joyce stared at him relieved he'd finally told the truth. But this night wasn't about him. It was about her future and she had to make sure the blame for everything fell to him.

Fred began to speak but Joyce cut him off.

"Barry, the women in the pictures. Answer me this. If they exhumed the bodies or had DNA on file from before, would they find your DNA inside them, from your semen?"

He began to tremble all over and she knew she'd pushed too hard. He reached for his notebook and started writing furiously.

"Barry," she said.

"Stop, just give me a minute. I don't know what's going on here. I can remember their faces and being with them but I did not kill them. I swear to God I didn't." He scribbled two pages of notes before he spoke again. Joyce dared not make eye contact with Fred. She didn't want interruption from her mission.

"How do you know, Barry?" she asked. "How can you be sure?"

His mouth opened to speak but no words came out. He flipped back the pages in his book. Closed his eyes, straining to recollect.

"Your short term memory is shot," she said. "And your memory from before the accident when you killed these women, when you knocked Helen down the stairs and tried to kill Danny, all of that is skewed. You're lying or you plain don't remember but you did it, Barry."

Fred tried to speak again but she grabbed his hand and squeezed. Barry was utterly lost and heartbroken. "Is Danny really my son?"

Fred sat forward. "Danny is *your* son? Jesus Christ."

"She told me he was," Barry said. He turned the pages back in the journal. "Joyce told me he was mine. A cruel trick that I would have a son I never knew about, then come across him later in life and love him like my own. That's what she said."

"A cruel trick that you tried to kill him," Joyce said.

"No, no I didn't. How many damn times do I have to tell you that?" He motioned to Fred. "She does this. She twists things around, manipulates people. She's trying to make me remember things that didn't happen because she's pissed I never loved her back. I remember that all right."

Bastard.

"Or she is trying to make you remember the crimes you committed," Fred said.

My knight in shining armor.

Joyce let him speak. "I'm not a cop and I'm not here to arrest you. But can you really say with a hundred percent certainty that you did not try to drown Danny, did not kill these women after you slept with them? Maybe it was an accident, like with the Rushmore girl." Fred had an angry bitter edge to his voice. Joyce would not want to be on his bad side.

"Please get out of my house," Barry said. He was writing in his notebook again. "Show yourselves to the door and get out of my house."

Fred and Joyce left him hunched over his page, taking notes. She would love to read those notes but no matter. Soon enough the police would have access to them. He had no way out. He was going down for his adultery, for treating her like she didn't matter, for never loving her back goddammit. The police could charge him with murder, but in her eyes it was semantics. He cast her aside again and again, cheated on Della, fell in love with that damn Helen. Love-of-his-fucking-life Helen.

She slammed the door behind her as they left. Let him hang for *those* crimes.

"Please take me home. I'll be there to testify and sign and say whatever you need to prosecute Barry but right now I just need to be alone."

- 5 -

A horn honked outside and Danny ran to the taxi. He'd been counting the seconds, praying the cabbie hadn't forgotten him. "Thank God you came back," he said as he jumped into the car. "I need you to take me to the city. I've got to save a man's life so drive as fast as you can."

The driver looked at him funny then realized he was serious. "I'm going to go around the other side of the lake, it'll be quicker. There's a road down here."

Danny remembered only a dirt path, but in the last fifteen years the town had built a road. As they drove through, the cab swerving with as much aggression as any Manhattan driver, Danny grabbed the door handle. There was a paved road now and a lot more houses than before. Had Danny known that, he would have gone to one of them to use a phone to get the taxi back quicker.

"You okay? What the hell did you do out here?" the driver asked. "Your head is bleeding. In the back. It's getting on my seat."

Danny felt his hair, saw red liquid on his fingers. It had all really happened to him again, just this afternoon. He slid his shirt down and saw bruises on his shoulders. But he was alive. Still. He was breathing. He was going to stay alive. Young Danny was going to go back and stay alive too and they would stop Joyce, not Barry. They had to figure out how.

"Sorry. I'm okay now. It's going to be all right as long as you can get to Barry Ford's house in time. 227 Beacon Street."

"I can do that," the man said as he accelerated even harder and the car took off onto the main road.

- 6 -

Jerry pulled into the spot in front of the Brundige lake house, where the taxi only moments before had parked. Barry stared at the dilapidated cabin. "You want me to play any songs for you, Mr. Ford?"

"No, no more, Jerry. I just wanted to come back here to see. To remember."

"I'll keep my headlights on for you."

Barry stepped from the car. It was pitch black out except for the headlights, and the flashlight on his phone. He shone it toward the house. Walking to the porch, he thought of the conversation he'd just had with Joyce and Fred. He didn't have all of it straight but read his notebook all the way here.

He smelled smoke and tried the door, surprised when it opened. There was a fire smoldering in the hearth. He shut the door behind him.

"Is anyone here?" No answer. "Hello?" He stayed, unmoving, listening. Not a peep.

Based on the graffiti, the trash, the scents left behind, he assumed someone was using this place as a crash pad. He figured whoever it was left when Jerry's car pulled in.

He hadn't been here since the day of Helen's death and Danny's disappearance. He walked to the stairs now, where Helen had lost her life. He sat on the floor at the foot of them, as he had that day. Barry closed his eyes and relived his agony. She was almost his. Their life was so close to being joined together. But then she was gone and it was over and nothing was ever really good again.

He traced his fingers on the floor where her blood pooled. He changed his focus to the door where Danny had run in and accused him. Toward the office where Fred had stood. *If only he had ended my life that day. I wish he had. I've hated living without you, Helen.*

He stood and added a log to the fire. He sat in front of it, watching the flames grow, feeling the warmth. "How did we get here, Helen? How did we go from being in love to this?"

She didn't appear or answer, though he wished she would.

"Joyce hooked up with your Fred," he explained, hoping that Helen was present even if she couldn't reply. "I can see it all over her face. She's smarmy and arrogant. The guy sleeps with her and just like that, she's trying to send me to jail. I don't know how to get out of it. I can't argue my way out my DNA being in those girls so what's the point? Might as well enter a plea. Who the hell cares anymore? Danny came back to make me do the right thing. He knows I didn't kill you, didn't hurt him. I guess that's all that matters in the end."

He waited but she still did not show herself. "I wish I could be with you, Helen. You know that's all I ever wanted. And you know in your heart I didn't murder those girls at the signings. If we had been together like we planned . . . Oh I think of it all the time. You, me, and Danny as a family. It would have been so nice. Maybe Fred would have understood over time, would have straightened himself out. He's not a bad guy, you know. Maybe he was then, he's not now. He loved you and Danny as much I did. As much as I do."

He waited again for a sign but there was nothing.

"I would never ever have cheated on *you*. You were my one true love. How can anyone recover from that? The way you left me, so suddenly, when our future was right there. So close I could touch it. The car packed and ready for us to—"

He recalled the big news suddenly, without even consulting the notebook. "You won't believe this, or maybe you will because maybe up there you find out all the secrets, but I'm Danny's biological father. Imagine that huh? Guess I was destined to be his dad no matter how fate or Joyce tried to fuck it up. And I suppose I was destined to lose him too. Can't get away from that. Not in the novel, not in real life."

He lost himself in the rising flames that reached out to him like fingers, summoned him.

"If I knew for sure you were out in the ether, watching me,

still loving me, I'd take a different road. Wouldn't show up at the police station and plead guilty to crimes I know I didn't commit. Please," he begged. "Helen, if you are here please, please show me. I'm at a crossroads and I need a sign."

A log slid of its own accord from the glowing stack, and descended into the ashes, causing a grand pop and crackle. Sparks flew out toward him and one glowing red ember in the exact shape of the original piece of sea glass hopped and landed in front of him. It glowed even after the others had lost their light.

He smiled. "You *are* here. I knew it. I knew you would believe me and that you'd wait." He stood up with great effort, using his cane for support. He left the fire to burn itself out. He didn't have the heart to snuff Helen's spirit.

Barry walked back to his waiting car. "Take me home, Jerry. I've got a very important task to take care of." He turned on the interior light in the backseat and wrote down everything that had just happened. He didn't think he'd forget it though. He'd bared his soul to Helen and she had given him the sign he needed.

"Oh and please play *Mr. Blue Sky*" he said.

"Of course, Mr. Ford."

Barry wrote about the log in the fireplace, about Helen, about her spirit communicating, as ELO brought him back to the happiest day of his life.

- 7 -

"Let me out here," Danny said as they pulled to the curb in front of the brownstone. He paid the driver.

"I hope you made it in time," he said. "Good luck."

"Thanks. I hope so too."

Danny leapt from the car and ran up Barry's steps. He knocked hard. No one answered. He pulled out his key and opened the door. "Barry are you here? Dad?" Both were names he'd used for the man in his two overlapping lives but his old life was all but forgotten now except for confusing entries in the upside down part of his notebook.

He walked through the house. Barry's notebook was gone

but the articles and pictures were spread on his coffee table. There was no way to tell from clues where he was. For all Danny knew, he'd already been arrested.

Danny rushed to Barry's office and his computer. He clicked the Safari icon and searched for Fred's office number. A landline phone, new but retro in the style of an old black payphone rested on a small table next to the desk. He dialed the number and after several rings, and a long greeting replete with pleasantries he didn't have time for now, he was able to leave a message.

"Dad, it's Danny. The grown up version. Listen, I'll explain it all but it's not Barry. I was wrong okay? It was never Barry. It was Joyce. Joyce did all of it. Pushed Mom. That's why she tried to kill me. She thought I witnessed it. She wanted Barry all to herself. And the other murders—"

A beep cut him off. Too long.

He called back. Waited impatiently then spoke to finish. "The other murders were Joyce too. Must have been. She was jealous of other women and she's setting him up. Please don't arrest Barry, he—"

Another beep. It would have to do. Leaving a message on a Friday night may not help him at all. He didn't have Fred's cell number and hoped he checked office messages on weekends.

He next searched for Joyce's home number. He wouldn't leave a message but if he got her on the line he may be able to stall her, or scare her. He had to try *something*.

"Barry?" she said, when she answered.

Right, the Caller ID.

"Barry, I'm here with Fred, what do you want? Do you want to confess?"

He hoped Fred was listening in, or she had him on speaker.

"It's Danny. I know it was you, Joyce. I know you killed my mother and tried to drown me, and probably killed those other women. I was wrong before, but you're going down for all this. Dad, are you there? Can you hear this?" he shouted.

She hung up the phone. He hit redial and it rang repeatedly until voicemail picked up. He did this four times and gave up. She must have discreetly hung up and shut the volume off. That meant Fred still didn't know.

Going to the police would do no good. "Hi, I'm Fred Brundige's time traveling son telling you that I just remembered my murderer. It was Joyce Tuttle after all." They'd toss him out on his ass. He had no proof about the other murders except a hunch now, a new view into Joyce's corrupt and demented mind which made her a hell of a lot more likely to have killed those women.

If they had any chance of fixing this, he needed Young Danny.

- 8 -

Fred emerged from the bathroom. "Did I hear the phone ring?" he asked.

"Salesman selling solar panels," she said.

"Oh."

He sat across from her on the chair, not all cuddled like they were last time he was over. "The police are on their way over to Barry's soon. How are you feeling?"

"Me? I'm glad they're getting him." It was a strange question. Was he trying to trap her, imply she was a co-conspirator?

"You've been close to Barry for a very long time."

"That doesn't mean I knew what he was up to, or that I was complicit in any of this. I don't like your tone."

"Of course not. I didn't mean that at all. Sorry if you misunderstood. I merely meant that you were close to him for so long, it must be scary and sad to see what Barry really was."

"Oh, yes. Yes of course it is. I guess I'm flustered. It's all a huge shock."

"Are you all right?"

He asked as a concerned boyfriend would, as anyone would. *I need to relax. Play it cool.*

"It's been a lot. First this strange man shows up on my door, then a little boy, then this relationship with you. It's wonderful— don't get me wrong—but unexpected. And now to find out Barry committed a string of murders. It's surreal."

Fred nodded. "I feel the same way. I'd resolved myself to

Danny's death. After so long, I finally accepted it. Then he was back. I want to put this all to bed and start my life over with Danny."

"And me too right? Me too?" She knew she sounded clingy and desperate, but Jesus, Barry was more than a man to her. He was everything. She'd thrown Barry over for this guy. Fred damn well better keep up his end of the bargain.

He paused. "Yes, yes of course you too. I didn't think I even had to mention that. I figured you'd assume."

"So what's next then? How do we proceed? After they take Barry away? Can we just take Danny and run off?"

He cocked his head, like he thought she was nuts. "It's not that easy, Joyce. It'll be a long process. It's not like they just arrest and convict Barry and put him away forever. There's an arrest and if they don't have DNA in the files they need to exhume bodies. Then he will go to trial which could take years. And surely there will be an appeal. There always is. And then—"

"What if he confesses though?" Her voice rose in pitch and she tried to settle herself. She'd been waiting her whole life to be someone's wife, someone's one and only. She was done waiting.

"If he confesses it will speed things up, sure."

"He already did, about Monica in Maine. Isn't that enough?"

He gave her the look again. Annoyance. It was annoyance. The type of judgmental glare her father used to give her right before he slapped her face and called her a spoiled selfish brat.

"This isn't about speed, it's about doing it right. Sure, if he confesses on paper to Monica Rushmore's death, that's a start. But you need to be around for the other charges. You were with him at the signings and may need to testify now or next year or in five years."

"Well that's goddamned stupid," she shouted. "He said he killed Monica. You know he was fucking your wife and then boom she was dead. He tried to kill little Danny. Who cares about the other murders? They have plenty to get him on right now."

He froze when she lost her temper. Shrank back from her.

I've gone too far. I've frightened him. She patted the couch. "Come here. Sit with me," she said with sickening sweetness she hoped he'd believe.

Fred shook his head. "I'm good here."

Think, Joyce. Think. Fix this. "I've got a lot of money put away. A lot of it. I stayed here because it's cozy but I could afford for the three of us to live nicely, off the grid for many, many years. Let's just do that. We'll find little Danny and run off. The police don't need us. We'll hide out. It'll be fun. An adventure."

She smiled but he didn't smile back.

"I have to go Joyce. I want to be there when they see Barry." He stood and began to leave.

She ran to the door, threw herself in front of it classic movie star style. "But you'll come back right? You'll come back and tell me how it went? And we'll be together?"

He gently moved her aside. "Sure, Joyce. Sure. Of course. I promise." She let him out, confident that he'd be back. It was all going to work out just like she planned. No worries.

She locked the door and moved back to her couch. She opened a drawer in the coffee table to reveal a stack of old letters from Barry, back from when people wrote them. It was tied with a pink ribbon. She untied the knot and flipped through them. She and Barry had slept together for only a few months, shortly after she started an internship at the magazine he edited. It was a wonderful time in her life. He was the boss and she admired him so much. He was a man of integrity and great intelligence. The kind of man she wanted to marry.

When he got her pregnant she assumed he would leave his wife for her. He never loved Della. She could tell. He only really loved *her*. He told her so when they'd made love. And in these letters.

She opened one now and smiled at the neat strong penmanship.

"*I hope you come home soon from New Hampshire. Sorry your aunt has cancer but you are a wonderful person for staying with her as she finishes her chemo treatment. I miss you. It's so quiet here without you. The afternoons, when we are supposed to be pleasuring each other, are filled with endless pages of other people's writings. I'd much prefer to be banging you on my desk. Let me know if I can come meet you in New Hampshire. It's hard being without you, pun intended. Regards, Barry."*

As she read this letter now and a couple of others, it was so clear now he was using her for sex. He never talked about a future, or marrying her, or exclusivity, but at nineteen sex was love. There was no distinction. She'd been in New Hampshire alone, hiding her pregnancy from everyone. There was no aunt, no cancer. Just a foolish girl who got herself knocked up by a married man who never, ever, ever fucking loved her back.

She'd planned to have the baby and surprise Barry. Present him with his child. He'd leave Della and marry her and they'd live happily ever after. But then she'd met the man in the bar who knew so much about Barry. "Take your unborn son and run while you're still able. If you're lucky you can outrun fate."

She thought it was a load of bullshit. The local fortune teller had told her she was having a girl and that her future with her daughter would be bright, and that her husband—she'd clearly said *husband*—would love her till the day she died.

When her son was born a month later, she began to question the fortune teller's prediction, weighing it against that of the stranger. What if the fortune teller's words, "He'll love you till the day you die" meant he'd kill her? What if the stranger was right?

But the idea of living without Barry . . . she couldn't comprehend that. She hadn't known him long but *he* was her fate and her future. She was sure of it. Maybe the only way to change the course the stranger had foretold was to give up the child. She'd considered the wrinkled red baby, its mouth puckering like a fish, waiting for her to feed it. She didn't even know this baby but she loved Barry. Her decision was made and she rang for the nurse. "Name him Daniel, after my father," she instructed. The nurse promised to tell the adoptive parents.

"Fucking cheat! Fucking using cheating asshole!" She screamed as she tore the letters, the ones she'd treasured all these years, into as many pieces as she could and then tossed them into the blazing fire in the hearth. "You ruined my life! I wasted my whole goddamned life on you for nothing! Tried to kill my own son because you couldn't keep your dick in your pants, and refused to love me!"

She stood up and regarded her Barry shrine: the photos on the walls, the boastful book covers that reminded her that her whole relationship with him was no more real than his fiction.

One by one she pulled them from the wall and smashed them on the coffee table, sending glass all over the room. Her cat howled and ran up the stairs for cover. She reached into the shattered frames and pulled out the pictures of them together, the artwork for his covers, the framed copies of awards he'd won, and tossed them into the fire. She grabbed a kitchen chair and stood on tippy toes until she had cleared both of her crowded walls of Barry.

Joyce observed her surroundings. The white drywall was covered in holes from all the nails. Didn't matter. She was moving. She was going to pack up and run off with little Danny and Fred no matter what he said about waiting for the trial, waiting for resolution, waiting for the right fucking moment to start their lives.

She was panting by the time she was done. Joyce gingerly positioned herself on the floor in front of the now raging fire. She was careful not to sit on any of the broken glass, not the big pieces anyway. Her hands were speckled with red dots where tiny shards had burrowed into her skin. She couldn't feel it. All she felt now was rage at Barry for using her, for ruining her life.

Her eyes glazed over and her heart slowed down as she watched the flames and smiled. She reveled in the destruction of the memories as the fire ate the love letters with their cream pages, fine black ink, and straight firm penmanship. The photographs curled into themselves and went up in flames, just as Barry's life would in very short time.

When there was nothing left but ashes in the hearth, she crunched the broken glass and crooked metal frames strewn on the floor with her boots as she walked to the desk and her computer. Tonight, she would scout out properties in desolate parts of the country for them to live together.

"Nebraska is a possibility. Or Idaho." She typed, "Nebraska

off the grid properties." Honestly she didn't even know for sure where those states were. *Up north, maybe in the middle or out west?* Fred was a PI He'd know how to set them up with aliases. And if Fred refused to go with her, if he insisted they wait, well then fuck him. She'd take the boy and live the life they were supposed to have. She'd helped Barry research setting up new identities for one of his books and could figure it out herself.

She smiled as she thought of Fred and his simple ways, his black and white outlook. Right or wrong, truth or lie, guilty or not guilty. Despite what he said, she could coerce him to come along. After all, this time she was going to get it right and for that she needed a husband. For once, her dreams were going to come true.

Yes indeed, the three of us can pack up and run off whenever we want. I'll pack a going away backpack for Danny just like Helen did. Our lives will come full circle. It's destiny for us to be a family and the last pieces just need to fall into place.

- 9 -

Barry toweled off after a long hot shower. He stepped into his bedroom and opened his bureau drawer. He selected fresh black socks and the best pair of underwear he owned. He checked both garments. No holes. He never saw the sense in spending too much on clothes. No one saw his underwear or socks so if he had a hole or stain, who cared? Same went with his wardrobe. It had been years since he'd bought anything new. His clothes were comfortable and that suited him.

Today though, today his appearance mattered. He put the socks and boxer briefs on then walked to his closet. Deep inside, a zippered bag held his tuxedo. He hadn't worn it in five years since the awards dinner when he won for . . . well it didn't matter if the title of the book wasn't in the forefront of his memory.

Didn't matter either that Joyce had turned against him. Among other things, he'd entrusted her to handle his finances, to work with his accountant at tax time and throughout the years to manage his income and expenses. Wouldn't surprise him if she'd cleaned out his accounts.

Helen and Danny were the only ones who ever mattered and they were both gone. He questioned now why he'd gone on at all. For Della maybe. Yes, for Della. For a moment he'd forgotten about good old Della. He'd stayed alive for her, made money for her, put on a good front and went through the motions because if nothing else, she was his wife and deserved it. He owed her that much for sticking by his side even though a big part of him died when Helen fell down the stairs and Danny was lost to the lake.

For the first time in many years now, he found himself at peace.

He set the garment bag on the bed, unzipped it, and smiled when he saw the crisp black fabric. He'd stored the white shirt and tie with the jacket and pants.

Slowly, he slid on the shirt and buttoned it. He reached into the small box on his desk and retrieved gold cufflinks shaped into an elaborate F. He snapped them in place, and then added the pants and jacket.

He stood in front of the long mirror. "I clean up good." He smiled. He felt remorse, regret, but mostly the relief at knowing soon it would be over. He was tired and lonely and sick of living minute by minute, day by day, and having each new event shrouded in confusion. Seeing Danny again after so long reminded him how much he had loved the boy and his mother, reminded him how hollow he'd felt since their deaths.

Barry tied his bow tie and checked the final product. He nodded approval. He headed back to the closet but thought better of it.

No need for shoes.

In the bathroom, he opened the medicine cabinet and removed the row of blades from his razor refill package. He was glad that he still used a double- edged razor, as the extra blades supplied an escape route for him without much effort to search for a method.

He peeked down the hall. The house was just a structure. None of it mattered to him. The place he was headed would be better and more welcoming. It wouldn't be filled with fancy furniture or imported marble, all the luxuries Della said they needed to make the house a home.

All he needed was his family.

He entered the Rainbox and flicked the light on. He shut the door and sat on the floor. He closed his eyes and thought of Danny and him on the beach all those years ago, picking up the sea glass, sorting it by color. Danny smiling, thinking he'd found jewels on the beach. In a way he had, Barry knew.

He removed his jacket, set it on the floor of the Rainbox. He unfastened his cuff links, which he'd added to the outfit only so he could snap them on one last time.

He folded his crisp starched sleeves up to the elbow.

Barry glanced at the glowing glass surrounding him. It was a dream he had created for all of them, a place in his mind where he could go back and change the past. He knew now it was only a fantasy. He understood that Danny was not a time traveler but a ghost, a scared and restless spirit who returned to make him remember, to find answers. Danny was surely at peace now that he knew Barry was not his killer. Now he was safely resting in whatever ethereal plane people went after they died.

He closed his eyes and pictured Helen and Danny standing side by side. Danny held his backpack and they stood outside by her car. It's how it was supposed to be. They smiled at him and Helen reached out her hand. "Come on, Barry, let's get away while we still can," she said.

Danny waved him closer.

He opened his eyes and inspected the razor blade, tight between the fingers of his right hand. He dug the blade deep into his left wrist, vertically as he'd read online. He switched hands and sliced the right wrist quickly before the pain fully set in and he was unable to complete the job.

Blood poured over his fresh white shirt and streamed onto his pants and then the bottom of the Rainbox.

"Maybe this is what the red sea glass was all along. Not a literal piece of glass but the blood of a man willing to die to return to his love. I'm coming back to you now, and we'll be a family."

He closed his eyes again, and in his mind saw himself running to Helen and Danny. As they embraced him, he felt life and joy course through him. The more the blood escaped from his body, the stronger Danny and Helen hugged him.

Until finally his spirit crossed from the Rainbox to the other side.

- 10 -

Fred stood in front of Barry's house at the bottom of the stairs. He wanted to enter but wasn't allowed. Fred watched the front door intensely, gritting his teeth. All these years he'd pitied Barry. Fred knew how it felt to lose Helen, and despite everything else he knew Barry loved her too. He still didn't get why Barry would have tried to kill Danny. That didn't make sense. He could wrap his head around the fact he'd fucked around on his wife and killed the women afterward to hide the murders, especially since he confessed to Monica Rushmore's death. But he couldn't shake the hunch he was missing something. He had no motive to kill Danny and that one piece made him question the rest.

Sure Fred had charged full speed ahead with the investigation. He couldn't argue with logic, circumstantial evidence, and the eyewitness account of Joyce. She'd gotten him all riled up. Her enthusiasm and the articles Danny dropped off threw him off.

Fred wanted so badly to get back the respect of his old peers that of course he'd run ahead half-cocked. After all, Danny *told him* Barry killed him.

But when he'd questioned Barry, watched his mannerisms, it just didn't fit. Barry didn't *feel* like a killer. He could spot a true sociopath or killer a mile away, at least back when he was in the game.

He cast his eyes down now. What the fuck was going on? No fucking thing as a time machine or his dead son coming back fifteen years later utterly unchanged. A pro could fake prints, could plant them if they knew how, could alter a picture. But why? Why dredge it all up if Barry wasn't guilty?

"Dad?"

He turned and saw Danny. In the flesh. Exactly as he was fifteen years ago. It took him a second to comprehend what he saw.

"Are, are you a ghost?"

The boy shook his head. "It's me. I came back."

Fred was scared shitless. All this time he waited for him to return. And those fingerprints and the picture—but he'd be damned if seeing his kid didn't scare the hell out of him.

He moved closer, under the lantern. The kid was solid, real. He saw a vein in his small neck pulsing, could hear him breathing. He had the same voice. Fred grabbed the boy's right hand and confirmed his identity, by way of a small triangle scar on the knuckle of his index finger. He'd been bitten by a goat in a petting zoo when he was toddler.

"Oh my God, it *is* you. Jesus Christ, it's you!" He picked the boy up and swung him around, kissed his cheeks. He even smelled the same.

He set him down and held him at arm's length. "How is this possible? You're not a ghost?"

The boy started crying then. "You look so different."

Fred hugged him long and hard and let the boy cry it out.

"It's okay. It's just a very, very good surprise. I wasn't sure if it was all a trick. But it's really you."

The boy nodded.

"Are you all right? Tell me you're okay."

"I'm okay, I just want to come home, with you. I don't like it here. In this time. I want to go back to before."

"How is it you're here?"

"The Rainbox. I came through the Rainbox."

"Jesus Christ. I guess you did. I guess you really did."

Fred stood back, felt dizzy from the excitement and wondered how the fuck this could be real. But it was and that's all that mattered.

"Listen to me, Danny. I know I was a shitty father but that's all gonna change now okay? Just gonna be you and me. I just need to see this Barry thing through. I got your articles and your message and the police are inside—"

A man walked from the shadows and stood next to his son.

"Who are you? Did you take my son? Did you hurt him?" Anger flared and he wished he had cuffs. He pulled Danny next to him. If this bastard—

"I'm him, all grown up," the man said. "It's a long story and it doesn't matter because we're going to go back and none of this will have happened. We don't have time to explain."

Fred stared at him then at his son. Same face, same everything except one was taller and older. His mother had Alzheimer's and an uncle was schizophrenic. Fred had spent most of his adult life with a phobia about losing his mind. He was sure it happening right now, unless this was a long-drawn out bitch of a nightmare.

"You can't take him back. You can't take him away from me. Not again. I can't live through it twice." He couldn't. If Danny left again he'd go home and blow his brains out. There was nothing left to live for.

"There was another life. A life when I was Barry's son. There were all these murders. All these same murders except Barry and Joyce were married and she was my mother. I told her about him, that he'd killed these girls and she confronted him. And then she fell down the stairs and died."

Insane, but he had no choice but to listen. Why not go even further down the rabbit hole? He'd listen all day long if it meant being able to hold his son in his arms.

"I didn't know what to do so I went into the Rainbox and prayed and cried and next thing I was back to when Joyce was pregnant. I told her to leave Barry. To run away from him. She didn't know who I was. I knew it would change things but I didn't want to go back to my life anyway. There was nothing for me. I figured when I came back I'd be in a different life.

"When I reappeared in the Rainbox I couldn't breathe. My lungs were full of water and I was dying . . . and next thing I was standing over myself, over him." He pointed to the boy. "Watching myself die under water. So I grabbed him, resuscitated him there in front of the lake and ran like hell. I don't even remember all of it except when we both magically walked back through the Rainbox in Barry's house. I brought Danny to a hotel and have been trying to piece together what happened."

"It's true, Dad," his young son said. "He saved me and brought me back. I saw Barry and Joyce and I remember what happened that day now. I'm so sorry but we were wrong. Barry didn't do it. That's why we came here. To stop you from going after the wrong person."

The young man spoke again, his voice cracking. "Barry didn't kill anyone. It was Joyce. She was with him at every signing and she was jealous."

That made more sense than anything. He should have seen it. *Joyce. Jealous selfish Joyce.* He thought of Barry's words. *She manipulates people.* He'd been duped, played. He should have followed his gut.

The boy looked up to him. "Where was Joyce when Mom was pushed?"

"She was . . ." Fred concentrated. Thought back beyond the tragedy, beyond the fight with Barry. "She went upstairs to help your mother pack. She said it to Barry in front of me. Mom ran upstairs crying and Joyce told Barry, 'I'm going up to help her. You deal with him.' Meaning me. Shit," he said. "Why didn't anyone ever suspect Joyce? Why didn't I think of her that day?" His answer was clear. He'd been a drunk hotheaded asshole who cared only that his wife was leaving him for another man. Tunnel vision.

"And she tried to kill you because she thought you saw?"

Young Danny spoke. "Yeah and because Barry loved me. Joyce wanted him to herself."

Fred's anger flared. Such a sweet boy who had done nothing but be lovable. And here was Joyce saying how excited she was to run off with Fred and Danny and start over again. Would she try to kill him again one day because he took too much of Fred's affection away from her? Probably.

"I bet if you compare her DNA to evidence at the other crime scenes you'll find it on the other girls," older Danny said. "Barry slept with them and Joyce killed them. Maybe they tried to fight her off. I came back to rectify what happened and the only way to do that it is to punish her."

Fred didn't speak. It was a lot to take in, he knew. None of it rational.

"You need to save Barry, Dad," Young Danny said. "You need to stop the police from arresting him. Please go get him."

Fred nodded. He was still confused but the concept of Joyce being responsible clicked with him. It would explain why Barry didn't remember killing them. Why Joyce flinched when they asked for her DNA. Why she was so eager to blame it on Barry. She was saving herself. When he pushed the sex aside and thought of her as a human, all the signs were right there.

"Will you be here when I get back? Promise me you won't leave. I can't lose you again." He ran up the steps to the front door before either of them could answer.

- 11 -

"How does this stop anything?" Young Danny asked. "How does keeping Barry alive and arresting Joyce, how does that change anything in the past? Did Joyce really kill all those girls?"

"I think so yes. Jealousy is dangerous. Can make people do horrible things. I don't know if any of this will change a lick of the past. Probably not, but it sets things right, at least in this dimension. Will keep new people from getting killed."

"Will I remember? When I go back will I remember? Then I can tell my Dad and it'll all be okay. He can get her there too. Can I go back right now and wake up and tell him?" He cried and Danny hugged him. "I hate it here. I don't like that my Dad got old, or that Barry is all messed up."

"I don't know if you'll remember. If you don't then this will play out all the same. It'll change history here only until you go back."

"I need to then. You have to find a way to make me remember," the boy said.

Before Danny answered, Fred walked out the front door. His face said it all. He spoke anyway. "He's dead. Barry. He took his own life. In the Rainbox. We were too late."

Young Danny burst out crying. Danny grabbed his hand. "Come on kid. We need to get you home. I need to get you home and we need to fix this."

"Dad!" the boy called to Fred who ran after them. He stopped running and tried to pull away to go to Fred.

"Come back! Please for God's sake come back! Let him go!"

"We need to get you home," Danny pleaded. "If he catches you he'll make you stay here and that can't happen. You have to go back."

The boy took a last look at Fred then ran ahead. "Okay let's go."

The two sprinted. Danny didn't know yet where they were headed but he needed to get away.

At one point, they lost Fred. "In here." They darted into an alley and hunkered down behind a dumpster. His lungs burned, his head throbbed. His heart beat so hard it hurt. The alley smelled like rotten fruit and urine but the worst sensation was the guilt Danny felt for causing Barry's death.

All of this was *his* fault. He'd fallen for Joyce's innocent act in two different lifetimes, had turned Barry in for crimes he didn't commit. Now he was dead. No doubt he died sad and scared, confused about what had transpired. "Fuck," Danny said. "Fucking A, I don't know how to fix this." He put his head in his hands. "I came back here and made things even worse. And except for saving your life I didn't change a goddamned thing. Barry will still sleep with other women and Joyce will kill them all and I can't fucking fix it. If you go back and you're not dead, what if you don't remember?"

The boy looked at him, a dim streetlight illuminating his smaller mirror image face.

Neither of them spoke for several moments. It took that long for their breathing to slow, to process it all.

Finally Young Danny said, "When I have dreams, once I wake

up, I usually don't remember them after a minute or two. But when I have nightmares, when really scary or sad stuff happens, those I remember. For a long time."

Danny considered that. The kid had a point. "When I first got here, I asked Barry about his memory issues. He said that really emotional events take root in the memory the best. He recorded everything, like I do, but he said the key to recall to make events stick was emotion."

"Barry killing himself is gonna stick with me for sure."

Danny nodded. "It is. It sucks. But I think you're onto something with your thinking."

"Joyce is my biological Mom, and she killed my mother and tried to kill me. That's really important and sad as hell but I need another big shock to make sure it all stays in my head long enough to tell Dad as soon as I wake up."

If you wake up.

"You're right. The more the better, but what else is there?"

"I want to see Bonnie again," the boy said. "Before I go back I want to see her again. I can't let her end up the way she did and if I see her right before I go back then it'll all be fresh in my mind."

Danny knew the kid was right. The more intense the memory the more that would stick. "Let's go."

▲▲▲

"I want to see Bonnie," Danny told the pimp. He wasn't hard to find. Everyone knew Bonnie, and her owner was just as popular. He stood on a street corner smoking an e-cigarette. Until Bonnie, Danny assumed the pimps he saw on television were just an overused cliché in how they operated and acted. But at least on this low end, it was just like the movies. Creepy guy takes advantage of girls and roughs them up and threatens them with corporal punishment or lack of drugs. No ethics, no concern for the girls' welfare. They were just a product he sold.

"What kind of shit do you want? Straight stuff, kinky?" He sneered down at Young Danny. "You're that kid in the diner right? I remember you two."

"That's us," Danny said. "We're her friends. Just want to talk. I'll pay you for her time. Double even. We just need a few minutes with her but we'll pay for an hour or whatever you want."

The pimp regarded Danny then the boy. "I don't want the kid involved. I have morals you know. There's a line."

Danny doubted that was true and bet if he paid enough, the pimp would do anything they wanted no matter how illegal or unethical. "We just need to talk to her and I'm not letting my little brother out of my sight."

The pimp deliberated the proposition. His eyes were glazed over and Danny assumed there was more than nicotine in the oil of that cigarette.

"You think you're gonna ride in here on a white horse and rescue her? Bring her home? You don't know how the street works." The pimp spit.

"We can't take her home," Young Danny said. "We're leaving and she can't come with us. We just want to say goodbye." The kid kept his voice steady. He'd grown stronger these last few days.

The pimp smirked. "The thing is Bonnie's dead so your last goodbye was your last goodbye. Happens to the best of them."

"It was your fault," the boy shouted. "You did this to her!"

The pimp took a drag on his e-cigarette. "She had a drug problem before she got to me. I just gave her what she wanted." He writhed his hips. "Gave her drugs and a good time too."

Danny punched him in the face. Lightning fast and hard. Felt like he broke a knuckle and he prayed he fractured the asshole's eye socket. The pimp collapsed. Danny kicked him in the stomach. Four times.

The guy stopped fighting. He wasn't dead but he'd be out of commission for a while. Danny saw a beer bottle on the curb and smashed it. He held the broken bottle over the pimp.

"No," Young Danny said, grabbing his arm. "We need to fix things not make them worse. Killing him won't make a difference."

"Thank you," a voice said from the shadows. She stepped forward.

"Bonnie!" Young Danny ran and hugged her. "You're not dead."

"No. Almost died on your birthday but it didn't take." She looked dead as shit. Dark circles under her eyes that even make-up didn't hide. Her face was thinner and paler than last time. "I didn't think I'd see you again. Thought it was in my head."

"Why did he say you were dead?" Danny asked.

She shrugged. "Doesn't want to lose a good worker I guess. Come with me." She held out her hand and Young Danny took it. "I've got a room a few blocks away."

Within five minutes they stopped in front of an old factory building.

"What is this place?" Danny asked.

"They used to build shoes here, now it's cheap apartments. Not very nice but it's warm, and safe if you're careful."

They walked through dirty glass double doors and down a long hallway. The apartment doors were scratched and dented. The hallways smelled like pot and cigarette smoke. Danny cringed.

They arrived at an industrial door marked *Stairs*. Bonnie turned the handle and they came to a small landing and a stairway. "Don't touch the railings. Germs. Come on. My room is down here."

Down two half flights of cement steps with peeling blue paint they came to Bonnie's room.

It wasn't an apartment or even a room at all but a cot in a storage section of the basement. She'd set it up as nice as she could. Hung curtains on the walls to lend the illusion of a window. A tattered pink rug sat beside her cot. "I don't bring Johns here. This is my place. It's not really a place but it's what I've got. The landlord lets me stay for a once a week—" she stopped herself, remembering young Danny's presence.

A couple of faded milk crates were stacked by her bed. A framed picture of her Mom and her sat beside a box of condoms. She picked the photo up and showed them, as she sat on her bed. "You remember my mom. Wasn't she beautiful?"

"Your mom lets you live here?" the boy asked, shocked at the idea.

"She split from my dad a couple of years after you drowned. Ran off with a musician in California. Never looked back."

"What about your dad?" Young Danny asked.

She shrugged. "He got a new wife, moved her in. They had a couple of kids in a couple of years and I was suddenly not wanted. I was a reminder of *her*. My stepmom said she couldn't wait until I went away to college so they could enjoy their new family without me. She didn't say it in front of me but I heard it, more than once. So I kept to myself. Hung out at the lake, always hoping you'd come out of the water and make everything okay. I'd sit out there and talk to you but finally I just ran away. Couldn't handle it anymore."

She moved closer to Young Danny. "I know you guys aren't real. That you're ghosts. Maybe my guardian angels right?"

"No, we're—" Danny began.

"Yeah," Young Danny interrupted. "Guardian angels. You're gonna be okay. We just wanted to visit with you and see how you were doing and tell you you're gonna be okay real soon."

She pulled off her coat then, even though it was still damn cold inside. She wore only a lingerie top underneath. Her right forearm was swollen and blue and green. "Not sure if I missed the vein, or the drugs are eating me from the inside out. Hurts like hell," she explained. "If I go to the hospital they might cut it off and then no one will want me."

The way she said it killed Danny. *No one will want me.* He wanted to tell her he loved her; that she deserved better than this terrible life. But there was little he could do to help her, not with mere hours left before they went back. Maybe not even if he had a lifetime here. It was too late.

"Can you fix this?" She held up her arm for them see, as if they hadn't both zoned in on it the second her coat came off.

Young Danny grazed it with his fingertips. "Yeah we can fix this."

She pulled a bin from under her bed and grabbed a faded sweatshirt. It was too big for her tiny frame but it covered her bad arm and her HOPE tattoo. "I don't have anywhere to go but here. It's not bad though, right? Kind of cozy. Made these to brighten up the place."

She pointed up to the ceiling where she'd hung origami cranes, dozens of them. They were high enough so he wouldn't have noticed if she hadn't pointed them out. "I learned how to make those in second grade. My mom and I made them together. You too, Danny. Do you remember?"

The boy nodded. "I do." He smiled but Danny saw tears in his eyes. "I'd go to your house and make them with you guys even though it was kind of girly." Danny remembered then too but it was hazy, filling in bit by bit.

"There's a lot of other origami stuff you can make but I only ever learned this one. I figure one day I'll get a book and learn a few of the other ones. Maybe sell those instead of, well, instead of this." She gestured to her body.

"I think that's a great idea," Young Danny said. "You're really good at it." They shared a smile. *A little kindness can change a life throughout all dimensions.* That was another line from *The Rainbox.* Another quote Danny had clung to, that he wished now he'd remembered before ratting Barry out.

"We have to go, but we're going to change all this," the boy said. "You just keep wishing and keep looking for me in the lake. I'm going to come out."

Danny reached into his wallet and tried to hand her all the money they had left.

"No really, I can't take money from you. That's not why I brought you here."

"It's almost six hundred dollars," Danny said. "This is part of what angels do. They take care of you, help you get what you need. Right now you need money."

She took it and shoved it under her pillow.

"Thank you. It was great seeing you again, Danny," she said to the boy. "I always figured you were here, with me. Watching. I'm glad I got to see you one more time."

"Me too." The boy hugged her. She still didn't quite seem to accept Danny was an adult version but her impact on the boy is what mattered most.

"Take care of yourself, okay? Don't let all the bad stuff get to you," Young Danny said.

"I won't." Bonnie shivered. Based on the color of her face Danny knew she was feverish.

"You should go to a doctor. About that arm," Danny said.

"I'm going to take a nap first. I'm so tired. I haven't had a night off in a long time. I'll go tomorrow. I promise," she told them. "I'll go as soon as I wake up."

He wondered if she would wake up or if this was her last night. If the infection in her arm didn't kill her, she'd likely use the money he'd given her to buy drugs and overdose. He reminded himself that none of it mattered. Once he went back . . .

They let themselves out. By then it was two in the morning. They could hang out in coffee shops or sleep in a subway station for a few hours if they needed to. Once the sun was up they'd head to Barry's house. By then hopefully the police would be gone and they could sneak in and go home.

SEVEN

- 1 -

Fred never went to sleep. He combed the streets within walking distance but couldn't find the Dannys. They could have taken a taxi or a subway or even a commuter rail in any direction and he sure as hell couldn't ask the police for help. As it was, Charlie had asked him who he was shouting for. When he'd said "my son" he got the usual reprimanding stare.

He'd gone home about three in the morning. His feet hurt and he had acid reflux from the ten o'clock gas station burritos he'd wolfed down. More than that though, he felt rage toward Joyce and toward himself for being an idiot. He should have known better.

He knew that she was counting on him to be stay by her side, and that would work to his advantage. It had been a long, long time since he'd used his undercover skills, his ability to transform, but he could do it again. He hoped Danny would come back to him but that was out of his control. What was within his control was what happened to Joyce. He had to play this close to the vest.

He fell into bed and dialed her number. "Hello?" she said.

Based on her husky voice and stuffed up nose, she'd been crying.

"Sorry I didn't call before now, but I assume you heard."

She sniffed. "It's all over the news. I can't believe he killed himself. I didn't want that to happen. I thought he'd just confess and go to jail and maybe because of his mental state could cop an insanity plea. Maybe end up in an institution. I didn't think he'd die."

He felt for her. No one likes it when someone you love dies but it was more her fault than anyone's.

"Are you all right?" he asked.

"No but I guess it's for the best. He must have been carrying around a lot of guilt all these years."

"I guess he was. I'm just glad he never hurt you. He could have killed you, you know. You're damn lucky."

"I suppose. I never saw him that way but he was a killer." She sniffled again. "Did you see his body? Was it horrible?"

"There was a lot of blood. A lot of it."

She was silent.

"They may need you back at the station tomorrow to close up a few loose ends," Fred said.

"Like what?" she asked. "What loose ends?"

He paused to think. "Well they need to know who his next of kin was, who they should alert. Private stuff only you would know. You were with him all those years."

"Oh yes, yes of course."

"Do you have a key to his place?"

"Yes. I needed one especially since his accident. He needed me." She was being defensive, as he expected.

"Of course he needed you. I don't know how he would have survived without you all this time. First Della died, and then he had his accident. The way you supported him shows me what a good partner you'll be to me."

He waited and listened and swore he heard her purr on the other end. Nothing worked better than an ego stroke.

"Thank you. Me, you, and Danny right? We're going to be a family?" she asked.

"Absolutely," he said, feeling justified in the lie.

"Do you want me to come over?" she asked. "I've had a bit of wine but—or you could come here?"

The last thing in the world he wanted was to fuck Joyce, in that way. "I'm beat but how about I meet you Barry's place in the morning? Let yourself in and start sorting through his things. I'll head to the station and see if they need anything from you."

"Are you sure it's all right if I go in? Isn't a crime scene?"

"It was a suicide. No signs of foul play. You'll need to go through his things. I guess it's on you to organize a funeral and all that too. Unless there's family."

She was silent again.

"Are you okay?"

"I'm fine. There's no family. It's all me. It's always been all me."

"And he's always been all you've had too," Fred said, just to be an asshole. "You did everything for him, made your life all about him. And now he's gone. I'm sure it's very hard on you."

She paused, got herself together and then said, "Yes but it's time for a new life. Don't have much choice. You, me, Danny, we'll start all over."

"We sure will. I'll meet you at Barry's about nine. That sound good?"

"Yes. Nine is fine. Maybe I'll go over earlier and start going through his things." She paused and then, "Have you seen Danny?"

"No but I'm sure he'll turn up. Let's just take it one step at a time. I'm not going anywhere."

After another minute or two, they hung up.

Fred rolled onto his back and sighed. *What a fucking crazy turn of events.* He stripped off his clothes and fell asleep in minutes.

- 2 -

Young Danny screamed as a rat ran across his foot.

"It's okay," Danny said, jumping out of sleep to swat the ground by the boy. He looked around the alley and at the sun peeking through the darkness. It was finally morning, and late enough to try to get into Barry's house to make their way home.

"I didn't sleep at all," Young Danny said. "Just sat and watched the rats and bugs and people walk by. I was afraid if I fell asleep I'd forget." As he sat up, he rustled from the newspaper shoved into his clothes for warmth.

"That was smart. I meant to stay up too. Sorry. We're lucky we didn't freeze out here. It's got to be thirty degrees. I wish we had warm jackets." Danny's body crinkled from the paper too.

As they spoke, clouds of their icy breath suspended before them, giving them a ghostly quality.

"It's okay. The sun is up. Can we go back now? I really want to go back."

"Let's go."

They stood up and brushed the grime off their clothes.

"We're out of money so we'll have to walk."

"That's fine. I want to remember all of it. I wonder if I'll re-member fifteen years from now, if I'll remember this day and you."

Danny shook his head. "I don't know. I have dreams from when I was kid I still remember, and things that really happened that stuck with me. Maybe. But this is different right?"

Young Danny talked as they hurried toward Barry's. He rubbed his arms and shivered when he spoke. "When you think back now, do you remember this?"

Danny stopped. "What do you mean?"

"Well, this now, this is a memory for you right? You at twelve?"

"I—I don't know."

"Try. Think about when you were twelve. Think about when you were pulled out of the lake? Do you remember all this before you were pulled out?"

Danny concentrated, sorting through his memories. Pain, agonizing pain, choking. Panic. The icy water. Pain in his shoulders, his lungs. Seeing Joyce above him, the silhouette of her hair. Then black. Nothingness. Flat line. No rescue. Just black.

What if it doesn't work? What if this is just a pre-death dream?

Danny started walking again, fighting the pain he now felt

throughout his body. Fighting taking exaggerated breaths to prove to himself he was still alive. Doing whatever he could to cover up what he'd just seen in his mind.

"I can't see anything," Danny said. "I don't think I can tap into all your memories that way. You know, because you're still here. Guess you'll have to find out for yourself."

"Should I change in there?" He gestured to a 7 Eleven.

"Yeah good idea. We need you back in the clothes you were wearing when I found you."

They walked into the store and Danny waited by the potato chip rack while the boy dressed in the restroom. He nodded hello to the clerk who met his eyes then continued to check the coffee urns.

When Young Danny emerged, he'd transformed into a be-draggled mess with only one shoe. "Guess I really have to stick to the outfit huh? I can hop."

He grinned at youth's comment. "You're almost home. You can endure one cold foot for a few minutes."

They left the store and crossed the street.

"Isn't that Joyce's car?" Young Danny asked, pointing to the dirty blue Mini Cooper parked in front of Barry's Brownstone.

Danny walked to it and touched the hood. "It's cold. She's been here a while."

"I don't want to see her. What if she tries to hurt me? Or kill me again?" the boy asked.

Danny put an arm around him. "She won't. She thinks you forgot. She knows you're her son now so I'm guessing everything changed. Joyce will probably be very happy to see you. And if not, I'm right next to you and I won't let anything happen."

"Are you sure?"

"Yeah. I've got your back. We need to get you home and she's standing in our way. Just let me do the talking and you play along. Whatever I say just follow my lead."

Young Danny nodded. "Got it."

They walked up the frosted slippery stone steps. The sun was a little higher in the sky now but still far from providing warmth.

Danny stood in front of the large door. His body had returned to pre-flashback mode, and his breathing was even. The pain had subsided. His fear though, that was huge. Once he got inside, he really didn't know what would happen. Would the Rainbox work again or was that a fluke? He wanted like hell to get out of this life and return Young Danny home but what if he couldn't? The idea of being stuck here, with Barry's blood on his hands, existing as two people at once, cursed to be pulled from death only to speed forward to the horrific future . . .

Young Danny reached up and knocked on the door, refusing to wait one more second.

The deadbolt turned and Joyce opened the door. She looked like shit. She clearly hadn't slept either. Her makeup was caked on, as always, but it didn't do its intended job in masking her appearance today. Her hair was greasy and messy. She wore jeans and a wrinkled sweatshirt.

She smiled, but her grief showed through. "Come in. Please come in. I'm so glad you two are here."

They walked in the house and she peeked outside. She shut the door behind them.

"Take your shoes off," she ordered.

"I need to wear mine," Young Danny said.

"No need for that now, Joyce," Danny said. "That was Barry's rule."

"Remove your shoes. Both of you." She hadn't noticed that Young Danny wore only one. Without any option they complied. "Just because he's dead doesn't mean he doesn't care anymore."

"You're right," Danny said. "We're being disrespectful."

The three of them headed to the living room and onto the furniture. "Do you think Barry really killed all those women?" Young Danny asked Joyce. "Did he kill my mom too?" He rubbed his shoulder. "Did he try to kill me?"

Danny wanted to smile and give the kid a high five. He'd turned out to be a terrific little actor. Fred would be proud of him.

"I'm afraid so," Joyce said. "But it's going to be all right now.

Nothing to be afraid of. From now on everything is going to be all right."

Danny looked at the boy and then to her. "Will you stay in this house? With Fred?"

She flinched. "With Fred?"

"I know you're dating him. It's okay. We approve." He looked to Young Danny with a follow-my-lead gaze. The boy nodded.

"You're my mother after all," the child said.

She smiled and knelt before the boy. "Did you know? That I was your mother?"

Danny spoke. "I figured it out when I came back. I told him last night."

"Well, see, it's all fate then," she said to young Danny. "It's all fate. This is how it was supposed to be. I should be raising my son don't you think?"

The boy nodded. "Will we live here?" he asked.

She scanned the room. "I don't think so. There have been a lot of memories here, many of them unpleasant. I think we should start a new life far, far away. Maybe buy a ranch out west with horses and cows and acres and acres of land. Tons of privacy. Wouldn't that be wonderful?"

"Joyce," Danny said. "You're being very strong. Very strong. You spent more than half your life with Barry. It must kill you knowing he's gone."

"Yes, yes it does. Of course." An empty cup of coffee and a bottle of Jack Daniels sat before her. She poured whiskey into her cup then leaned back in the chair.

The Dannys shared a glance from opposite sides of the couch.

"I did everything for that man. I loved him very much. Too much I guess. I never married, didn't keep my only child. I devoted myself to him totally, assuming one day he would wake and see what was right in front of him. See the sacrifices I made for him."

She downed the contents of her mug and set it on the table, missing the coaster. Danny hadn't realized until then how drunk she was. He wondered if she'd spent the night here.

"People think I'm heartless but I'm not. I am not. My heart was filled with love for Barry from the first time I met him. He was my unattainable goal. My only goal." She pointed to Young Danny in the exaggerated way drunk people do. "Don't you ever love someone that much, Danny. It'll only end in heartbreak. You do everything for them. Everything goddamned thing they ask, and even things they don't ask for. Because you know them—I knew him better than anyone did. Better than his publishers or Della." She threw her arm up in revulsion. "Big old Della. She didn't know Barry. At all. She took his money and bought nice things. Had no fucking idea about the man she was married to. I did though."

"And he never loved you back?" Young Danny asked.

She shook her head. "Well, in a way he did. After Della, after his accident, he told me all the time that he couldn't get by without me. That I was everything to him. But it wasn't the same. I wasn't *everything*." She turned angry for a second and pointed again. "Your mother was everything. Your adoptive mother, that is. Helen, Helen, Helen. I was so sick of hearing her name. He loved her ghost more than he loved me. He was always chasing that damn woman's ghost."

"I think he loved you very much," Danny said blocking the tirade. He didn't want her to go on and on and confess because then she truly may want to hurt them. If the Rainbox didn't work, he didn't want her blurting anything out now. Better she save it for the police.

"Did he?"

"Of course he did. Maybe not in the same way he loved Helen but she was a fantasy. That's all. She was *his* unattainable love. If he'd managed to have a life with you, I'm sure he would tire of her and choose you. Anyone would." He reached over and squeezed her hand.

He winked to Young Danny.

"Joyce, I need to go now. Back in the Rainbox. I need to go home," Danny said.

She stood with difficulty and swayed toward Danny. "You

can't take my son with you. I can't lose him twice. He's all I have left of Barry."

"I'm not going to leave you," Young Danny said.

As if she didn't hear, Joyce continued. "I gave you away to keep things simpler between me and Barry, to make myself more desirable. You know, single and free. And Barry, the bastard, through fate I guess if I'm gonna be all philosophical—" She sat back in her chair and closed her eyes for a moment. "Sorry, a little dizzy. He manages to fall in love with that woman and say he loves Danny as his own. Can you believe it? I wanted to say "As your own? He *is* your own, you moron. And if you're gonna love anyone it should be me. Me! I'm the one who gave birth to him for God's sake!"

She rested back in her chair. Silent again.

Young Danny stood up. "Guess we were meant to be together. Mom." He took her hand.

Danny smiled. *What a kid.*

"Let me walk Danny to the Rainbox. I'll stay here with you forever but I need to say goodbye to Danny."

Danny saw a change come over Joyce. She was suddenly soft, warm almost. Not fighting, not demanding, just trusting. No doubt this is the side Fred had seen of her. It was a rare side to be sure, this vulnerability, but it was exactly what they needed.

"I'll be right back, Mom," Young Danny said. He kissed her forehead.

Danny realized then it wasn't all an act. On some level the boy did feel a level of attachment to her as his real mother.

"Come on," Young Danny said. "Let me walk you to the Rainbox and say goodbye."

They walked down the hall in silence. It wasn't until they reached the Rainbox, entered and shut it, that they spoke. Blood stained the grout on the floor of the Rainbox, puddled at the edges of the fake drain.

"That's Barry's blood," the boy said. "Because of us."

He put an arm around the child. "Not just because of us. And you know what, it doesn't matter now. Pretty soon we're going to

change all this. You're going to go back and this reality, this lifetime, it won't be real. Barry won't be in pain and he won't die . . ."
Danny got choked up as he said it because it was *his* fault Barry
was dead. Not Young Danny's. He'd been an unwilling participant
and had been jerked around by Joyce. Even if they were successful
in reversing it all, *he* had caused Barry enough pain that his only
way out was death. He prayed this worked, prayed he wasn't lying
to child, prayed he truly could undo this life path.

"You did a great job out there with her. I'm proud of you,"
Danny said.

The boy's eyes clouded. "If Joyce knew I was her son then,
do you think she still would have tried to kill me?"

Danny wondered the same thing. "I hope not."

The two stood in the box, the lights glowing around them in
greens and blues. Danny pulled the piece of red sea glass from
his pocket and placed it on the soap dish. He felt a vibration start
under his feet, pulse its way through him. "Hold my hand."

"What will happen to us? To you? If I go back what happens
to you?"

"I don't know. I don't belong there, not like this, but I truly
don't know."

The vibration increased, coursed through his body like an
electric shock. Young Danny closed his eyes tight. "I feel sick. I
think I'm gonna throw up."

"You're okay, just keep holding my hand. You'll be back soon."

"My chest hurts," the boy said. "My chest hurts. I can't breathe."

Danny felt it too. The vibration grew more intense, rattled
him and Young Danny so fast everything grew blurry.

Please work. Please work. Please work.

"What are you doing in there?" Joyce yelled from outside the
door.

Hurry. Hurry. Hurry.

"I'm scared!" Young Danny screamed. "I don't want to die!"

Danny squeezed his hand harder.

The vibration intensified.

"Just hang on!" His words came out as a deafening buzz. He

couldn't feel his mouth move. Just violent jolts of electricity and pain.

And then it all went black.

- 3 -

"What are you doing in there? Why won't you answer me?"

Joyce pounded on the door of the Rainbox. The door didn't have a lock on it yet she couldn't open it. "Let me in right now! Danny, come back to me! Don't let him take you away from me. Not again. Danny!" She smashed her fists on the door.

From within she heard a sound she couldn't identify. Loud. Not thunder, not banging, not wind. *Like a tornado.* When she was a child, her parents had taken her to a wedding in Kansas. During the vows of the bride and groom, the tornado hit. Everyone ran, trampled over each other, to the church basement. There she sat huddled between her mother and father as the rumble grew louder. She buried her face in her mother's lap as the wind spun and roared, attacking the world around them. It was the scariest thing she'd experienced in her whole life until now.

"Danny!" She banged harder.

Suddenly there was silence. She tried the knob. It turned.

She opened the door and peeked inside. The Rainbox was empty except for a stain where Barry had ended his life.

Joyce slouched onto the floor. Barry's blood was still tacky in areas where it had congealed, brown and flat in others. She moved and her butt stuck to the floor a bit. The idea of it sickened her.

Danny was gone, again. Barry was gone. Who did she have? Fred? So what. Without Danny to raise together, what was the point?

"The point is I'm not going to jail. I'm without Barry and Danny but I'm not going to jail."

She reached up to the empty soap dish and felt for a small lever under the dish. A hidden drawer opened and revealed several items.

Joyce pulled the drawer out all the way and dumped the contents onto the blood soaked tile.

With a shaking finger, she sorted the trinkets, smiling when she saw the token of her first kill. Monica Rushmore. Joyce had hidden behind the counter while Barry screwed that pubescent slut. Listening to him mere feet away broke her heart. That's how he'd sounded with *her*, the handful of times they had made love. He was so passionate, so enamored.

She began to leave the store but silence overtook the moans of passion. Barry swore, shouted words to himself about killing Monica. He ran out and disappeared down the street. She was about the do the same when she heard the girl gasp and cough. When Joyce walked into the back, to the Time Travel Box, Barry's conquest held her throat and coughed. *She's not dead.* That first time Joyce killed, there was no thought. It just happened. She was driven by a jealous rage, furious that girl could bed Barry but she couldn't any longer. He'd lost interest. What did Monica have that was so great? He's mine, the thought, as she grabbed a piece of magic rope from the floor, another prop. Death was quick. The girl was too weak to struggle.

And after, Joyce felt good. Not guilty, not sad, but calm and vindicated. No one belonged with Barry but her. She couldn't make him leave Della but she could do her best to keep the distractions away. She tossed the rope back down and began to walk out but stopped at the counter and grabbed a white lucky rabbit's foot with a green ribbon that read *Rushmore Magic*. A remembrance of how free she felt. Barry would assume of course that he killed the girl and she wondered if he'd ever tell.

Well, he never did until just recently when confronted. He still assumed he was responsible. He died thinking he was a murderer. For a second Joyce felt a twinge of guilt, but it passed as quickly as it came. She set down the rabbit's foot and picked up the next item.

A necklace from Claudia Daley. A locket with a picture of the girl's mother. The police hadn't mentioned it as missing but Joyce knew all about it. Had ripped it off that bitch's neck as she was begging for her life. A picture of her mother. What a crock. A good mother would have taught her daughter to stay away from married men. She fingered the broken chain, the tarnished silver heart. "He was never yours, Claudia. I hope you enjoyed him while you could. I hope he was worth it."

Next she retrieved the school ring from Mallory Dennis. University of New Hampshire. A lovely blue stone. That was a bitch to get off that girl's chubby finger. Joyce never understood why Barry fucked that one. She had a pig face. She wasn't a fat girl; it was just her face and those sausage fingers. Of course with Barry it was about validation more than anything. He celebrated all his debut signings with an extra-marital dalliance.

Alice Shannon didn't have jewelry but she had a library card. "Beggars can't be choosers," Joyce slurred. She was really feeling the effects of last night's drinking, and this morning's.

There were two other trophies from dead girls, ones Danny and Fred didn't know about. Girls Barry probably didn't even remember because his adultery was not limited to book signing nights. He was on a quest to bed as many women as he could after Helen died.

After the Rushmore girl he behaved himself for a good long time. But then there was Helen. Her death broke his heart he'd said. Joyce rolled her eyes now thinking of it. Oh how pathetic he'd been after he lost Helen and Danny. It was like Joyce became invisible after that.

She didn't kill every woman he ever bedded, obviously. Joyce was petite and not strong enough to pull it off. She wanted Barry to herself and was pissed when he chose others over her, again and again. Once in a blue moon her jealousy got the best of her, especially when the tramps were small or she could catch them by surprise.

Joyce leaned back against the edge of the Rainbox now and reflected. She smiled. "I wish I had been strong enough, or had a gun. There would be a hell of a lot more trophies in here if I did." She spied her own hands. Little fingers, little body, but not lithe. Never lithe or skinny. She'd been born stocky and would die stocky. It's just how things were.

"If I were big like Della, with big man hands . . ." She whistled. She picked up the items all in one hand. "This would be a much more impressive take."

A wave of dizziness and nausea overcame her then. She reeled from it and closed her eyes. "I'll just rest for a few minutes, then I'll get up, put all this away. I'll be rich and I'll adopt a baby and no one will ever take him away from me." With that plan set in her mind, she let the liquor ease her into a restful sleep.

- 4 -

"I can't believe you got me to agree to come here. I swear, Fred, if this doesn't pan out, I'm really done with you." Charlie popped a third piece of Nicorette into his mouth. "You have any idea the kind of liability we could face from Barry's death?" Charlie glanced from the road to Fred.

"The police didn't interview him, didn't accuse him. It was all Joyce, and me. Barry reviewed old reports and pictures, that was all. He swore he didn't commit the crimes. Sure, maybe he questioned his guilt because of his memory issues but he never actually confessed to anything but the Rushmore girl and he insisted that was an accident. Negligent homicide at most. He was dead when the detectives walked in to question him."

"I just—I just can't even believe I'm going there," Charlie said. "Can't believe I'm even entertaining that this time you have it right. A whole new hundred percent guilty suspect." He shook his hand, banged the steering wheel. "Because your little boy, who is magically still eleven years old—"

"Twelve. He just turned twelve," Fred interrupted.

"For fuck's sake, Brundige. Your son who is still magically twelve years old told you now he remembers that Joyce tried to kill him. A jury's gonna love that. And if that ain't enough, *you* suddenly remembered that she was upstairs helping your wife pack so she must have pushed her. Do you have any idea how ridiculous that sounds?"

Fred nodded. "Of course. But you know about Danny's picture on my computer. You saw the fingerprints. I can't explain it and I know we don't have any evidence. I just want to go there and talk to her while she's fragile. She's going to be off kilter about Barry and may be a little loose lipped."

They pulled in front of Barry's house as another car was pulling out. "Good timing at least," Charlie said. "You think she killed those girls? Not asking about proof but you think she did it? You think she's capable?"

Fred considered for a moment. "I always trust my gut. Everything about Barry didn't fit, except the fact that all the circumstantial pieces did. His personality wasn't right. But Joyce—There's something not right with her. She's manipulative and jealous as hell. Possessive."

"And you're fucking her?" Charlie asked seriously.

"I was. I'm not now. But I'm not a cop remember? It doesn't matter. Has nothing to do with anything. It's been a long time and she's crafty. Manipulative like I said. I should have known better but I've been wasting my time on these PI gigs spying on people and digging up dirt. I was out of practice, what can I say?"

"Fair enough," Charlie said. "But let me do the talking okay?"

They left the car and ascended the steps. Charlie knocked. No answer.

Fred tried the door. "It's our lucky day."

They walked into Barry's house. "There's her purse and a bottle of liquor on the table. That's a good sign," Fred said.

"Whose shoe is that?" Charlie asked.

Fred stopped by the door and saw one lone child-sized shoe. He reached to pick it up. "This is Danny's. The right Reebok sneaker. The partner to the one found by the lake fifteen years ago."

He handed it to Charlie. "What the fuck?"

Suddenly Fred felt the past and present colliding and crashing around him, weaving a web of confusion and despair around him. "I think he's gone back. Through the Rainbox." A lump formed in his throat but he stifled it. This was *not* the time to fall apart.

"Can't be," Charlie said. "I don't know what to think anymore. I can't remember a shoe from fifteen years ago any better than you."

Fred stared him down. "I can remember the last thing I ever saw of my son, the only thing he left behind at the lake. I'm sure the partner to this is still in evidence."

Charlie snorted and set the shoe down. "Well then welcome to the goddamned Twilight Zone." He looked down at the shoe again. "You think he disappeared back through the box? That's your theory?" he asked doubtfully.

Fred shrugged. "Getting harder to deny it all isn't it?" It was rhetorical.

Charlie mumbled yes and that he needed to retire, as they quietly stalked through the house.

"You hear that?" Fred asked. It was a distant and faint rumbling sound.

"Yes, let's go see." Together they walked down the long hall, following the increasing sound.

"Someone snoring?" Charlie said.

As they drew closer to the open door of the Rainbox, the noise increased.

Joyce lay against the interior wall, passed out, snoring away. Her right hand held a few items. Others had fallen from her grasp, onto the blood-stained floor.

Quietly Charlie stooped down next to her. Fred did the same. "Don't touch anything," he said.

"I won't."

Charlie pulled a pen from his pocket and poked at the items on the floor. "Holy shit. These are objects that were missing from the victims. Never revealed to the public. Only listed in the police records."

Fred nodded. "You believe me now? You believe she's guilty now?"

"What's going on?" Joyce blurted out, suddenly awakening. "What are you doing here?" The men stood in unison. She gazed up at them through unfocused eyes, then at the contents in her hand and on the floor. "These aren't mine. They're Barry's. I just found them in here. In the soap dish. These aren't mine I swear."

Charlie glared at her. He was old now but still intimidating as hell when he wanted to be. He didn't say a word and neither did Fred.

"They're not mine. You can't prove anything. You go ahead

and exhume those bodies and you'll find Barry's DNA in every one of them."

"I have no doubt that's true but he's not my suspect anymore. I have a better one now," Charlie said.

She began to rise but felt back down. "My foot's asleep. I need a minute. You can't be serious. Tell him, Fred. Tell him I wouldn't do it. Tell him how I spent my life taking care of Barry, doing anything he needed. Sacrificing everything—" She shifted her leg, tapped it to get the blood flowing. "You tell him, goddammit that I was a good companion to that man!"

Her voice changed from loving and sad, to cornered and angry. "This doesn't mean anything! All this shit. I don't know what any of it even is. You can't prove I took it or I was there with any of these women. Any of them! You can't prove I ever even saw any of them before they were killed."

Fred and Charlie exchanged a glance. "Then how do you know these came from the victims?" he asked.

She began to open her mouth to fight but stopped. "I want a lawyer," she said.

Joyce spit at Fred but it didn't reach, only fell back onto her leg.

"Joyce Tuttle," Charlie began. "You are under arrest . . ."

EIGHT

October, 2000

Fred sat on a rock and started crying. He'd fucked everything up. Everything. If he'd been a better husband, Helen wouldn't have wanted to run away with Barry. None of this would've happened. He looked to the left, saw the group of searchers and Barry and Joyce. He saw Charlie, who turned away.

Couldn't blame the guy. Fred smelled like liquor and sweat. His breath was foul and the taste in his mouth made him want to puke. He needed to shave and change his clothes but none of that mattered to him.

Everyone had been here all night trying to track down his lost son, while he was passed out drunk in his Jeep, a jealous useless piece of shit father. He punched himself in the side of the head. God, he'd give anything to take back all he'd done wrong. He wished Barry's damn Rainbox was real. Probably a lot of people read the book and made that same wish. If you could just go back and change what happened —Jesus, no wonder Helen loved him. On top of everything else, the guy could write. He was rich, handsome. *Fuck.*

He walked to the part of the lake around the corner, where the shoe was found. It was still there. The lonely left shoe of Danny's new Reebok. He held it up to the sun, the dim light just peeking over the horizon. "Danny, if you can hear me, I love you. If there's a God out there, please send him home. Please. I promise everything will be different."

He saw ripples in the water then. They were faint. Probably water bugs but he ran closer.

Please God. Please!

He leaned over the shallow water and saw the sand below transform into a shape, then a boy. His boy. Pale and unmoving but it was him. "He's over here!" Fred screamed.

He reached down and grabbed Danny by the shoulders, pulled him from the water. He threw him to the ground, listened to his heart. Nothing. "He's over here! I found him!"

Fred raised his head and saw people running toward them.

A paramedic took over, gave Danny CPR.

Charlie stood next to Fred, Barry and Joyce on his other side. All of them watching, probably praying like he was. No one said a word, just watched the boy's chest go up and down from the CPR. Listened as one paramedic talked to the other.

There were others there too. Neighbors, people from town. Father Preston. Fred knelt down next to Danny on his open side, squeezed his hand. "Danny, wake up. You're gonna be okay. Wake up, son. You can't leave me. You need to come back and make things right."

Danny suddenly moved, starting coughing up water. The paramedic rolled him over. More and more water poured from his lungs as he gasped for air. The paramedics slapped an oxygen mask onto him. One went to get the stretcher and then the two men heaved him up onto it.

Danny's eyes darted around in panic at the people standing around him. He reached for Fred's hand and squeezed it. Fred kissed the boy's forehead, tousled his hair. Danny flinched and Fred noticed blood on his hand. "Hey, he's got a head wound too."

"We need to get him to the hospital and get him seen. We can't risk secondary drowning." They grabbed the edge of the stretcher.

Fred pulled himself from his shock and noticed everyone hugging each other, smiling, crying with joy and relief. He was crying too.

Barry smiled at him and they had a polite nod between them. Joyce stood without emotion. Weird. She'd come off as strange to him when he'd met her yesterday.

Danny yanked his mask off. "You need to leave that on, son," the paramedic said trying to replace it.

"Captain Bachman," Danny croaked, to get his attention.

Charlie ran to Danny. "What is it, son? Whatever it is can wait."

"No, I need to tell you now. Before I forget. Please."

The crowd grew silent in anticipation.

The paramedics nodded. "Just for a minute."

"Joyce did it," Danny said. He was weak but belted out the words. "She pushed my mother down the stairs and she tried to drown me."

Everyone turned to Joyce. She cringed.

"Are you sure, son?" Charlie asked.

Danny pulled aside his wet sweatshirt and t-shirt. "She scratched me hard when I tried to get away. Check her fingernails."

Fred thought that was a pretty sophisticated thing for a kid to say but there were a lot of police and crime shows on TV now.

Charlie stormed over to Joyce who was staring at her fingers. Two of her long nails were jagged and broken on her right hand.

"Did you try to drown Danny Brundige?" he asked in about the harshest voice Fred had ever heard.

"No, of course not. Barry loved that boy more than anything. I'd never hurt him!" Her voice rose in pitch, usually a dead give-away a person was lying.

Barry pulled away from her. "Did you try to kill him, Joyce? Did you kill my Helen?" Barry's recent look of elation over the finding of Danny was now replaced with terror and heartbreak.

Fred let the "my Helen" thing go.

"No, Barry. I didn't touch her. Or him. You loved them both more than anything. I would never—"

"Loved them more than you? That's it wasn't it, Joyce? Did you push Helen down the stairs? You've resented her and Danny the whole time I've known them and I've dealt with it. You tried to sabotage us repeatedly because I didn't love you. But killing? Did you kill her?" He walked to Danny, held his other hand. "Try to kill this wonderful little boy?"

All eyes were on Joyce, who showed only anger. "I want a lawyer," she said.

For a moment or two, no one reacted expect the paramedics who loaded Danny into the van. Fred jumped in too.

He turned and looked out the back doors, right before they closed, to spy Charlie slapping handcuffs on Joyce. "Joyce Tuttle you are under arrest . . ."

Then the doors slammed shut and Fred turned back to his son. "It's a miracle, Danny," Fred said.

The boy's eyes were red and swollen like the rest of him and the mask was back on. He was breathing evenly and he had an IV running. One of the paramedics sat next to Danny adjusting tubes and monitoring his vitals. The other flipped on the sirens and rushed toward the ER.

"You were missing for a long time, Danny. You know how long?" Fred asked.

"A week?" the boy said quietly from under the mask.

Fred laughed. "No, not quite that long. Overnight though. Can't imagine you were under water all the time but we didn't know where you were. We were worried sick. Me mostly. But listen, when you come home it's gonna be just us. I'm gonna take a leave from work and rebuild our relationship okay? I'm sorry for how I've been but that's all changing."

The boy nodded.

"Do you remember what happened, Danny?" the medic prodded. "We need to find out how long you were under, if you know. Or where it happened. Where did Joyce hold you down?"

"It happened right there. Last night. Right in that spot."

"That would've been twelve hours. Couldn't have been then," Fred said. "Let's ask him later when he's rested up. All that matters is that he's alive, right?"

"Yes, at the end of the day that's really it."

He pulled his mask off again. "I feel weird, Dad. I had all these dreams. I went through the Rainbox and into the future and Joyce was a murderer and Barry died and Bonnie was a prostitute—"

The paramedic replaced the mask. "You can tell us all about it later. We need to get your oxygen levels up."

"What about me, Danny? Was I in the dream? What was I in the future?" All the things the boy said made sense given what he'd seen right before he went under water. Well, maybe not the part about little Bonnie but he wondered what Danny's subconscious said about *him*.

The boy smiled, touched the mask and the paramedic nodded. He probably wanted to know too. "You were still my dad and you loved me and you believed me. You said everything was gonna be different now. It was just gonna be us and we were gonna be okay."

He put the mask back on. Fred smiled.

They would be all right. No one could bring Helen back but Joyce would go away for a long time. He still had his son and a new beginning for them to both look forward to.

The ambulance roared into the hospital parking lot and the entrance.

"I guess I'm the dad who loves you whatever time we're in," Fred said. He gave Danny's hand another squeeze then hopped out to let the medical people help his son.

NINE

Fred checked his reflection in the mirror. He adjusted his tie and smiled. Tonight was the annual Policeman's Ball. It was a celebration for all the cops and their families to get together knowing they'd made it through another year. This was a rough year for everyone. The bombing had rattled their town. Stupid kid decided to put a bomb under the arena at the high school football stadium. Fifteen people dead, sixteen if you included the bomber. Fred didn't include him because that happened a week later, when the scumbag was in custody. Sitting in his cell, no doubt proud of himself and all the attention he was getting.

Typical nutjob basking in the havoc he caused, thinking it made him a hero. Ready to cost the taxpayers millions of dollars in court costs and appeals when the city had enough trouble funding the school budget. Fred took care of it. Was always the one who did the dirty work for the force, the behind the scenes action no one else wanted.

In this case, the perp hung himself. The clerk had forgotten to take his belt away when he was admitted, though he swore he did. And the guard who was supposed to be watching him was in the bathroom. In cases like these, usually there was a public outcry, an investigation. *How could this happen? Was there foul play? He didn't seem suicidal.* For anyone else the headlines would have rallied against the police, cried brutality, cried for someone's badge.

But in Bradfield, no one said a word. Everyone was just as happy the guy was dead. Dead now, not ten years and millions dollars of government funded court costs later. You mess with children and the climate for justice changes.

Whatever the actual reason for Fred's promotion, his ascension to Captain was noted only for his years of hard work on the force, in stopping crime and keeping their lovely city safe, or words to that effect.

Tonight was the dinner, and they would announce the retiring of Charlie and Fred's promotion to take the job.

"I'm so proud of you," Cindy said, peeking over his shoulder in the mirror.

"And I'm proud of you," he said, turning to face her. She was as beautiful as she'd been back in high school. Any lines on her face or extra weight made her even more attractive, more lived-in. He smiled.

After Helen died, when Danny had gone missing and almost drowned, she'd stepped right in and helped him and Danny to rebuild. Set them both up with good grief counselors. She urged Fred to go to AA and he'd conceded. All the nights he was straightening himself out, she'd stayed with Danny. The boy said he was old enough to stay alone but he quickly grew to love Cindy. Back then he said she was "Dad's cool friend," who taught him about clues and evidence and gory stuff most women shied away from. A couple of years later, at their wedding reception, Danny had called her, "Dad's cool wife."

"Look at us," Cindy said. "You're going to be a police captain and I run the forensics department. Who knew we'd end up here?"

He hugged her, gave her a nice long kiss. "What would I do without you?"

"Dad!" Danny called from downstairs.

"Come on, being a father never takes a break."

Fred took Cindy's hand and led her down the stairs to where Bonnie and Danny were celebrating their own accomplishments.

- 2 -

Danny sat on the floor of his room. It used to be the den but Dad knocked a wall down and combined it with the spare room. Together they'd added a bathroom. For the last two years, he'd been living in this big room with Bonnie. She'd moved in with them when she was fifteen. Her mother had moved away to California. Not long after, her father remarried and the stepmother didn't want her. It was a crazy situation but thankfully Dad and Cindy had welcomed her in.

Through high school, Bonnie had been Danny's best friend and nothing else. But once they started college, a local school where they commuted home each day, they'd fallen into a relationship that had been right under their noses. He supposed he was probably in love with her since they were in first grade and knelt side by side receiving their First Communion.

They'd been engaged for a year and had been saving money for a down payment on a house for three. They were closing on a new house in three days, just a half mile away on the other side of the lake. They'd been digging through all of Danny's and Bonnie's things for weeks, scrounging through old pots and pans in the garage and basement.

"Hi Danny."

"Hey Dad."

"Wow you're all dressed up, Fred." Bonnie said. "You look so official." She noticed Cindy then who walked in behind him. "Great dress!"

"Thanks," Cindy said.

"We clean up nice for old folks," Fred said. He laughed when he saw Danny surrounded by open boxes. "You called?"

"Yeah, can I have the dartboard? You don't really use it right?"

"Not without you. Sure, you can have it. We can play when we come for dinner five nights a week right?"

Bonnie hugged Fred. "Six nights a week. We can't go cold turkey from seeing you."

Danny smiled at Bonnie. She was about the sweetest person he'd ever met. Not just because he was marrying her but she was. She taught kindergarten and volunteered in a women's shelter twice a week. What a catch, he thought. *Damn, I'm lucky.*

"Okay, we're taking off now. When I come back you're going to have to call me sir," Fred said.

Danny rolled his eyes. "Have a good time. Hopefully when you get back, we'll have sorted through all this." He waved an arm to the mess around him.

After they left, Bonnie joined Danny on the floor.

She pulled open a box marked "Books."

From the top she pulled a swollen, faded book. "Hey, it's *The Rainbox.*"

Bonnie handed it to Danny who smiled. "Wow. I forgot I had this." He flipped through the warped pages. "That was a lifetime ago, huh?"

"You loved this book so much. Loved Barry too."

"Yeah." He read the inscription aloud. "To Danny-the son I always wanted. Whatever happens, we will forever have our Rainbox-Love Barry."

"That's sweet. You never talked to him again after, after everything did you?"

"No. He was at my mother's funeral. I felt bad for the guy. He really loved her, just as much as Dad did. He lost her, and me, and then Joyce. He was such a good guy. All those years he kept Joyce as his assistant and then she goes and kills my mother and tried to kill me, just out of jealousy."

"And wasn't she convicted on another other murder too? A girl in Maine?"

"Yeah that's right. I forgot about that crime. Barry left her for dead but she was still alive when Joyce finished her off. My dad didn't want me to know about it but it was all over the news. I think the DA got her to confess to that murder to avoid the death penalty."

"That's how I remember it too, but we were still kids so I wasn't sure. I know she'll spend her life in prison, where she belongs."

"Exactly. Who knows what would have happened, what other people she may have killed if I hadn't been rescued? If I hadn't been able to remember and tell them Joyce was guilty?"

"It's scary to even think of it. So what do you remember now of the near death experience dream you had? It's been fifteen years but when you first woke up you were talking all kind of nonsense."

Danny leaned against a pile of boxes. "It's funny, parts of the dream are still so clear. Like, I remember Barry had a bad limp from an accident and he kept forgetting stuff. He had brain damage. And I was there as me and as older me. It was really bizarre."

"You were dead for thirty minutes they said, from what they could tell. I think the brain concocted a bunch of strange stories while you were gone, trying to sort out what was happening."

"I guess." Danny tried to recall more. "I remember I was so sad, I just kept telling the grown up me I wanted to go home and see me my dad."

"Did you really see me as a prostitute?" she prodded, laughing.

"Not like that, Bonnie." He frowned. "It was tragic. You were—Oh my God, I just remembered. You had a tattoo across your chest. It said HOPE all in capitals. I don't remember much about you except that you were so damn skinny, and that tattoo. I think I spent half the dream crying or on the verge of tears."

"Doesn't sound like a good near death experience at all." Bonnie held his hand.

"It wasn't. No bright light or feelings of euphoria. It sucked and I really just wanted to come home. I missed you and my Dad so much. You know what's really crazy? In the dream Joyce was my biological mother and Barry was really my dad. I overheard them or, I don't know. It was like watching a movie where I could see all of it, from up above, and some parts I was really in."

"What was the last thing you remember before you woke up? I wonder if it's changed from what you remembered fifteen years ago."

Danny was as shaken thinking about it now as he had been throughout the years. The death of Barry still crushed him, even though it wasn't real. He still woke up sporadically with mixed memories of this life and that one and yet another one that didn't come from anywhere. Many a night he'd woken up crying, seeing Dad walk from Barry's house, telling them he'd killed himself. Many a night he'd recalled Bonnie with her skeletal frame and track marks, the infected broken veins in her arm, and the origami cranes.

Those were secrets he kept to himself. It would do no good to share all that pain with Bonnie. She was too innocent to be marred by the images in his head.

The rest of his time he'd spent unconscious blurred together in no order and with no discernible meaning: recollections of him in his scout uniform selling candy bars, seeing a dinosaur movie in a museum, eating at a diner on his birthday.

"The last thing I remember was going into the Rainbox, the one at Barry's I saw when I went to his house that time. We went in, me and the older me, and Joyce was banging to get in, shrieking for us to come out. And there was all this light and I felt like I was being electrocuted. And I just kept screaming I wanted to go home."

"And then you did," she said.

"Thank God." He was relieved it was all behind him. That it wasn't real. Just a damn bad nightmare whose elements flooded him every so often.

"And then I did. Right. Then I was here. Right out front. A few hundred feet away. I'd never really left."

Bonnie let go of his hand and did a search on her phone. "You know, Barry has a new book out. A story collection."

"I heard about that on the radio," he said.

"He's doing a signing in town on Sunday. Starting the tour with his local store. Maybe we should go. I think it would mean a lot to him to see you again, and to you too."

He smiled. "Wow, seeing Barry again, after all this time. You know I would like to go. Not like Dad would care after this long. He never really blamed him anyway for what happened. He said Mom was awesome and Barry couldn't help loving her."

"It's true," Bonnie said. "Your mother was amazing."

"Fine, if we can get through all these boxes by Sunday, we'll go see Barry." Danny knew come hell or high water he'd go to that signing. Fifteen years was long enough.

- 3 -

"Can't see a damn thing in this rain," Barry said as he drove through the city traffic to find a parking spot. "You think they'd reserve me a spot."

"There's one down there, just past the diner. I've got an umbrella. We're fine," Amy said.

With the wipers swiping full blast, Barry could just make out the neon sign and the small spot between a Jeep and a BMW. It took some maneuvering but he squeezed his Accord in.

He looked across the street to the line of people outside the store, all with raincoats and umbrellas. "Can't believe this many people are here for me. For my book. I took all those years off; it's nice to see the fans are still out there."

"It is nice. I'm your fan." Amy smiled.

He smiled at Amy in the pink light of the Joe's Diner sign. Meeting her was one of the biggest breaks he'd ever gotten. After Della died of cancer, he was drifting around depressed. She was his wife, his assistant, his best friend. She forgave him for his affair with Helen and the incident made them stronger as a couple. She'd been as blown away by Joyce's involvement as he was. They'd both lost her as a friend when she went to jail. They'd turned to each other.

When Della got the cancer diagnosis, they fought it together. They hoped for the best and accepted the worst. When she passed away, he was beside himself. Depressed. Saw no reason to continue on.

He'd drunk a half bottle of his most expensive bottle of Scotch and headed outside to his new motorcycle. Barry had been in full-blown suicide mode and was just holding the door handle. Suicide note written and signed, will notarized leaving everything to Danny Brundige, the closest thing he'd had to a son.

And then his house phone rang. Amy Rickels, the speech therapist he'd called two weeks ago about research for his new book on memory loss, *The Forgotten Man*. He didn't know who the caller was then of course, and toyed with continuing to walk right out that door and end it all. But a feeling he couldn't ignore urged him to turn around and answer it.

"Hello?"

"Barry, it's Amy Rickels. I'm sorry I didn't get back to you sooner. My husband passed away." She paused. *"Unexpectedly. A motorcycle accident."*

Barry contemplated the keys in his hand. *A motorcycle accident.*

"Are you there?" she asked.

"Yes, yes I'm here. I'm sorry for your loss. Do you want to get a cup of coffee? To talk about it?"

She was quiet for a moment.

"I know we haven't even met," he continued, *"but I'm feeling down myself tonight. You have no idea what your calling at just this moment did for me. I'd like to sit down and talk to a friend and right now I'm about as lonely and friendless and I've ever been."* He waited, hoping she'd accept.

"Yes. I would actually. I'd love to sit and talk. I don't like being here without him," she said.

He looked around his empty brownstone. He could certainly relate to that.

"I know a good diner. They make a hell of a meatloaf and their milkshakes are—" he stopped himself before saying "to die for." Instead, *"Milkshakes are damn good too."*

"I'd like that," she said. *"Half an hour?"*

As he told her the address, he removed his motorcycle key from the ring. He sold it the next day. They met and soon became best friends, kindred spirits.

A year ago they were married. Maybe they'd saved each other's lives. For sure they had rescued each other from lives of unhappiness and loneliness.

He stepped from the car with the umbrella then went around to her side to open her door. He took her hand and together they walked across the street to Bradfield Books.

▲▲▲

Barry sat at the signing table. Amy sat beside him, greeting each customer before he did, writing their names on a Post It so he'd get the spelling correct. She was a gem all right.

He'd forgotten how exciting these events were. Most of his joy came from the actual process of writing the books, but seeing his fans' excitement, knowing his words, the worlds he'd created, had become a part of their lives, even if only for a short time, cemented his choice of vocation. Not that writing was ever a choice. When he wasn't penning new novels or stories, spending most of his day in a land he'd imagined, and transcribing the lives of his characters as they happened, he was a cranky malcontent.

God bless Amy for standing by his side. She'd written her own nonfiction book about the difference in memories that were real, dreams, or created by the imagination or suggestion. It turned out there wasn't much difference at all where the brain was concerned.

So in a way, every word he wrote became real, sort of. He smiled at that. Maybe he didn't have a child, the one true regret in his life, but he had his tales and that would have to be enough.

The crowd dwindled and the wind and rain outside picked up.

He checked his watch. The store had him scheduled another half hour but he doubted he'd see any new faces. Not in this weather.

"I'm going to use the ladies room," Amy said. "I'll be back in a minute."

No sooner did she walk away, the front door of the store blew open. The storm propelled a young couple through the entrance. The man and woman were drenched, and the man shook a broken umbrella. He wasn't the first one to lose one tonight. Half the customers walked in cursing the wind and their inside out and broken umbrellas.

The young man leaned it against the wall and shook his head like a puppy after a bath.

They both walked toward Barry. Faithful fans. Nothing like them. The man slapped a book down on the table.

The Rainbox. An old bedraggled and water bloated, faded copy of his first novel. The one that had put him on the map as an author. Barry smiled. "Wow, haven't seen this in a long time."

"Do you remember me?" the man said.

Barry looked up from the book. He didn't recognize the face. He glanced to the young woman beside him. She was very pretty and familiar but—He had Déjà vu again. It happened a lot and he always rode it out but this was so strong. The same scene had happened before. He was sure of it. Or maybe not, he thought as the sensation passed.

"I do remember you," he said, but he could not put names to faces. "Do you want me to sign your book?"

The man and woman looked to each other and he could see pain and dejection in the man's face.

"You already did," he said.

Barry opened the book. In his own writing he saw the inscription. *To Danny-the son I always wanted. Whatever happens, we will forever have our Rainbox-Love Barry.*

"Oh my God!" A surge of joy overtook Barry. "Danny!" He moved his gaze to the girl. "And you're Bonnie aren't you?"

They nodded, smiling broadly.

He ran from around the table and hugged Danny, hard. "God I missed you. What a fine man you've grown into. And you, Bonnie. You were a little wisp of a thing last time I saw you. Now you're a lovely grown woman! I'm sorry I didn't recognize you, Danny. I should've but you're all grown up."

The crowd of onlookers stared. "Everybody this Danny. From *The Rainbox*." He threw his arm around him. "God I loved this kid like my own son!"

Danny leaned into him. "And I loved him like a dad."

After Helen's murder Barry had kept the identity of Danny secret out of respect for Fred. After so many years though, enough time had passed.

Bonnie moved in front of them. "Let me get a picture."

The flash blinded Barry for a second but when the light cleared he was relieved to find Danny and Bonnie still there. Others in the store held up their phones and took photos as well. Danny held the pose which was fine with Barry. He didn't want to let go.

"You have no idea how good it is to see you again." Barry said. It was as if all the prior years had melted away and his boy was back.

Amy came from the back of the store then. "Amy, this is Danny. *My* little Danny all grown up." His voice rose from excitement. He knew Danny wasn't really *his* but it didn't hurt to indulge himself just for the night.

She hugged Danny. "It's so nice to meet you. I'm really glad you came."

"Nice to meet you too," Danny said.

"Sorry, this is my wife Amy. Della passed a couple of years ago."

"I'm sorry," Danny said. "I didn't know."

Barry shook his head. "How is your father? Did he remarry too?"

Danny nodded. "He married his high school sweetheart. After Mom died she was really good to us, came over all the time, got us both through it. She's been a great mother to me."

"I'm really glad. So you and Bonnie are still friends. I'm happy to hear that."

Bonnie held out her hand and a small diamond engagement ring. He knew that ring. It had been Helen's. He felt a wave of melancholy, of nostalgia, but it passed when he saw the love in Bonnie's eyes. "We're engaged."

"I'm just about done here, can we all go out? Catch up on all the lost years?" Barry asked.

"There's a great diner across the street," Amy said. "Kitty corner to the library."

Danny and Bonnie laughed. "We love that place," Danny said. "Why don't we head over and get a table and you can meet us there when you're done?"

They said their goodbyes and Barry watched as the young couple walked out of the bookstore, hand in hand.

"They say you can't go back in time and change events, but in the end everything ends up right where it should be," Barry said as Amy and he took their seats to finish out the last few minutes of the signing. "All those books I wrote about time travel and see? Without anyone changing fate, usurping God, as I wrote in *The Rainbox*, it all ends up just fine in the end."

Amy squeezed his hand. "It certainly does."

TRACY L. CARBONE

Tracy L. Carbone is the author of six novels and two short story collections. She is the editor of the Bram Stoker Award nominated anthology *Epitaphs: A Journal of the New England Horror Writers*, and co-editor of *Cemetery Riots: A Collection of Dark Cautionary Tales*. A lifelong resident of New England, Tracy now lives and writes in the sunshine and warmth of Southern California.

shadowridgepress.com